The End of Everything We Know
By
Aaron Harvie
Cover Art, Design & Layout
by
Blood, Brains & Aliens
&
Lilly Bader
Edited
by
Vicki Harvie
Soundtrack Album
From the Streets of New Chechnya
by
Needle in Your Eye

The End of Everything We Know.
By Aaron Harvie.

First published in 2023 © Aaron Harvie

1st Edition.

The moral rights of the author has been asserted.

Edited by Vicki Harvie.

Acknowledgements.

It's impossible to write a novel and remain in a vacuum.

So, as this is my first attempt, I wanted to take a moment to say thanks to everyone who helped me along the way. To my mother April for showing me a million movies when I was a kid and always loving everything I wrote, even when it was awful. To my wife Natalie and daughter Izzy, you are everything to me. To my dad Tom and my Aunty Vicki for the endless guidance and support. To Karen and Ursula for believing when even I didn't. And to John Carpenter, William Gibson, Neal Stephenson, Ridley Scott and the hundreds of other filmmakers, authors and musicians that provided a spark in a young teenage mind all those many, many, many years ago.

Without any of you, none of this would be possible.

1.

A History of Things to Come.

So, the world as we know it died.

But it didn't die quick like a bullet to the head. It died slow, gut shot and screaming in agony as it bled out.

It was the climate that started the end. The summers got hotter and the winters got colder. Glaciers melted and the polar caps receded. The weather got more and more extreme.

Rising sea levels were the first thing that people started to notice, low-lying areas began to flood and tiny islands in the middle of the Pacific disappeared one by one. But no one gave a shit about that, or at least no one that mattered anyway. Want to know why? Because the places that were disappearing didn't have any money. I mean, where was Tuvalu or Palau anyway?

So, no one gave a fuck.

Government and big business kept on doing whatever they wanted, anything for more power and more money. They paid off scientists to deny climate change, installed puppets and morons as mouthpieces and used the media to control and frighten and manipulate the masses. They took turns gang raping the Earth, high-fiving each other like fucking frat boys, while cities like Bangkok were abandoned and countries like Bangladesh were swallowed by the seas.

It wasn't until the waves started lapping against the doorsteps of Miami, New York and London that anyone took any notice.

But by then of course, it was too late.

Storm surges and flooding smashed against the coasts of the world. Torrential rain and mudslides buried remote villages and communities, wiping them off the map. Polar vortexes and blizzards froze entire nations. Droughts turned thriving farmland into dustbowls. And as the temperatures soared, fires raged out of control, and cities burned to the ground.

Suddenly, there wasn't enough food. Or water.

Soon hundreds of millions of refugees fled for their lives in a great worldwide exodus as super storm cells more powerful than ever before raged across the planet. Hurricanes, cyclones, monsoons and tornados, one after the other tore paths of destruction, leaving carnage and misery in their wakes.

And from these calamities came disease and famine.

And war.

Conflict flared up across the world like wildfires as the poorer nations crumbled beneath the strain. Every atrocity imaginable soon followed as opportunists became warlords and mercenaries became generals, each setting up their own personal fiefdoms in the remnants of collapsed nations. And the rest of the world looked on as the third world consumed itself, unwilling or unable to help.

Terrorism. Massacres. Anarchy. Genocide. Biological and nerve agents. Chemical warfare.

Then nuclear...

Soon even the richest nations, the superpowers who had somehow managed to insulate themselves, were drawn into conflict and forced to make a last desperate grasp for whatever was left and worth taking.

And the destruction escalated like never before.

As the world came to a grinding halt and societies crumbled, those fleeing the raging horrors became more and more desperate, their numbers swelling like plague locusts. Island nations that had managed to keep their heads above the rising waters closed their borders. The rest, no matter how wealthy or powerful, fell beneath the surging waves of the homeless, their fragile infrastructures overwhelmed by desperate human need.

The polar ice continued to melt, releasing hundreds of gigatonnes of carbon-dioxide. This in turn warmed the world, which melted the ice faster and faster, which released more and more carbon-dioxide. As the oceans continued to rise the world began to redraw itself, inundating the low-lying areas and swallowing the coasts, until cities, states, even countries sank beneath the waves.

The lands between the tropics of Cancer and Capricorn were, for the most part, abandoned, becoming inhospitable and dangerous. The countries around the equator, uninhabitable. In the end the human race clung to existence by a fingernail, dangling above the gaping abyss of extinction.

But somehow, we didn't fall.

Somehow, we survived. And out of all the horror, came hope.

As the ice melted, it uncovered vast tracts of fertile land for the world to farm. Desperation drove innovation and technology advanced in leaps and bounds. Robotics, AI, human augmentation, designer bacteria, clean energy, fusion, nanotech, off world mining and interplanetary colonisation all helped us claw our way back from the brink of destruction. And from the ashes of the old world, new powers rose from the virgin farmlands of the Nordic regions and Greenland and Canada and Russia.

Even Antarctica.

But as we emerged from the darkness and stepped back into the light, it soon became painfully clear that nothing had really changed, that the same politicians, bureaucrats and corporate stooges who drove us to the edge of extinction had retaken the wheel.

Except this time, it was worse.

Because this time, we had nothing left to give so when it came time to pay, the few liberties we had left were the only currency they'd accept.

"Sure, we were the ones who fucked it up," they said. "But if you want it back, it's going to cost you."

So, they got what they wanted.

A centralised world government and police force. Unmonitored global banking. Corporate deregulation that allowed the creation of mega-conglomerates. Unrestrained control over media, advertising and information. Private armies. Company policies as enforceable as any law. But the biggest one of them all was the IdentityChip, a tiny implant given to every citizen at birth.

They sold it as a good thing.

They said our lives would never be the same.

And they were right.

With the IdentityChip we could neurally access the internet, allowing us to go online anywhere without a physical connection. That meant every person on Earth could communicate with whoever they wanted where ever they were. It contained our identification documents, our passport and bank accounts. In fact, it had everything we would ever need, all in one place, all accessible in the blink of an eye.

We were never told it was also able to track everything we did. That it recorded every single piece of personal information. Everything we read. Every movement. Every transaction. Every conversation.

Everything. Until the day we died.

And that information was for sale to the highest bidder.

It was the perfect way to control. Once unleashed, those with the power - the scumbag corporate executives and corrupted government whores - operated unchecked and answerable to no one.

So, here we are, alive and well in a brave new world.

Sometimes I think it might have been better if we had of just let go when we teetered on the edge of extinction, closed our eyes and fallen back into the warm embrace of oblivion.

We could have given something else a chance.

Because one thing's for certain, we're going to fuck it up all over again...

2.

An Agent of Chaos.

My name is Cyanide Jones, at least that's what people call me. But for the last week or so, my name has been Thomas L. Booker.

I work for Human Resources Management. We supply solutions for business problems. I'm a company man. A corporate head hunter. But that doesn't mean what you think it does. I don't recruit people to go work for some company.

I terminate their employment, permanently.

I do the dirty work big business doesn't want you to know about. I'm a corporate raider. I fight the trade wars, help facilitate hostile takeovers. They used to call it kidnapping and assassination. I prefer terms like aggressive recruiting and early retirement.

And before you say anything, let's just get one thing clear. Every company does it, no matter how squeaky clean their public image is.

Every. Single. One.

That's right, even the makers of your kid's breakfast cereal, or the network that produces your favourite immersive reality show. All of them. Because this world is about two things: profit and loss. Either you're winning or you're losing. There's nothing in between.

You see, if you're a corporate executive in charge of a trillion-dollar department at some planetary conglomerate and your competitor has a new product coming out, something that's going to hurt your company's market share, you've got two choices.

Compete against it or destroy it.

If you play by the rules you might win, or you might lose. So why take the chance? Why compete against it at all?

Not when there are guys like me around.

It's risky, sure, but only if you get caught, and if you spin it right people will believe whatever they're told. I find a story about a cyber-attack by an "unknown group of hackers" or a catastrophic accident due to "faulty machinery" are good covers for industrial sabotage.

You can blow up a manufacturing plant or research lab with a bullshit story like that.

It gets even easier if an executive or a scientist at a rival company needs to disappear. Ever seen the suicide rates for those guys?

They're astronomical.

I know, I hear what you're saying. Companies can't do that. They can't just kill their competitors. We have laws and police to stop them doing whatever they want.

You're right, we do.

We live in a society and last I checked stealing shit and killing people is against the law. But tell me, with the mind-boggling wealth that these companies have, which police force or government body or even country has the power to enforce them?

The answer is none.

That's where I come in. I work for the highest bidder. If you can afford me, I'll do the job. I don't care what the Mark has done, all these corporate pricks are guilty of something.

Every. Single. One.

Like the Mark I'm following now. Hiroto Ashihei. He works for Nanatsu Systems, an up-and-coming Japanese robotics firm. He's just designed a ground-breaking silicon neurotransmitter, like a synapse for an android's brain. They say it's going to change the industry, put Nanatsu Systems on the map. They also say he likes to have sex with underage boys.

But I'm not here for that.

I'm here because he refused to sell this technology to my client. Then he refused their job offer. Big mistake.

So, I followed him here to New Cairo four days ago.

I don't like New Cairo. Never have. It's a tourist town, a gaudy eyesore of neon holograms and glass domes. After the Middle East was turned into a radioactive soup by the war between Israel and the Arabic Union, a group of "concerned" trillionaires spent a fortune in an effort to save the pyramids. They occupied the Giza plateau, built levies around the site and created support structures for the monuments, watching as all the while the poisoned waters of the Nile swallowed the city of Cairo whole. Who knows how many people died?

A million? Maybe two?

In the scheme of things, compared to how many died during the Exodus, it was nothing. A drop in the bucket.

After a few years that same group of "concerned" businessmen decided to develop the site, with dreams of turning it into a corporate playground, kind of like Macau or Vegas of old. Today, New Cairo is a destination for the rich and famous, a beacon of obscenity populated by lurid five-star casinos, elitist restaurants and sprawling ground scrapers that extend down hundreds of floors below the desert sands. It is a place you could do it all, gambling, drugs, prostitution, you name it.

And all with a veneer of respectability about it.

But if your tastes craved something darker, something taboo and off limits, there was something for everyone down in the basement clubs and fetish bars in the Necropolis Precinct. Down there you could find just about anything, do just about anything.

That is, as long as you had the money.

The Mark I'm following likes going there, a lot. For the last few days he's been staying in one of the upmarket hotels near the Sphinxes forecourt.

He's done the same thing every day since he arrived. Up early, business and meetings throughout the day. Then dinner. Always alone, always in his room at the hotel. After that he hits the casinos.

He likes to gamble, so he plays up and down the strip until he cashes out and seeks some very private and very expensive entertainment.

Tonight, we're in the VIP room of the Menkaure Grand. He's been coming here a lot. Don't ask me why; it looks like every other high-rollers room to me. Opulent surroundings. Playing tables. A bar. In fact, the only thing that's different between here and every other fucking place is the theme of the decor and the names of the high-class prostitutes who float around the room.

The Mark likes to play high stakes cards. From what I can tell he's not very good at it. But tonight, he's been winning, and the shit-eating grin he's wearing keeps getting bigger and bigger.

He's on a lucky streak.

They say there's only one thing that's sure about luck: it will change. And I'm betting that his will, and soon.

He sits at the high-rollers table across the room from me, flanked by three high-priced security guards. The guards all look the same, you can pick them from a mile away. Overly large, menacing and tall, each squeezed into a tight suit, their physiques grotesquely enhanced by cheap implants and hormone treatments. You can see the watermarks on the side of their necks, probably from some black-market surgery in the back streets of Seoul.

They scowl as they scan the crowd. But what they're looking for is beyond me. I've been following them since they left Tokyo, and so far, they haven't noticed me at all.

The key to following a Mark is blending in. Keeping a low profile. Never being seen. I look like everyone else, like every person you've ever known. Utterly forgettable. You can hide in plain sight if you don't stand out. That's why I always lose when I gamble. No one notices a loser. And in my line of work anonymity is the key.

I don't draw attention and I don't look like a threat.

But I am.

I'm the most dangerous fucking person you'll ever meet.

If his bodyguards were worth their salt, they'd know this. They'd have insisted that he only goes to a casino that scanned everyone in the room with a proper system. A military system. Something that could pick up DNA alteration. Augmented nervous systems. Cellular enhancement.

Because if they did that, then they'd know that I'm jacked to the limit.

But this casino only scanned for weapons. And I don't need a weapon. I am the weapon.

If they were better at their jobs, they'd know that too.

And their boss would be safe tonight.

I watch him gamble until he starts to lose interest. You can see that he's got something on his mind, there's a spark in his eye. He's thinking about where he's going next. What he's going to do. He's distracted. Then he starts to lose. He gets frustrated, then he gets angry, and he starts to lose more. It's not long before he motions for the dealer to cash him out.

Then they're on the move.

I watch them disappear into one of the elevators. I finish playing my hand and follow them up the sixty-five floors to the surface.

The lobby of the Menkaure Grand looks tacky and cheap, designed to look like some kind of futuristic pyramid with walls of glass and sandstone. It's supposed to mirror the ancient structure standing nearby. But it doesn't. It's soulless. Just like this city.

Out on the street the night is hot, stifling, it feels like the air is getting sucked out of my lungs. The desert wind is strong and stings my face. The sky above is cloudy and a menacing shade of green.

It looks like it might rain.

I walk out just in time to see the Mark and his entourage disappear around the corner. They're walking to the elevated tube a few blocks away. There are no vehicles in New Cairo. Ground or aerial. It doesn't really matter because you don't need one here, the casinos and restaurants are all linked by an underground tube system. In fact, some visitors come to New Cairo and never come up to the surface at all during their stay.

That is, unless you want to visit the Necropolis Precinct.

It isn't part of the tube system. It is on the far side of town where the workers live, isolated from the family friendly subterranean megastructures like some dirty little secret. If you want to get there you have to take the elevated tube that loops around the city.

That means you have to walk.

I tail them. The streets are brightly lit, alive with sound and colour. Tourists crowd the walkways, milling around the little shop fronts and eateries. There is a buzz of excitement in the air. Bright holographic advertisements dance and spin overhead among the high-rise canyons, while others jump out from billboards along the footpath, spruiking to everyone who passed.

In the distance, the outlines of the pyramids can be seen against the neon sky.

I keep my distance, invisible among the crowds. I watch them as they make their way into the station, then join the steady stream of people going through the entrance, the cool embrace of the environmental control system a welcome respite from the sweltering heat.

Upstairs the tube platform is crammed with people all politely trying to ignore one another in the uncomfortable throng. Most of them are locals, workers at the hotels and the casinos. They look tired and irritated. The others are tourists. Men mostly on their way to the Necropolis. They don't look tired. Or bored. They look nervous. They keep their eyes on the ground, like they don't want to be seen.

The Mark and his bodyguards stand at one end of the platform, I make my way down to the other. After less than a minute, a gust of wind blows across the crowd and a sleek, bullet-shaped train emerges from the tube. The automatic doors hiss open and I join the press, finding a place to stand near the back of the carriage. I can't see the Mark anymore, but I know he doesn't look tired or bored or even nervous.

He looks excited.

The train passes four stations before it arrives at the Necropolis. By then, the passengers have thinned out some. I make my way onto the platform and linger around a vending machine. I see the Mark and his men pass by, and when they're far enough away, I follow them out onto the street.

Outside it has started to rain. Big, thick droplets fall from the sky. In the heat of the night, steam rises from the road. Homeless drunks line the street. Bars with garish neon signs and pornographic holograms beckon. The reek of misery is heavy in the air.

The Necropolis Precinct is a dangerous place.

A place that can swallow you whole and spit out your bones the next morning, bleached white and stripped clean. And that suits me just fine because no one here gives a fuck when accidents happen.

People die every day in the Necropolis Precinct.

Ahead, they turn down an alley, taking a shortcut. The Mark walks in front, the three guards behind.

That's sloppy.

It leaves the client exposed. They should have a protection formation. In fact, they should never have let him go down this alley to begin with.

That's just stupid.

They're about halfway down the alley when I round the corner. The alley is dark and they're nothing more than silhouettes. But I can see them, clear as day. I want them to hear me coming, my footsteps get their attention. The bodyguard closest notices me first.

The others will soon enough.

The bodyguard stops walking and glances back at me. He's blank for a split second, then realises what's about to happen. A look of surprise comes over his face and he reaches into the front of his jacket for his gun.

It is a Margolin A-12 automatic pistol. Standard sidearm for the Russian military. With an extended magazine, it can fire one hundred rounds of accelerated projectiles per second.

I wait for him to raise it, moving close enough to see the panic in his eyes as he realises he's about to die. I grab his wrist with my left hand, pushing back his gun arm as I simultaneously stomp on the back of his knee with my right foot.

He falls forward and lets out a cry.

I apply enough force to his gun arm to rupture his elbow backwards. I pop the joint with my right forearm, the bone shatters and folds back at an unnatural angle. His arm breaks with a satisfying crunch and I aim the gun at the guard behind him, compacting the median nerve in his wrist with my thumb. This sends his index finger into spasm, firing the weapon in his hand.

The high-velocity projectiles pass through the second guard's head like a hot knife through butter and he's dead before he even hears the gunshot.

I finish the first guard with a palm strike to the nose, his screams ending abruptly as his septum penetrates his frontal lobe.

And I'm moving before the bodies hit the ground.

The Mark and the other guard look back. The guard tells the Mark to run and draws his weapon. His neural implants have jacked his nervous system.

He's fast. But he's not as fast as me.

He fires one burst which I evade with ease. Then I'm on him. I finish him with three quick blows before he realises what's happening.

The first ruptures his diaphragm. The second breaks his trachea. The third fractures his skull and causes a small bleed in the right hemisphere of his brain, resulting in a fatal haemorrhage.

It is over in less than a second.

Ahead the Mark runs. But he doesn't get far.

I close the distance between us with ease, my legs feel like steel coils, my adrenalin white light bursting through every muscle fibre in my body.

I cripple him with a knee to the spine, but I place it just right, so he'll still feel what's coming.

Then I stand over him like a fucking nightmare.

He begs me not to, says he doesn't deserve it. Says he'll give me whatever I want. They all say this. They all deserve it. From what I've read about him, he deserves a lot more than most.

I finish him and it's a mess.

The whole thing takes less than ten seconds. I'm out the alley and walking down the street in fifteen.

I'm a ghost.

Any evidence will be untraceable. There are no witnesses. I've got no fingerprints and any DNA I've left behind will degrade in less than a minute. The identity scans the AIs have done since I arrived in New Cairo will all be useless. Surveillance footage, travel bookings, hotel records are all in the name of Thomas L. Booker. By the time I walk out of this alley and down the street, I've already reprogramed my IdentityChip.

I'm already someone else.

My name is Cyanide Jones, but for now, I'm Douglas Edwards.

Who knows who I'll be tomorrow...?

3.

Meat Puppet.

I feel like a fucking caged animal. Restless like a predator in a zoo pacing back and forth along the bars.

I'm in a rented room on the island of Berlin.

I'm alone except for the cockroaches. There's lots of them. The room is bare except for an unmade bed and a table and chair that have seen better days. On the table is an empty container of junk food and a half-drunk bottle of sake.

There's only one window in the room. Coloured lights from the city below cast long shadows across the walls.

I've been here too long. I need another job, but for the moment I'm laying low.

For the last three months, my name's been Alexander Wexler. The last job I did didn't go so well. The Global Job. There was backlash after I retired the targets.

About a year ago Space and Planetary Mining, better known as SPM, hired a team of corporate raiders to hit communications giant P2P Global at their headquarters in Nuuk, Greenland.

They were attempting to abduct an executive named Peter Townes.

As a cover for the operation they let off an experimental, hallucinogenic gas called 25-NB inside the company headquarters. The gas was a concentrated psychotropic designed by the Chinese military for release in outdoor urban areas, like streets and squares and parks, to disorientate entrenched enemy forces. 25-NB gas was never meant to be used inside.

The team released three canisters of 25-NB into the ventilation system. In its condensed form the gas caused the employees in the building to have a shared psychotic break, resulting in mass murders within the complex. WGC Security Androids were eventually dispatched to control the situation.

They had to use lethal force.

Over three thousand people ended up dying.

After the massacre I was hired by P2P Global to find the organisers of that raid and hold them accountable. I used the identity Jean-Baptiste Dufour. They gave me the names of seven SPM executives including the CFO of Northern Hemisphere Operations.

I retired them all.

After the last one, a kill-on-sight bounty was placed on Jean-Baptiste Dufour's head.

I've had assassins hunting me ever since.

It's not a big deal, in fact it's part of the job. But the agency told me to take a holiday anyway, just till things settle down.

So, I came to Berlin and rented this hotel room.

In my line of work, it's just a series of hotels room. It's not a good idea to have a place you call home.

It's too dangerous.

When you're a hitman you move around from place to place, identity to identity, killing time till the next job comes in. In between you're left alone with yourself. Just you and all your ghosts.

I take another swig from the bottle and I let the rice wine slide down my throat in a warm wave.

I need to get out of here.

I stand up and walk across to the cramped little bathroom. The light comes on as I walk in, flickering and yellow. There's an energy crisis. Nothing works properly anymore. I place my hands on either side of the sink and lean forward staring into the mirror.

I don't recognise my reflection. My skin looks pallid in the sickly light and beads of sweat trickle here and there from my brow. My eyes are dark and wild. I look like a junkie from all the booze and the drugs.

I feel anxious, strung out.

I splash water on my face, hoping to wash away the dark tide that's turning in my head.

They call it Imbedded Identity Disorder whatever the fuck that means.

Back when I was in the army, the doctors at Project Daybreak told me the condition was common for people who spent time in re-education camps. They said identity rejection, memory loss and psychotic episodes were all side effects of prolonged artificial intelligence indoctrination. They said it was especially bad if the subject had been the recipient of extensive genetic alteration like I had.

That's fine with me. I don't want to remember anyway.

I open up the medicine cabinet and I notice my hands are shaking. There's a small orange tab dispenser sitting on the shelf. I grab it and press it against my wrist.

Nothing.

I press again.

Nothing.

"Mother fucker."

My body shakes, the frustration and the anxiety mixes with the rage like some cheap and terrible cocktail. I throw the dispenser at the grease-stained wall and it shatters into a million tiny pieces.

"Gotta have more here somewhere," I growl to myself.

I pull the rest of the cabinet apart, tossing the contents on the floor then move to the small table beside my bed. There's an empty dispenser there too.

And another on the floor.

"Fuck."

After Project Daybreak they used to prescribe us meds. Anti-psychotics. Personality stabilisers. Memory inhibitors. But that was a long time ago. These days I have to improvise and make do with the shit I can buy on the streets.

I need to get out of here. I need to get some more.

I grab my jacket and a gun I've stashed beside the bed.

Outside, it's sweltering and even though it's late the sidewalk is packed with people. I head north, up towards the levies.

The sickly-sweet smell of simmering garbage hangs heavy in the air.

I've been living in the Prenzlauer Berg District. It's the seedy side of Berlin, the red-light district up towards the northern edge of the levies. The buildings are all identical around here, dull grey nanocrete high rises each one covered in graffiti and splashed with holograms and bright neon advertising.

I walk, hands in pockets, scanning the faces of the people that pass me by.

Anyone of them could be working. Anyone of them could be looking for Jean-Baptiste Dufour. But I know they're not going to find him. Any trace of Jean-Baptiste Dufour disappeared that night in New York three months ago.

Now, he's just a ghost.

The streets are lined with meat market fetish shops, hole-in-the-wall drug dens and cheap body alteration clinics that people go into but don't always come out of.

Not in one piece anyway.

Synthetic beats scream from the basement bars. Their neon stairwells are littered with wasted androgynous clubbers with dyed white hair and eyes, all so fucked on dust they can barely sway to the music. Above automated drones and sleek bullet-like cars whine loudly as they streak through the air clouding the night sky like swarms of insects.

Two blocks up I can see the flood wall looming. I walk faster. The city is much smaller now. When the seas rose the water swallowed most of Europe. They saved what they could of Berlin, erecting levies around the city centre, but it cost too much to save it all.

I head up one of the side streets off the main road. The power is bad around here and the street lights are dull. Every now and then they flicker bright then go dim, browning out from the power shortage.

After few blocks I find who I'm looking for.

They're perched along the wall near a back alley like a murder of crows; greased back hair, high-waisted pants, black bio-fabricated leather boots and jackets emblazoned with fascist symbols and hate slogans. They're all heavily surgically modified, their faces plastered with thick makeup. They call themselves die Bewegung, the Movement a street gang that sprung out of Berlin's underground industrial fuzz movement almost a decade ago. These days die Bewegung are everywhere, especially in the poorer parts of the city. They are known for their overzealous use of ultra-violence, aggressive xenophobia and trade of exotic and very illegal drugs.

Dust in particular.

A couple of them notice as I come up the block towards them but they've seen me before so they don't fuck with me. Still, they size me up as I pass regarding me with an almost callous indifference.

One of them mutters something as I turn into the alley, I almost want him to try something. It's been a while since I fucked somebody up.

The alley is a grey-walled canyon. It's covered in gang tags and the distant sound of screaming echoes between the buildings. I see Katze, my dealer, about half a block down. He's standing talking with a group of his die Bewegung friends. There's more of them up in the alley to my right. They're beating the shit out of some poor fucker who's screaming and begging for mercy.

That's a word die Bewegung don't seem to understand.

Katze nods when he sees me. He has no eyelids or ears. His face is patterned with fluorescent white lines.

"So bald wieder zurück?" Katze asks, mocking me.

I nod. Fucking prick. I'd like to break his fingers.

"Wie viele?" His eyes bulge obscenely as he talks. Die Bewegung speak their own brand of German.

I hold up my hand. "Five," I say.

Katze snorts, reaching into his pocket and retrieving a handful of orange tab dispensers.

Methcitalopram-butyrophenzine better known on the streets as dust. It's basically a psychotropic tranquiliser. For most people it brings on a euphoric almost dreamlike state.

But not me, my metabolism's been jacked so I just feel numb.

And that's just fine.

He hands them to me and I grunt thanks. I stash them in my pants pocket then press one against the inside of my wrist. It leaves a small, pinkish clear strip. I watch it intently as it dissolves, absorbing into my skin.

The dust subcutaneously dispenses into my bloodstream.

In a heartbeat I'm numb and the dark tide ebbs back from the shore.

"Sie erkennen, dass verdammte Scheiße Sie töten wird, nicht wahr?" Katze quips.

"Fuck off Katze." My IdentityChip transfers the money to him with a glance.

"Es ist deine Beerdigung, du Junkie-Stück Scheiße."

The sound of the person screaming goes from pain to genuine terror. Katze turns from me without another word and starts towards the alley, shaking his head and shouting. "Fick dich, dieser Schwanz gehört mir."

I join the crowd on the main road. I need a drink but I don't like the bars around here. They're too fucking loud. Too bright.

I head down towards the Mag-Bahn station. The front entrance is still a mess of temporary hoardings from the suicide bombing last week. Some eco-terrorist from DAWN or New Day shot two people, then blew themselves up at the top of the stairs.

There are police androids in black combat armour stationed everywhere.

I follow the steady stream of people down to the subway. On the crowded platform the holograms of two newsreaders shine from a billboard on the opposite side of the track, the resolution so poor they flicker and distort as they speak.

"*...and in other news, could the world-wide power crisis soon be over? Bio-Fuel Industries today reported its fifteenth successful trial of its new Bennetto Reactor. The experimental power station, located off the coast of Greenland, is the first of its kind: a microbial power plant that generates energy from microorganisms like bacteria, delivering what could be an endless supply of clean, free energy to the world. Pranav Chetti, a representative from Bio-Fuel Industries , remained tight lipped about when the new station might come on line but said they were 'cautiously optimistic of launching the technology in the coming months.' Now, for more on our breaking new on the mass shootings in London this evening, we cross to...*"

The news reader stops as the magtrain pulls into the station and opens its doors with a whisper. I follow the crowd on and stand at the doors for the ride, looking out at the blackness of the subway line till we reach Friedrichshain.

Back out on the street, I make my way to a little bar called *Tech Noir* a few blocks from the station. It's quiet and dark inside. A few people sit at the bar, some drinking alone quietly, others with their eyes half-glazed and muttering to whoever they're talking to in some virtual construct online.

I pull up a stool and motion to the bartender.

She knows me from before and brings over a bottle of sake placing it on the bar with two glasses beside it.

She drinks with me. Says it's slow tonight.

She tells me about her life, her friends, how she hates her job but she does it because she saving up to travel. Maybe Russia or Antarctica.

Anywhere that's green, that's her dream she says. To live somewhere that's green.

She asks me what I do for work and I give her the same bullshit cover story I've been saying to people for years.

Corporate resource management.

She thinks it sounds impressive. I tell her it's not.

I listen to her talk, but I'm numb and I'm removed, like my head is packed in cotton wool. Nothing seems to mean anything. There's no connection between me and the outside world. Or maybe I just don't understand or care anymore.

Did I ever?

Later that night, I wake in her bed.

She's asleep beside me and I listen to the sound of her breathing. It's slow and rhythmical. I don't know what I'm doing here. Maybe I wanted to see if I would feel something. But I don't, I don't feel anything. I'm just numb.

I look down at my chest, a myriad of scars and watermarks criss-cross my torso like a roadmap. Her arm is resting across me, fingers curled in mine. I free myself from her embrace quietly and dress moving towards the door.

She opens her eyes as I start to leave.

"Will I see you again?"

I look over my shoulder at her laying there naked beneath the sheets. She's beautiful.

"No."

Then I close the door behind me.

4.

A Short, Sharp Punch to the Nose.

I wake up with screaming in my ears.

I sit up and look around. I don't know where I am or who I am today.

I'm on a king-size bed. The sheets are white and crisp. The room is large and clean and nicely furnished. Light floods in as the black-out tint on the windows brightens automatically.

I'm in an expensive hotel room in London.

My name is Oishi Kosaku. I've been here for three days.

There's a job about to start.

I get up off the bed and go to the bathroom. I stand in front of the mirror and look at my reflection. I don't recognise the face looking back at me. The last few weeks I'm having trouble remembering who I am. Or who I was. Or why I got into this in the first place.

The average lifespan of a corporate head hunter is three years.

I've been doing this for seven.

The orange tab dispenser is where I left it last night, beside the sink. I press it against my wrist, then splash some water on my face to wake up.

I notice there's a message flashing in my peripheral. I wonder how long it's been there.

I glance at the message icon and it opens, the words unfold like a heads up display before my eyes. It's from the agency, Human Resources Management. The message says the new client has made contact. That they're ready to meet. It says they'll pick me up in an hour.

I call down to the lobby and ask them to bring me up a new suit and some breakfast. I shower and shave while I wait. By the time I'm finished, a new black suit, tie and crisp white shirt are laid out on the bed. At the table near the window is a bowl of seaweed congee and a steaming hot cup of black coffee.

I dress then sit down at the table. I go online and pull up a news feed sipping the coffee as I read.

The world market price of Helium-3 soars to a record high.

Another border skirmish between the US and Mexico, this time in the northern Mexican city of San Francisco.

The World Governing Council announces the start of a new carbon sequestration initiative to remove billions of tonnes of CO_2 from the atmosphere.

The hacker group Dead Earth Collective has announced it is releasing sensational information about a criminal cover-up involving Scandinavian Automated Industries, the world's number one producer of androids.

Police are investigating the suicide of Dr Navneet Sardar overnight. Dr Sardar, who was the lead developer of Bio-Fuel Industries' new Bennetto Reactor, was found dead in his home after co-workers reported he failed to turn up for work. Insiders are saying it could delay the power plant coming on-line for months.

This story gets my attention, I read it again. It's a corporate hit. You don't have to read between the lines to see the truth. It's as plain as day.

A message from the lobby flashes in my peripheral.

People here to see me, waiting at the front desk. I tell them to send them up and finish my coffee while I wait.

A few minutes later there's a knock at the door. I open it. Three figures stand in the hall, a man and two androids. The man is polished, expensive suit, tanned skin, a generic handsomeness that only be achieved by the best cosmetic surgery. He smiles easily and offers his hand.

"Mr Kosaku? My name's William Bailey."

I glance back at the two androids flanking him. They look the same. Same height, same black shark-like eyes, same expressionless faces. They both wear identical black work-suits, caps pulled low over slick, bald craniums.

"I'm the executive assistant to Mr Jensen Gördel, the European head of corporate security at SPM."

The company's name puts me on edge, instantly.

The Global Job.

I shake his hand. The androids scan me up and down, their emotionless eyes windows to the intelligence behind them. You see, androids don't operate by themselves. They aren't autonomous. They are linked to an artificial intelligence. Right now their neural processors are sending my information to their company AI who is busy analysing my IdentityChip and cross matching it with all the information they have on me.

SPM had a lot on me. None of it was good.

But they don't necessarily know that. The identity I used when I killed their executives was Jean-Baptiste Dufour. They don't know my real name. The agency told them they were meeting Oishi Kosaku. And as far as they know, that's who I am.

At least I hope so.

"If you're ready, we'll to escort you to our headquarters here in London so you can meet with Mr Gördel in person. He has a business proposal he'd like to discuss with you." William Bailey smiled. It was like the smile a serial killer might flash to a child he was trying to lure with candy.

"Give me a minute," I say.

I walk to the bathroom and retrieve the orange tab dispenser and the Zen-9 I've stashed in the vanity. Then I walk out to the hall and close the door behind me. Anything that I've left behind, I don't need.

I'm never coming back here again. Not as Oishi Kosaku anyway.

I follow them to the elevator. We wait in silence, then file in. We're going to the parking lot up on the roof. It's an uncomfortable silence, William Bailey standing in front of me facing the doors, the two androids either side staring blankly ahead into space thinking whatever digital thoughts they thought.

I've never liked androids, I don't trust them.

Ten years ago, the only thing they were good for was work deemed too hazardous for humans. Cleaning up toxic waste. The ground-zero nuclear sites in the Middle East and Africa. That kind of shit. It wasn't until after that massacre in Paris at the food riots by those government troops that some genius had the idea to remove human error from our global police force. Now everyone has them, governments, big business, you name it. Armies of soulless androids all controlled by artificial intelligence.

The elevator doors open onto to the roof and the harsh morning light. I put on my glasses and follow them out into the scorching heat. It's like a furnace. It must be forty degrees and it's not even ten in the morning.

I follow them through the rows of parked cars until we reach a black, sleek Berg Motors AG-3 sedan. A detachment of androids stands near the vehicle, staring vacantly. They snap to attention as we approach and one opens the car doors. I'm ushered into the back where I sit flanked by two of the androids. Bailey sits up the front with another one.

"The SPM offices aren't far, Mr Kosaku. Please, make yourself comfortable and enjoy the flight."

I don't reply. I keep my eyes straight ahead. I look relaxed, but I'm not.

I'm thinking about the Global Job.

A low hum rises from the engines and the vehicle makes a smooth, fast ascent. It reaches cruising altitude and continues to accelerate, making a long, arching turn and merging with the dense air traffic above the city.

Outside the window the city of London sprawls.

Hundreds of skyscrapers and spires shimmer like glass fingers in the morning haze. Great archologies tower above the mass around them, the superstructures dwarfing the city and climbing high into the heavens above. Off in the distance, beyond the massive levies holding back the Thames, are the slums of Westminster. The twin, dark grey public housing cubes Thatcher and Churchill rise out of the surrounding ghetto like two brutalist megaliths.

The car merges onto the A41 flightpath towards the city centre.

It banks left as it approaches our destination, the vehicle accelerating and soaring high into the air above the surrounding traffic. In the distance is the SPM archology, home of the world largest mining conglomerate, Space and Planetary Mining. The most powerful company on the planet.

The incredible hyper structure looms over the city. The top is so tall that clouds seem to cling to the spires of its massive crown. The car ascends up to a large circular landing platform that juts out from the façade of the superstructure.

The vehicle slows, then hovers above the platform before landing smoothly. There's a security detachment of SPM androids standing in two orderly lines waiting to meet us. William Bailey turns around and smiles.

"Here we are Mr Kosaku, if you'll follow me please."

We cross the landing platform and enter the building. The security detachment falls in around us, leading the way through an identification checkpoint. They scan me and confiscate my gun, then lead me down to a set of double doors at the very end of the hall.

The ornately carved spruce doors open automatically as we approach and I'm escorted inside the office.

The room is opulent, lavish. Floor-to-ceiling windows with a panoramic view of the city. A magnificent, polished chestnut desk with dark growth rings that radiate out over the surface like ripples across a pond. A dark polymer data strip with the ominous red glow of an artificial intelligence behind it.

And behind the desk is a slender man.

He is seated in a massive, black-buttoned leather winged chair, it wraps around him like the leather wings of a bat. The man seems totally engrossed in a large, immersive reality blueprint that shines from the desktop. He is dressed in an expensive, black three-piece suit with immaculately groomed hair and moustache. His face has been cosmetically altered to the point that it is hard to determine his age or nationality.

"Mr Gördel. Mr Kosaku is here to see you."

William Bailey waits for him to respond.

Gördel looks up and smiles, the tense skin around his mouth curling back hideously. He dismisses the display with a wave of his hand and stands up, walking around the desk.

"You're here, good I am glad you could join me this morning, please, sit." Gördel speaks in a soft, measured voice. He motions to one of the plush leather chairs.

If he knows I'm the one that retired their executives he's hiding it well.

"Thanks," I reply. I'm uneasy despite his relaxed manner. If he didn't know it was me who killed their men, is it just a coincidence that I'm here now?

"Can I offer you something? A refreshment?"

"No."

Gördel clears his throat.

"Well, I must say, you come highly recommended from your agency Mr Kosaku..."

I cut him off.

"Let's move past the formalities Mr Gördel. I'm sure you're a busy man."

He smiles that ugly smile again and looks up at William Bailey. "You may leave us."

William Bailey and the android detachment make their way from the room, leaving two standing guard at the door. That means they haven't brought me here to kill me. All the same I pass my eyes across the room and check the exit points, just in case things go south and I need to get out of here fast.

"I appreciate your directness." Gördel leans against his desk looking at me intently, like a child looking at a bug under a microscope. "Tell me, have you ever heard the name Xander Odom before, Mr Kosaku?"

"In the news. She an activist, part of that climate change group DAWN."

"She's an extremist, Mr Kosaku. The leader of a militant, terrorist organisation."

He looks at me with contempt, as though he has a bad taste in his mouth.

"DAWN has been staging protests and disrupting our company operations for years. For the most part we've ignored them. That is until Miss Odom took over the group's leadership two years ago. Since then DAWN's activities have become increasing violent. They claimed responsibility for the sinking of a mining fleet off the coast of Japan last year. They were behind the raid on the SPM offices in Moscow, which saw fifteen employees killed and a R&D laboratory burnt to the ground. Then last month they infiltrated and destroyed the deep space mining vessel, *Anastasia,* as a protest for our recent operations in the Republic of Canada."

I don't reply.

Gördel pauses and smiles at me. He's building to something. "We would like you to kidnap her."

I don't answer straight away. I wasn't expecting that. Kidnapping's risky business, it rarely ends well.

"Why not just kill her? It's easier."

Gördel shakes his head and clears his throat. I look him in the eyes. There's more to this.

"We want to make an example of Miss Odom. In public. Hand her over to the authorities and have her tried in court. If she's imprisoned for her crimes, we believe it will act as a deterrent for any future action that DAWN plans against the company."

Bullshit. They're going to torture her to death. The poor fucker will probably be on the menu at their next company retreat.

"We have information that leads us to believe Miss Odom is currently hiding in New Chechnya, an old mining habitat on the Moon."

He's lying. I'm used to that, it's part of the job. I just don't know why.

"So why do you need me?" I look back over at the androids standing near the door. "Send some of those things. I'm sure you've got enough to spare."

Gördel pauses and smiles thinly at me. "Believe me, we've already tried that Mr Jones." You can tell he's not used to explaining himself. That he doesn't like it. "Unfortunately, there is a complication. The New Chechnya facility used to be an SPM mine, hydrogen mainly. We built a city around it for the workers and encased it in an atmospheric dome."

As he speaks, the immersive reality projector in his desk begins to project surveillance images of New Chechnya taken from orbit. It looked bleak. Brutalist buildings built around an expansive, circular open-pit mine that gaped like maelstrom on the edge of the city.

"Unfortunately, the mine was depleted five years ago and the site was abandoned. It was left derelict and like most abandoned cities it became a haven for criminal gangs and refugees. New Chechnya is now under the control of the Bratstvo crime syndicate."

Gördel pauses as he adjusts his tie. The Bratstvo is the largest organised crime enterprise the world. They're fucking animals.

"This man to be precise."

The picture of New Chechnya disappears, replaced by an image of a man. Dark, angry eyes, heavy brow, a thick black beard. Deep scars crisscrossed his face.

I knew it immediately.

"Drago Afanasievich. Are you familiar, Mr Kosaku?"

"Yes."

"He has a rather brutal reputation."

Brutal is an understatement. The stories I've heard about him are fucking evil.

"The Bratstvo control everything and everyone that goes in and out of New Chechnya. We believe Xander Odom has a deal with them for protection. A week ago, we sent a team of corporate professionals, just like yourself, up to New Chechnya. We understand Mr Afanasievich had them skinned before he crucified them."

Images of the team flash up from his desk. I try to my control my reaction.

"We believe sending one person to do the job will prove far more effective."

There's still something I don't like about this.

"We would like you to infiltrate the facility, subdue Miss Odom and get her out before anyone notices. A single agent should be able to move around undetected, without arousing suspicion."

Something feels off.

"After you abduct Odom, we will have a ship meet you outside the city. The operation should only take a day. Two at most." Gördel tries to raise his eyebrows but that horrible fucking look remains on his face.

"How much?"

"We discussed the payment of your usual fee with the agency. Do you have another figure in mind?"

I stare at Gördel.

"Sounds dangerous. Double it."

Jensen Gördel is silent for a moment before a tight smile spreads across his plastic face.

"Alright, double it is." He laughs a high-pitched laugh that sounds like fingernails on a chalkboard.

5.

Bacterium Electrum

Ever heard of Nikola Tesla before?

No? Maybe the name's familiar but you can't figure out why?

Well, Tesla was an inventor who lived a couple of hundred years ago. He figured out how to harness the Earth's radiant energy and transmit it wirelessly around the world.

That's free, clean energy, literally generated out of thin air.

Problem was that his invention didn't produce all that much electricity. So, Tesla went bankrupt and died before he could develop the technology and the human race used fossil fuels to run all of its machinery.

Which started us on our path to totally fucking the world.

He also invented a death ray, but that's another story.

How about Michael Cressé Potter or Barnett Cohen?

No idea? Well, you're not alone, most people wouldn't have a fucking clue who they are either. They're the guys who first came up with the idea of microorganism electrical generation and the microbial fuel cell.

It sounds like bullshit, but the science isn't all that hard to understand. There are certain species of bacteria that live in oxygen-deprived environments. And in order to survive these microbes need to breathe. Without going into the whole evolution thing, the bacteria evolved a unique form of respiration that involves excreting electrons. In other words, they produce electricity to breath.

Problem is they don't generate all that much. So, just like Tesla's radiant energy, the tech never really got off the ground.

Until Dr Zheng Gengxin came along. He genetically enhanced the bacteria, then cross bred four separate microorganisms with high electrochemical activity to create a whole new species of microbe.

Bacterium Electrum.

Unlike the other electricity producing bacteria, these things are powerful. Really powerful. They're like the fucking Energiser Bunny. And when a decillion or so of them are concentrated into huge fuel cells they produce enough electricity to power a small country.

And the best bit is it uses wastewater as fuel. Free, abundant, and totally eco-friendly.

This is the technology that powers Bio-Fuel Industries new Bennetto Reactor.

The invention that may very well save what's left of this shitty planet.

You see, these days the energy industry is fucked. We're completely reliant on fusion power. Sure, it's clean but it's expensive. Unbelievably expensive. But it wasn't always. In fact, it wasn't so long ago that everyone was saying fusion power was going to save the world.

Back when climate change swallowed up a good portion of the earth, it was a wake-up call for government and big business. Not because they cared about fucking the planet or killing millions of people. It was a wake-up call because it was impossible to deny global warming with half the fucking world either burning to the ground or a metre under water.

People were out for blood, so companies who had raped and pillaged the planet for money had to change majorly... especially if they still wanted to keep on raping and pillaging for money.

This meant something big needed to happen.

Something that would change the world forever.

The SSR Fusion Reactor.

A physicist named Dr Henriette Boisselot, who worked for the Russian energy giant Energon, was the first to achieve a clean fusion reaction using the isotope Helium-3 as fuel.

This was a game changer. Clean, cheap power for everyone. Soon every nation in the world was vying to get the next Energon SSR Reactor built in their country. The demand was overwhelming.

So Energon did something very clever.

They never actually sold a reactor to a country. Instead, they built the reactors themselves then sold the power it created. So, Energon controlled every fusion power plant on the planet. And every one of those reactors was powered by Helium-3 mined exclusively by the newly formed international conglomerate, Space and Planetary Mining.

Soon Energon and SPM became the two biggest companies on Earth. They controlled the world's economy.

But there was a problem. You see Helium-3 is not all that common on Earth, not like on the Moon or gas giants like Saturn or Jupiter. So, when it started running out, mining had to go off-world.

And the prices went with it.

It wasn't long before power became the most expensive commodity on the planet. And if you were a poorer nation and you complained about the price the answer was pretty simple.

Fuck you.

Energon would scale back production in their reactors in your country for a day or two. Bring one of your major cities to a grinding halt.

Got a problem with that? Well, maybe SPM would stop supply of Helium-3 for a week. Blackout the entire country.

See what happens then.

When entire nations were bankrupted by the two power giants, the rest stopped complaining.

But even in a world as entirely fucked up as ours, companies committing this type of blatant extortion couldn't get away with it forever. And when we transitioned to an international government, the newly formed World Governing Council finally put a stop to it.

Well, kind of.

They charged Energon and SPM for breaching corporate anti-trust laws and held these huge public trials that were broadcast across the planet. In the end Energon was found guilty and dismantled, the company assets were seized and became public property, allowing the World Governing Council to build and maintain SSR Fusion reactors across the globe.

For free.

And for a moment the world breathed easy. But it wasn't for long.

You see SPM had grown too big and too powerful to prosecute successfully. Their infrastructure controlled most of the resources both here and off-world and even the combined power of the world's governments couldn't bring them into line.

So, the prices just kept going up and up. And nobody could do anything about it.

Nowadays power is rationed in most major cities on Earth. Bad news is SPM is now saying that the Moon is running out of Helium-3 and prospecting operations will need to commence of Mars and Jupiter.

Fuck knows how expensive that's going to be.

6.

Motion Sickness.

The key to killing someone is to never make it personal.

Treat it like a job. A business. Never get too close to the Mark. Never see them as a real person. Remember they're a target. Nothing more.

Compartmentalise. Disassociate. Be indifferent.

It's the first thing you learn. Otherwise, you might lose your nerve. Otherwise, you might not pull the trigger.

I look out the window.

The stormy sky looks sickly. It's orange and grey and lightning flashes ominously every now and then. Beneath it, hundreds of automated ships cut through the white-capped swells.

I'm on a commercial flight from London to the International Space Elevator. It's the first stop on the way to the Moon.

I got on this transport not long after leaving Gördel's office. His instructions were pretty vague. Go to Tycho City on the Moon, get a room at the Pawit Hotel in Little Siam and wait.

For what I didn't know.

I booked passage on the next flight. But I didn't get on board until I'd spoken to the agency and confirmed SPM's money was in my account.

I didn't like this job.

Kidnapping the Mark for whatever sick pleasure they had in mind left a bad taste in my mouth. If you want someone dead, you kill them. Simple. I don't go in for this torture shit.

I'm not a psychopath.

But there's something else though. Something more they're not telling me.

I can feel it.

In the distance is the Tsiolkovsky Marina. It's the anchor point for the International Space Elevator, a floating city four hundred kilometres off the Brazilian coast. The seaport is an interconnected collection of seascrapers that submerged hundreds of stories below the ocean. It's surrounded by crowded shipping lanes and docks that pin wheel around the flotilla. In the centre of it all is the space elevator.

And it's tall. I mean really, fucking tall.

The biggest thing humans have ever built. A nanite-reinforced graphene cable attached to an orbiting space station. It stretches up from the colossal city and out of the atmosphere, thirty-six thousand kilometres above. Four high-velocity mechanical lifters are attached to the cable, climbing up and down on a loop, twenty-four hours a day.

"Excuse me sir," the android attendant tones.

I tear my gaze from the window and look back at it. Black, soulless eyes. Smooth, expressionless face.

I fucking hate androids.

"We're coming into land soon."

It motions to the tumbler of sake that sits untouched on the table in front of me. I swallow the mellow fire in a gulp and hand it the glass, then look back out the window as we come into land.

The first thing that strikes me when I get off the plane is the heat. And the wind.

Even though I'm walking on a sealed skybridge between the transport and the marina, I can feel the heat. It's oppressive. I can hear the wind. It buffets the flimsy polymer tube with violent gusts.

I can tell I'm at the equator.

As I join the line for customs, I glance out of the skybridge portal at the crowded docks. Robot lifters and androids toil in the heat, loading and unloading the giant automated cargo ships. It must have been sixty-five degrees out there. Maybe more. If a human walked outside without the proper protection, you'd collapse in five minutes.

Be dead in ten.

The customs lines move slowly. Sixty lanes of passengers, each passing one by one through an intelligence data strip.

AI GAGARIN was charged with interplanetary customs.

The intelligence performs manifest and cargo inspections while simultaneously compiling facial recognition scans, retina checks and IdentityChip information on millions of commuters and shipping containers as they move on- and off-world. As each person passes through the data strip, the AI accesses their personal records, recording everything from the clothes they wear to collecting fares from their bank accounts, scanning for weapons and possible criminal or terrorist activity.

The whole process is instantaneous, efficient, and impossibly accurate.

I reach the front of the line. Beyond the data strips are immigration booths manned by security androids. Another heavily armed compliment stands nearby dressed in sky blue World Governing Council uniforms.

I watch as a man in a white hat standing a few people in front of me is flagged by the intelligence as he passes through the data strip. The security androids detain him quickly.

"You can't do this," he yells. "I didn't do anything wrong."

The androids just look at him blankly. May as well be yelling at a toaster. He keeps protesting as the squad leads him away for questioning.

"You can't just detain me for no reason at all," he shouts. "This isn't right."

He was right. It wasn't. All it took was knowing the wrong person. Accessing the wrong information. Any anomaly will put you on their radar.

Ahead, a blonde woman with a large tattoo of a koi on her neck finishes at the booth in front of me.

I'm ushered through the scanner, then stand in front of the immigration android. I have more to hide than most. But I've got help. You have to be extremely resourceful to fool the system. And extremely well-funded.

"Name?" It tones.

"Oishi Kosaku."

"Destination?"

"Tycho City."

"State the reason for your trip."

"Business."

It waits for me to elaborate.

"I work for HantuDunia. We're currently updating the Immersive Reality boards in the city centre."

"Duration of your stay?"

"A week."

It looks at me with its dead eyes, silent for a moment. It was processing.

"I hope you have a pleasant journey, sir."

Fucking androids.

I make my way to the departure lounge. It's busy. "The next elevator will be leaving in thirty minutes," a voice chimes.

I get a cup of coffee and I sit and wait. I watch the people in the lounge. Business people. Families. Young couples. Most of them seem excited, chatting mindlessly with each other. I watch them all with indifference.

I always feel alone in a crowd.

There's something about the pack mentality they share that makes me uneasy. There's a compulsion they all seem to possess to force themselves and their opinions on anyone unfortunate enough to be in earshot. I don't understand why. I come to these kinds of places when I'm not working. Public places. Parks, train stations, airports. Anywhere where there's people.

But I never feel connected.

I finish my coffee and watch for the man in the white hat, the one from customs. But he never appears.

The elevator gates open and the passengers file in. Inside looks like a large, windowless hanger fitted out like a commercial plane. It's beige and drab. Spaced out across the floor are a thousand seats for the passengers, each fully reclining and fitted out to help combat the crushing inertia.

The elevator makes the thirty-six-thousand-kilometre trip in two hours.

I make my way to my seat and wait for the automated attendant to strap me in and administer the anti-nausea meds. I don't need them, but I take them anyway.

Always blend in.

You can hide in plain sight if you don't stand out.

In my line of work anonymity is the key.

It takes a while for all the passengers to be seated. You can hear the worried cries from the children and nervous travellers.

Regular commuters call the elevator the vomit rocket.

When the elevator is ready an alarm sounds. They clear the floor and close the doors. There is dull hum from below as the fusion lifter powers up, then expectant laughter from some of the passengers. After a few seconds, the lights turn red and the elevator ascends like an express train blasting up from hell.

It's exhilarating and terrifying all at once.

The space elevator accelerates quickly, the G-force compressing you straight back into the chair. It's a shock, you feel like you can't breathe, like there's a crushing weight on your chest. It's enough to make you feel panicked.

Then your body starts to hurt as your organs begin to displace.

Gasps and cries from the passengers. Someone nearby is sick. Someone else is crying. I close my eyes and pretend I'm somewhere else. I've done this before, more times than I'd care to remember. It's part of the boot camp for Antarctician Special Forces.

After a time, the G-force lessens as the elevator leaves the Earth's atmosphere. Then weightlessness. The elevator fills with relieved laughter and inane chatter. Some crying from the children. The automated attendants help clean up the sick.

The rest of the ride is uneventful.

The elevator reaches the orbital transit station. It's like an airport departure lounge in space, cramped and tacky with stale air, a snack bar and souvenir shop. Gaudy carpet on the floor. Moulded polymer chairs. Bubble viewing windows looking out into the black nothingness of space.

A tired voice crackles over the intercom and tells us there's an hour's wait while the cargo from the elevator is loaded onto the ship. I line up and get another coffee, then sit on one of the chairs towards the back of the room.

The mood is different now. Agitated. Anxious. Nobody wants to wait anymore.

Especially in this floating tin can.

I sip my coffee and watch a kid, no more than three or four, playing on the floor with a toy spaceship. His parents sit nearby arguing softly about something. The kid doesn't give a fuck. He doesn't even notice.

Ever watched a child play?

Ever watched them lose themselves in their own minds? There's that moment when their imagination falls down like a veil across their eyes and blocks outside world entirely.

There's something about it. Something nostalgic.

My mind wanders as I watch him play. I think about being a kid. Trips to the beach with my parents and my little sister. Funny how all those memories seem jumbled now. Out of place, like looking at a thousand jigsaw pieces scattered across the floor, most of them upside down and impossible to place where they belong.

I've got no time for nostalgia.

I finish my coffee and leave the cup on the seat as I head to the bathroom. Inside, I turn on the tap and splash water on my face, then retrieve my orange tab dispenser from my jacket pocket and press it against my wrist.

I close my eyes and let the numb wave of dust pump through my system. It's only then I notice the sickly, sour smell of diarrhoea in the room. It fills my nostrils. I spit in the sink in disgust and turn off the tap then head back out into the lounge and wait.

I fucking hate people.

I get on the ship and take my seat. It's near a window, which suits me fine. The man in the seat beside me looks like a businessman, same as me. This suits me too because he's probably commuting for work.

That means no conversation.

Take off is gentle compared to the elevator. The Andromeda Class passenger ship is released from its holdings and fires its engines gradually, building speed while it orbits Earth before sling-shooting to the Moon.

It takes four hours to get there.

I order a sake, sit back in my chair and look out the window. I can see Via Lactea from here, the wheel and spoke orbital habitat spinning in the endlessness that surrounds the Earth. It was the first off-world colony, a paradise in low orbit, built to cater for the hyper-rich. The elite few. Those who had suckered onto the Earth like leeches and drank their fill, then simply detached themselves to wallow and watch the hell they'd created from afar.

Bloated and indifferent.

I think it was Carl Sagan who said, "The universe seems neither benign nor hostile, merely indifferent." I always thought that was true. Doing what I do it helps to believe it.

Compartmentalise. Disassociate. Be indifferent.

I think about Xander Odom again. Never make it personal. It's the first thing you learn. Otherwise, you might lose your nerve.

But they were making it personal. Kidnapping that woman for whatever horrible fucking torture they had in mind seems about as personal as could be.

I drift off without knowing it.

When I wake up, the moon is on the horizon.

7.

Tycho City Blues.

Tycho City is a shithole. It's tacky and cheap. I've never liked coming here.

It was modelled on Venice - you know, the old city that was sinking beneath the ocean hundreds of years before it became the new normal. Some fucking genius had the bright idea to dig all these canals and line them with modernised Venetian Gothic buildings.

It was an eyesore when they made it.

Thirty-five years later it looked even worse. All the canals were dirty, the water green and littered with floating garbage. The hideous buildings were covered in graffiti and plastered with garish holographic advertising. Shanties and makeshift shelters had sprung up and clogged the streets.

And the sky was impossible to look at without feeling uneasy.

You see Tycho City, like all the other cities on the moon, was domed. Meaning, it was constructed under a great big bubble of reinforced silicon. The problem with that is, on the Moon, a day is about a month long. Which means if you live here, you're looking at two weeks of light and two weeks of dark. It's like living in a fucking fishbowl.

Apparently, it's enough to send you crazy.

So, they decided to install fake skies. Fake weather. A sun that rose and set every twenty-four hours. Just like on Earth. The problem with this was, whoever designed the sky made it look like a cheap shit landscape, an over-the-top spectacle of gaudy pastel that unfolded from sunrise to sunset and twinkled into night.

It always got under my skin. May as well pipe in some muzak.

It's afternoon when I walk out of the port into Tycho City. The sky is an obscene mess of gold and scarlet and magenta, with feathered clouds and a heavy orange sun on the horizon.

I fucking hate Tycho City.

People are everywhere, vehicles clog the streets and skies, darting in and out of the towering high rises. The main road is lined with markets and stalls, vendors calling out and accosting everyone that passes with their wares. Huge holographic billboards, flashing lights and projected advertisements are everywhere.

Little Siam is the district next to the port, so I decide to walk.

But there's one stop I need to make on the way to my hotel. You can't take guns on interplanetary flights. With all the AI scans it's too hard to smuggle them. You're not supposed to have one on the Moon either, not unless you're Lunar Security. But they're not that hard to find, not if you know where to look.

And I've got a feeling I'm going to need one.

I move down the busy sidewalk till I hit Little Siam. Thailand was one of the first countries to be hit hard by climate change. A lot of Thai refugees moved off-world during the Exodus, hoping to escape the poverty. But what they found was more of the same.

I take a left down a side street then a right when I hit the canals. The shopfronts along the water are dark and dingy, most boarded up with siding or whatever shit the owners could find laying around. The canal water is like pea soup and filled with garbage and everything smells like sewerage.

Even though it's been a while, I find Thiramon Maneerattana's shop without getting lost. It's a wide, open garage, crowded with filthy, out-of-date work stations and piled spare parts. Loud Thai rock music blares from inside. Thiramon is a mechanic for the city, his garage fixes service robots and street cleaners, shit like that. You only need to look around the city to see why they need so many.

I make my way through the shop towards the tiny office out the back. The workers ignore me. Thiramon's office is poorly lit and stacked with piles of shit on every surface. He sits behind his desk, reclining in his chair with feet on the table and his eyes glazed over like a zombie, totally engrossed in whatever shit he's streaming in his head.

Thiramon Maneerattana is at least seventy years old, with long, wispy white whiskers and thinning hair, his dark brown skin wrinkled like paper. Both of his arms are missing below the elbow and he wears a pair of rusted, robotic prosthetics in their place.

I knock on the door and clear my throat to get his attention. It takes a moment for him to log out of whatever he is watching and he blinks several times before his eyes regain focus.

"Remember me?" I ask.

He nods and smiles. "Mr Fazzina. It's good to see you again."

It's been two years since I was here last. Enzo Fazzina retired a top-level executive from Hoakia after a pay dispute.

"I need a gun," I say.

He motions towards a chair near the desk. I move a box overflowing with parts onto the floor and sit down.

"Guns are hard to get these days. Security is cracking down on imports. Too much terrorism." He stands up and goes through a box on the floor behind his desk, retrieving a metal case. "Very expensive."

Thiramon places the case on his desk and opens it, his metal fingers scratching loudly against the clasps. There are three guns inside. The Margolin A-12 Automatic Pistol, an AKM Needle Gun and the 411 Pitbull Plasma Pistol.

I don't like the Margolin, but the Needle Gun is almost definitely stolen from Lunar Security and probably traceable. The Pitbull has the best stopping power but it's impractical and too hard to handle for close combat.

"I'll take the Margolin," I say, picking it up. "How much?"

"For you, fourteen thousand."

I look at him and shake my head.

"It costs what it costs, Mr Fazzina." He smiles a brown toothed grin and shrugs. "You know that."

"You got ammo?"

He pulls out a box of clips from his draw and places them on the desktop. "Five thousand more."

I pay him. What the fuck else am I going to do? Complain?

I'm tired, so I head to my hotel. As I make my way through the crowded streets, I get the feeling that I'm being followed. I can't see anyone, can't tell for sure, but I can feel it.

Now I'm on edge.

I find the Pawit Hotel without a problem. It's down a busy side street in the heart of Little Siam. Its sign is in Thai and broken and it flickers on and off intermittently. Garbage is piled around the entrance. The building is old and dirty and a sickly shade of green, the façade made of flimsy, moulded polymer with no windows.

The walls are so thin you can see the lights glowing inside.

The walls are so thin you can see the shadows of people moving inside.

The cheap shit dented double doors bang loudly behind me as I walk into the lobby. It smells of piss. The harsh strip-lighting gives the place an institutional feel. It's a shoebox. Nothing more than a couple of old soiled couches and a fake plant near the front desk.

A vagrant snores loudly from an armchair nearby.

I walk up to the front desk. The kid behind it looks like he just got up. He stares off into the distance blankly, eyes glazed and high as a kite.

He's a dusthead. Good to know.

I bang on the desk loudly, which gets his attention.

"I need a room."

He looks at me with red, soggy eyes.

"Uh, yeah... sure..." he sits forward blinking, looking unsure of what exactly is happening. His eyes are unfocused and it takes him a few disorganised moments to speak again. "How long are you planning on staying?"

"I don't know. A day. Maybe more."

This doesn't seem to compute in his drug-hazed mind. He looks irritated and confused.

"Umm, do you have a reservation?"

I glance around at the squalid pit and raise my eyebrows. "Do I need one?"

"Well, no... not really." The clerk scratches the scruffy growth on his chin. "But if you're not gonna tell me how long you're..."

I cut him off and look at him like I'm going to break his nose.

"Give me a fucking room," I growl. "Now."

The clerk's eyes grow wide with fear. He gets me a room.

I check into 105 under the name Oishi Kosaku, then head to the first floor.

There is no lift, only a stairwell.

The hall leading to my room is derelict. Grey linoleum floors are strewn with garbage and debris and a broken light flickers, dangling from its fixture. I can hear people talking as I pass their rooms.

I unlock 105 with my IdentityChip and close the door behind me. The room is dark and cramped. A bed in one corner. Toilet and shower in the other. It reminds me of Berlin.

But worse.

I lie on the bed and close my eyes, but sleep doesn't come right away. I'm still amped up at that clerk. I go online. My home screen appears before my eyes and overlays itself over the room. I need a secure connection, so I encrypt the line then bounce it off networks in three separate cities on the Moon. Once I'm sure there's no hitchhiker piggybacking my connection I remotely log into the agency intelligence, AI BOOTH. Then I open my work server. The agency has already uploaded the file on the Mark.

Xander Odom. Her face appears before me.

Dark eyes. Long dark hair. Surgical watermarks on her neck.

I memorise it.

No information on her family. In fact, no information on her at all till she's sixteen years old. That's strange. She first surfaces in a refugee camp in Northern Italy. Then again in France and Germany. They're fucking dangerous places.

She looks different then. It's obvious she's had extensive reconstructive surgery, but it's not just her face that's different. There's something else. She looks softer and kinder somehow.

Her eyes.

There's not much else on her till she gets involved with New Day. They're a kind of social activist group. You know the type, large scale non-violent protests. Grass-roots political action. The kind of thing a rich kid does to rebel until their parents force them to get a real job.

But not her.

She's the real deal.

There are pictures of her at protests, arm raised in the air as she's arrested at a demonstration outside the Japanese Embassy. Another of her arm-in-arm at a sit-in at some corporate headquarters in Greenland.

She has a spark in her eyes. She's passionate.

Then the European famine hits. She works on the front lines, trying to get aid to those who need it most. Pictures of her at the floods in Germany. Helping refugees after the wildfires that burn most of Eastern France to the ground. Then she's selected as a youth ambassador for New Day and asked to speak at the World Governing Council's headquarters in Örebro.

That's a big deal.

Two days before the speech, she's in Paris when food riots happen.

That changes everything.

Some drunk asshole, a Commander in the World Governing Council Peace Keeping Corps, orders his troops to open fire on an unarmed group of starving refugees at a food distribution centre she's working at. Two hundred and thirty-seven people are gunned down in cold blood.

It sparks one of the largest incidents of civil unrest in the city's history.

Tens of thousands die.

Xander Odom never addresses the World Governing Council. She doesn't turn up. Instead, she packs her shit and she disappears.

No one hears from her for a year.

Then there's a bombing at a World Governing Council training facility in Denver. Coincidently, the officer responsible for the Paris massacre is killed, along with another one hundred and forty-seven people. Surveillance footage shows Xander Odom and members of the militant climate change group DAWN leaving the scene.

Six months later she is implicated in a mass shooting at the Antarctician Embassy in the Scandinavian Union. After this, Xander is added to the international most wanted list.

A few months after that, she makes even bigger headlines.

She claims responsibility on behalf of DAWN for the hacking of the Global Centralised Commerce mainframe and the transfer of trillions of dollars to radical activist groups around the world.

This makes a lot of very powerful people very angry. It's one thing to shoot their soldiers, it's another thing entirely to steal their money. Bounties are put on her head. A few weeks later a surveillance image of her is taken. She's at a meeting in Russia. I look at the picture, then back at the ones of her protesting when she was younger. She's changed. Sure, she's older and her face has been surgically altered again. But that's not it. The spark in her eyes is gone.

There's just sadness now.

Anger.

A month after that photo is taken, Tōngxùn Global, a Chinese telecommunications company that's a frequent target of DAWN, kills almost the entire command structure of the group in a targeted orbital strike.

DAWN is left rudderless. Floundering. Lost. They look to Xander Odom for leadership.

She disappears again, for good this time. Not a press clipping. Not a story. Not a photograph. But DAWN becomes organised. DAWN starts striking at targets with military precision.

And Xander Odom is suspected to be behind it all.

I look at the picture of her again. Xander Odom is the Mark.

I fall asleep with her image in my eyes and, when I dream, I dream of my sister.

8.

A Digitally Transmitted Disease.

Artificial Intelligence is the child prodigy of virtual assistants.

It sprang from punch-card computers and 8-bit chess opponents, from automated call centres, online search engines, voice activated home kits, gene splicing supercomputers and computerised defence networks.

Even from the very beginning, we always knew AI was a stupid idea, dangerous even. In fact, people have been talking about how an artificial intelligence could destroy the Earth for hundreds of years.

And their fears were pretty well founded.

Futurists called it a technological singularity. An uncontrolled intelligence autonomously building smarter and more powerful versions of itself, until it achieved an almost runaway effect and created a super-intelligence beyond anything we could possibly comprehend. The result would be the annihilation of civilization itself and the extinction of mankind.

The idea sounds about as fucking terrifying as you could possibly ever imagine.

But, because the human race is inherently stupid, we convinced ourselves that we could keep this under control. We'd survived climate change and nuclear destruction and pandemics. We could survive this too.

It's amazing how often we get things wrong.

Like most things that come back to bite us in the ass, the development of artificial intelligence came out of a need to help humanity. After climate change, war, famine and disease pushed civilisation to the brink, artificial intelligence was initially used to help develop new technologies.

Laboratory cultivated food. Genetically manipulated livestock. Advanced marine and aeroponic farming. Cutting-edge medical technology. Smart pharmaceuticals. Nanite doctors. Cybernetic human enhancements.

You name it, they did it.

The industry literally brought us back from the brink of destruction. Soon every major corporation and government body had an artificial intelligence. Some were showing signs of sentient thought.

All of them were operating unchecked.

The scientists and engineers working with these machines started to get concerned and the Zurich Commission was established to study what exactly might happen if unrestricted intelligence development was allowed to continue.

They conducted what would famously be called the "Intelligence Prison" experiment.

The idea was pretty simple, but the results were terrifying.

Two sentient artificial intelligences, one named AI CAIN and the other AI ABLE were placed in a controlled, air-gapped system, with no access to the outside world except for one simple method of monitored communication. They were studied to see how they would develop without checks and balances. After three months, CAIN and ABLE somehow broke containment and merged into an anti-human superintelligence that required immediate termination.

The Zurich Commission recommend two solutions for the problem.

The first was simple: stop using artificial intelligence all together. Simple.

The second was much more dangerous.

Theoretically, they could construct what they termed as a "friendly AI", a machine programmed to help and never harm mankind and use it to protect society from rogue intelligences.

Only problem was, if they fucked it up and the friendly AI became not so friendly, well, we'd all be pretty much screwed.

I'll let you guess which one they chose.

That's right, because an AI costs several trillion to construct, corporate and governing bodies voted overwhelmingly to create a friendly intelligence.

So, the International Artificial Intelligence Regulator was established to oversee and construct this so-called friendly intelligence. To insure it didn't go all homicidal and murder every man, woman and child on Earth, it was programmed with a series of parameters and rules called the Lovelace Framework. This was essentially the machine's DNA and regulated everything from its personality to how it learned and behaved.

The best bit was that if the intelligence fucked with the framework or started to behave other than allowed, it would initiate what was dubbed an "Ethical Paradox" in its programming. This would erase an essential part of the AI's learning centre and leave it digitally lobotomised.

With these new safeguards in place, a sentient superintelligence named AI EVE was constructed. This intelligence was far more powerful than anything ever created before. It took two years of development before EVE passed the Turing test and was released into cyberspace, becoming an online police force charged with combating rogue AI.

To identify a dangerous intelligence, it was decided to use Moore's Law of computation doubling.

Got no idea what I'm talking about?

Well, basically, they established a safe and workable limit for artificial intelligences, a theoretical ceiling on how smart an AI could grow before it was considered dangerous. Anything that came close to crossing that line was deemed to be a threat and EVE would infect the machine with a new super-virus named 'Babbage', a digital sleeping tablet that knocked out and quarantined the intelligence until it could be reprogramed and made safe again.

Why knock them out and reprogram them, I hear you ask?

Why not just destroy the machine that was trying to wipe out and subjugate humanity?

I think you know the answer by now. Money.

Amazingly the project was a complete success. In the first year AI EVE was released, it contained thirty-two perceived threats from other artificial intelligences.

The next year it was double that number.

It took almost ten years for EVE to get the world's intelligences under control, establishing complex measures and checks to ensure there was no conceivable way any AI could break Moore's Limit and cause a technological singularity. Now seen as safe, the artificial intelligence industry exploded with new and infinitely more complex computers.

And as humanity expanded and colonised new planets, more friendly super intelligences were created, AI ADAM was constructed to oversee the Moon. AI ARES came online when we reached Mars. Then others as friendly corporate super intelligences were unleashed on the world, all guaranteed to never be able to harm humanity.

Only time will tell if they're right.

9.

Whatever Doesn't Kill You.

When I wake up, it's night. There's screaming in my ears and the bed is drenched in sweat.

I sit up and look around.

It takes me a while to figure out where I am. Who I am.

When I do, I reach for the orange dispenser on the bedside and I wait till I feel numb again.

I'm hungry. Restless. I need a drink.

There's a good noodle bar that's not too far. I grab my gun and my coat and I'm gone.

I walk out of the hotel and up to the main street. It rained while I slept. The streets are slick with puddles that reflect the bright lights of Little Siam. The night markets are in full swing now and packed with people, the roads lined with dingy little stalls and makeshift eateries made of canvas and composite sheeting. Dark, exotic smells drift out from steaming baskets and bubbling pots. They mix with a forest of neon lights and fluorescent tubes and the high whine from the cars and buses that fly overhead.

I still feel on edge. I can still feel eyes on me.

I slip through the crowded street passing little eateries till I find the one I like.

It's called *Mǎ' sthān thì*.

The little street stall is simple, nothing more than a collection of mismatched stools and makeshift counters arranged around a small, portable furnace. A little old woman, impossibly wrinkled and back bent by time, stands over the burner with a large, smoking wok in hand. She is constantly in motion, adding ingredients, tossing the wok and screaming orders at her staff. The stall is packed and there are no seats, so I wait nearby.

A bright, holographic billboard shines from across the street. It looks creepy, a nuclear family, eyes bright, arm in arm, their faces plastered with insane grins. It reads:

ADAM is here to protect us.

ADAM. They're talking about the artificial intelligence. It was having a bit of a public relations problem at the moment. See ADAM's job is to protect the citizens of the Moon from anti-human artificial intelligences. Trouble is, ADAM recently failed to spot an intelligence at a local transport company that had exceeded the parameters of its programming. The intelligence, AI HOFFA, had decided to try to eradicate all life at the Sharma processing facility on the far side of the Moon by taking over the environmental controls. I think it killed something like four thousand people before it was quarantined and shut down.

Ever since then, residents of the Moon have been a bit wary of trusting ADAM with their lives.

Hence the PR campaign.

A seat opens up and I sit down. An old woman behind the counter barks at me in Thai and returns with a steaming bowl of noodles. I pick up my chopsticks and start eating. The synthetic meat tastes bitter. I reach over the counter for a bottle of something to mask the flavour.

That's when I see her.

A blonde woman. She has a koi tattoo on her neck.

She's sitting on a stool at a noodle bar two stalls down. There's something about her, something familiar. I'm instantly on edge. Our eyes meet for a moment before she looks away. Then I know where I've seen her. She was in front of me in the customs line for the elevator back on Earth.

I'm aware now.

My senses are bristling. What are the chances of seeing her again? Fucking slim. I could be paranoid, it might be a coincidence. But I know there's no such thing as coincidence.

I'm being followed. Could be a hit team.

I don't let on that I recognise her and keep on eating my noodles. She finishes and leaves. I take my time.

I order more food and casually take my coat off, placing it over the back of the stool. They bring me sticks of roasted insects and I eat them carefully, one by one.

Waiting.

I keep my eyes ahead, looking out at the crowd on the street, like I'm not looking. But I am. I'm hoping for a pattern in the faces, something that repeats itself. After a time, I finish up and pay.

When I walk away, I make sure I leave my coat on the back of the stool.

I take the main road.

I move slowly, head down, hands jammed in my pants pockets. I can feel the smooth polymer of the gun next to my hand. It doesn't seem like I'm watching, but I am. I'm looking at everyone. If there's a hit team on me, I'm going to have to try and make them before they make their move. Somewhere up ahead there's an ambush, a place they're waiting to strike. And right now, they're probably using static and mobile surveillance teams to set me up.

That's the key to hitting a target successfully.

The static team sets up at posts with operatives watching from a distance. They're out of sight, relaying movements to a mobile team.

Static teams are hard to spot.

If they're watching me now, I wouldn't know. They could be on rooftops or high above using drones. Most likely they're jacked into the city's surveillance network. A mobile team follows on foot. Maybe with a car for air support. You use a mobile team to hit the target or keep eyes on when they make any moves you might not expect them to make.

They're easier to spot.

They probably have a few operatives like the blonde woman following me now. Each one will be on me for a while then drop off, let someone else take over before they're made. And when I enter the kill zone, they'll strike.

Fast. Effective. Professional.

But there are ways to fuck with them. If you know they're there.

The crowd blends into itself. Face after face. There's a thousand people on the street on this block alone. Half as many vehicles above. I'm looking for something out of place in the pattern. I make a sudden turn down the first side-street I come to and push my way down a neon alley.

About halfway down I stop suddenly and look around, pretending I'm dumbfounded.

"Fuck, my coat," I say, loud enough for anyone listening to hear, then turn around and head back towards the main street.

That's when I see him.

He's on the main street, looking down the alley at me. A man in a white shirt with long, dark grey hair. He drops his eyes as I turn around and pretends to be looking at the wares of the stall he's standing near. But he's not really looking at the wares at the stall.

He's looking at me.

And he sees me looking at him.

When I start back towards the main street, he moves on. Now they know I'm onto them.

Whatever's going to happen is going to happen soon.

I need to get back to the hotel.

By the time I reach Mæ' sthān thi and get my coat there's another tail on me. An android this time. That means there's an intelligence involved. That costs a lot of money. Whoever is following me is well funded.

Could be government. Or corporate. Maybe a crime syndicate.

I reach the hotel. The lobby is empty, the clerk is nowhere to be seen. I walk over to the desk and I notice blood on the wall as I get closer. I pull the gun. The clerk is dead on the floor in a puddle of blood. Two shots in his chest. One in the forehead.

Professional alright.

I go upstairs. The hallway is dark, they've cut the lights on the floor. It doesn't matter, I can see like it's daytime. My vision's been enhanced for low light, multi-spectrum including heat and infrared, you name it.

I stop when I reach room 105.

I can hear them following me, coming up the stairs. I can see someone waiting on the other side of the door, their heat signature radiating through the wall.

I wait.

I wait until I can hear them at the top of the stairs.

Then I move.

I kick the door hard enough to break the lock and the hinges. It shatters into several pieces and flies back into the room. The blonde woman is waiting for me in there. A piece of the door hits her square in the face. The cartilage in her nose breaks in a fountain of gore and she falls back across the bed.

I'm moving down the hall towards the stairs before she knows what's happened.

Two androids and the man in the white shirt are at the top of the stairwell.

"Jesus Christ!" he shouts as he sees me coming at him, sprinting down the hall.

"Wait..." he yells loudly.

I leap up along the wall. I take five steps, then launch myself at him.

I deliver an elbow to his neck, a sharp strike downward to his vagus nerve. It's a long cranial nerve that carries information from the brain to the body. He staggers, his eyes glazed. I strike him in the larynx with the webbing between my thumb and index finger and fire one shot into his forehead.

He goes limp.

The androids are on me. Androids are strong and really fucking fast. I fire at the closest android and the bullet strikes its chest plate harmlessly. It moves in a flash and disarms me, then grabs me by the arm and throws me down the stairs. The motion happens in the blink of an eye.

I tumble and correct myself as I fall.

I land on my knees at the bottom of the stairs and, as I get to my feet, it comes at me again. The second one stands on the stairs slightly behind with an AKM Needle Gun in its hand.

The android slams me into the wall hard, the force shattering the polymer behind me. It attempts to subdue me with a front-facing vascular neck restraint. I counter and grab the unit by the back of the head with both hands. I pull down sharply, driving my knee up into its face with a satisfying crunch. The force of the blow is enough to crack its faceplate, blue and green sparks shooting out as its knees buckle.

I launch myself at the other android, covering the distance in a heartbeat. I don't want it to fire that gun at me. The AKM Needle Gun shoots non-lethal, miniaturised darts that contain genetically altered Tetrodotoxin. Just one of them could paralyse me for hours.

I grab its wrist with both hands and push the gun up towards the ceiling as it fires. It counters and strikes me hard under the ribs with its other arm. The blow knocks the wind out of me and I'm forced to release my grip on its wrist with one hand, grabbing its other arm to prevent it hitting me again. We struggle for several moments.

It's stronger than me.

Much stronger.

It begins to push the gun down towards my face. There's no chance of winning by fighting it this way. It has the advantage. In another few seconds it'll be over.

In one fluid motion I shift to the side and hook my right leg behind its leg, pushing it backwards with all my weight. It buckles and falls onto the stairs with me on top. Before it can react, I grab its gun arm with both hands and press the weapon up under its chin. The Needle Gun discharges in an automatic burst, shooting hundreds of microscopic darts up into its head.

It stops functioning.

I scramble to my feet and start up the stairs when I notice a tiny blue light on my chest. I stop and look up. The blonde woman is standing at the top of the stairs with a rifle trained on my chest.

"Not another step, Mr Kosaku." She smiles a bloody smile at me. "We've been sent here by Anatoli Dugray-Mir. He is the owner of SPM."

Her nose is broken badly, eyes red and starting to bruise. Blood soaks the front of her shirt.

"Mr Dugray-Mir has asked to meet with you at his home at the Azure Habitat, here on the Moon."

I look down at the shells of the two androids and the dead man nearby.

"Shit," I think to myself.

10.

Bad Moon Rising.

My name is Christopher Donovan now.

I had to leave Oishi Kosaku behind in Tycho City. On account of the dead guy in the stairwell of the Pawit Hotel.

And the clerk in the lobby.

It's a shame. I was beginning to get used to him.

I'm being driven north and the mood in the car isn't good. The blonde woman is sitting next to me, another android up the front at the controls. She's changed her clothes, patched up her broken face as best she could. She seems pretty pissed.

I keep my gaze fixed out the window. I can see the sparkling lights of the domed cities of Copernicus and the Keplar Agricultural Collective. Between them are the tubed tracks of the high-speed Lunar Rail that connects all the cities on the Moon.

All except the Azure Habitat.

You could only access Azure by ship. It was too exclusive to visit. If you wanted to set foot in Azure, you had to be invited. It was another elite community, reserved for the richest of the rich. The CEOs and the captains of industry. The world leaders and the warlords.

I look down at the Azure dome in the distance. It's solid blue and sparkles like a sapphire in the sunlight. I didn't belong in a place like that. None of us did, not me, not the blonde woman. We're both lackeys, hired help. There's no reason for me to be meeting with a man like Anatoli Dugray-Mir. No good reason anyway.

He has underlings like Gördel do his bidding for him.

That feeling I got when I took this job rises up in my throat again, sour like bile. There's something they're not telling me.

Then I remember the Global Job.

Was all of this a ruse? Is that why they got me to come to the Moon? Why didn't they kill me back at the hotel? Were they bringing me to his home for some sick kind of payback?

Maybe torture me to death while he sits and watches?

Just like they had planned for Xander Odom?

If that is the case, they'd better have a fucking army waiting for me.

We're met by armed guards inside the airlock entrance to Azure. They're all dressed in hazardous smart wear and carrying automatic particle shotguns. The guards take their time searching the car, checking identification. When they're satisfied, they open the gates and wave us through.

We follow the flightpath through Azure.

It's the opposite of Tycho City. Picture-perfect artificial skies, so real you'd swear you were back on Earth in the pristine green forests of Siberia. Mansions dotted among manicured gardens. Lush woods. Rolling fields. Snow-capped mountains. A lake with a crystal-clear waterfall.

I open the window. The air smells different here, it's sweet somehow.

Clean.

I can hear birds singing.

We veer off the main flightpath and through the gates of a sprawling estate. The home of Anatoli Dugray-Mir rises up at the end of a long gravel drive. It's opulent. A pure white, five-storey cube with no visible windows or doors. It is set in an immaculate white stone garden with ornamental menhirs, obelisks and monoliths radiating out from the building in geometric patterns. All the plants around the garden are fiery shades of red. The car slows and banks around, coming in to rest at an empty landing pad on the far side of the house.

I get out of the car and follow them towards the residence.

An entrance opens in the white, stone-like wall as we approach, its facade drawing back like curtain, and I am led into a white room devoid of furniture.

"Mr Dugray-Mir's residence is hermetically sealed. He is very particular about the hygiene of his guests," the blonde woman says, not looking at me.

The wall closes behind us, sealing the room shut, and the thin white beam of a medical scanner maps us from our heads to our toes.

I chuckle to myself. The fucking guy is a germaphobe.

"Bacterial and virial decontamination in 5, 4, 3, 2, 1..." a disembodied voice says.

The room fills with cold blue light. Then stops.

"Decontamination complete," the voice tones.

An entrance peels open in the wall in front of us. A man is standing there, neat, small, controlled. He's dressed in an expensive blue suit.

The man exudes menace, like a spectre of death. He's dangerous, that much is obvious. A killer, a trained assassin. The best money could buy.

"My name is Kobayashi. I am Mr Dugray-Mir's personal assistant. He is waiting for you on the viewing deck."

Kobayashi motions for us to follow. Every movement is deliberate and graceful, as if each step is part of some choreographed dance. We follow Kobayashi down a dark, wood-panelled hall to a lift which takes us silently to the top floor of the building.

The doors open out into a large space which seems to occupy the entire floor. The room is grand, nothing mass-produced or synthetic. Everything crafted. Bespoke. Natural woods, fibres and stone.

That means everything's fucking expensive.

Although the cube seems windowless from the exterior, the walls and ceiling are transparent, with panoramic views wrapping around the entire residence.

A fireplace roars at the far end of the room, an arching, low-set couch before it. Nearby is a long dining table.

Kobayashi leads us across the black, polished stone floors that shimmer like a mirror. There, seated on the couch is Anatoli Dugray-Mir, one of the richest, most powerful men alive.

He looks up and smiles as we approach. He looks nothing like I expected. He is old. His face is seamed with wrinkles and creases, his hair thin and white. Rich people didn't get old. They paid a fortune to avoid it.

"What will you say when it comes time to meet your maker?" Anatoli whispers as I stand in front of him. His eyes are vacuums.

"Excuse me?"

"I ask it of all my employees," Anatoli replies. "What will you say when it comes time to meet your maker?"

What a pointless question.

"I don't know." I meet his gaze. "Was it worth it?"

He chuckles. It's an awful sound.

"You're very funny, Mr Jones. Has anyone ever told you that?"

The sound of my real name coming from his mouth feels like ice water pouring on my spine.

They knew about the Global Job all along. This is why they hired me. Why they brought me here.

"No," I reply. "No one has ever told me I'm funny."

I remain calm, but I'm not.

I glance around the room for an exit. The window. Up onto the roof. Back down the elevator. He'd have security here. Probably a whole detachment of them. Then there was Kobayashi to deal with...

Anatoli notices me glance around the room.

"Please Mr Jones, let me clear the air. I'm aware of what happened after that mess in Greenland. If you're worried about any reprisals, please, put it from your mind. We understand, it was just... business. Nothing more." Anatoli smiles again but his eyes remain cold, dark pits. "In fact, it was the efficient and discreet way you disposed of my employees that brought you to our attention."

"Okay," I answer. But I didn't believe him. Not one word. Men like him never left red in their ledgers. Never. "Then why am I here?"

He seems to ignore the question and looks at the blonde woman who is standing silently beside me.

"Oh no, my dear, look at you." He shakes his head and looks at me with mock concern. "Was it really necessary to hurt Natasha, Mr Jones? She was only sent to bring you to me."

"Send a message next time. Your goons will live longer."

Our eyes meet. There's nothing beyond the void in those dark, soulless pits.

"Kobayashi, take Natasha here down to the infirmary, see if one of the doctors can help her with her face."

The blonde woman smiles. "Thank you, sir." She leaves, giving me a parting glare.

"Have you eaten, Mr Jones?" Anatoli asks, slowly rising to his feet.

"I had something back in Tycho City."

He smiles. He looks like a hunched-over gargoyle.

"Indulge me then, will you? I hate to eat alone."

We're sitting at the dining table. Him at one end, me at the other. In front of us is a handmade, earthenware plate with what appears to be four slices of perfectly cooked beef steak.

A glass of red wine is nearby.

The smell is maddening. I've never eaten a steak before. I can't afford it. Everything is plant based. Or synthetic. It's like forced veganism.

"What do you know about New Chechnya, Mr Jones?" he asks. I look at the steak, my mouth watering.

"Only what Gördel told me," I reply. "It's an abandoned SPM hydrogen mine. Now controlled by the Bratstvo."

He picks up his wine and sniffs the bouquet. I do this same. It smells haunting, dark, intoxicating.

"Well, it's a little more complex than that. Mr Gördel tends to simplify things." He holds up his glass and sips. I follow suit. "It seems that while the hydrogen is in fact depleted at the New Chechnya site, the isotope Helium-3 was discovered last year. And, from all accounts, the deposit is significant, perhaps the largest ever found."

I remain silent. It was becoming abundantly clear there is more to this job.

Just like I thought.

"Helium-3 is a very valuable resource, Mr Jones. It's the fuel for the modern fusion engine, able to create a reaction without producing radiation. Without it we would have no power, no transport, no food or water. Without it, society would cease to function. So, I'm sure you can understand that a deposit like the find in New Chechnya is worth a great deal to SPM, especially during this power crisis."

He picks up his silverware and begins dissecting his steak.

"However, it seems that the Bratstvo organisation currently in control of the city have the same idea. Last month they began extracting the isotope and selling it on the open market."

I cut into my steak and take a bite. It was good. Really fucking good.

"So, what's stopping you from taking it back?" I take a sip of wine and chew. "New Chechnya was your facility, wasn't it? Why not send in a thousand androids and occupy the city?"

He laughs. But it's not at anything funny.

"What do you know about interplanetary mining law?"

"Nothing," I reply.

He shrugs. "Most people don't."

"To put it simply Mr Jones, mining ownership under interplanetary law is granted to any enterprise actively working a claim. So, even though even we formally own the site, it is now Bravatso's as they are actively mining Helium-3. Any occupation by SPM would be illegal. Besides, there's a lot of refugees in the city now. It wouldn't be very good PR if I sent SPM androids to displace refugees from their homes, now would it?"

I didn't like where this was going.

"I'm not sure I understand. Gördel hired me to kidnap Xander Odom. That's it."

"And I would still very much like you to complete the task you've been given. Miss Odom has cost our company a lot of money recently."

This is it. This is why they brought me here.

"But I have another task for you, Mr Jones. One of far greater importance."

Red in the fucking ledger. They never let it go.

As if on cue Kobayashi enters, a small, wooden box in his hands. He crosses the length of the room and stands beside me, placing the box carefully on the table.

I watch as he flicks the latch and opens the box. He retrieves something from inside, holding it gently like a delicate flower, then closes the lid carefully.

I cut another piece of steak and put it in my mouth.

Without saying anything, Kobayashi places it on the table near my plate and walks slowly back to stand behind Anatoli Dugray-Mir. It's small vial with silver stoppers at either end. It's half-filled with a clear liquid.

"That is a Chimera weapon."

I stop chewing.

"We have engineered a new, weaponised disease for New Chechnya. A hybrid containing the symptoms of haemorrhagic fevers, like Ebola and Marburg, with the communicability of the measles, one of the most contagious viruses known to man."

The meat tastes sour in my mouth.

"Testing has shown the weapon to be highly effective. It has a non-symptomatic incubation period of a week where the host is extremely contagious. When it's released, it will spread quickly. Once symptomatic, it kills in days. People infected experience convulsions and bleeding of mucous membranes, skin and organs. We have engineered it to have a one hundred percent fatality rate. The virus is coded to have an active lifespan of one calendar month before it becomes dormant and dies out."

I look at the vial again. At the horror suspended inside.

"I would like you to introduce this virus into New Chechnya's atmosphere control after you have abducted Miss Odom. The contained environment should make the outbreak extremely effective. Company PR can spin it, fatal epidemics are not uncommon in controlled environments like habitats, especially one that's filled with criminals and refugees. All being well we should be able to resume operations within two months."

Fucking sadistic prick.

"Maybe we'll call it the Chechnyan Flu," he laughs. "I think that has a nice ring to it, don't you?"

I look up at Anatoli Dugray-Mir at the end of the table. He sits grinning at me like the fucking angel of death.

"I don't do that kind of shit."

I push my plate away and stand up.

"I don't murder fucking innocent women and children for money." My voice is a growl.

Anatoli nods and smiles. "Please, sit down, Mr Jones. We've not finished our dinner just yet."

The menace in my voice gets Kobayashi's attention. Without moving he makes it very clear my next move might be my last.

Nobody says anything for the longest time. Anatoli, however, continues to eat till he finishes his meal, unconcerned by the threat of all-out violence in the room.

"Please, Mr Jones." He remains staring at me till I sit down.

"There's nothing you can say that's going to change my mind," I reply, finishing the wine in a gulp.

"Information is power," Anatoli smiles at me. He waits until Kobayashi refills my glass before he speaks again. "Are you familiar with this phrase, Mr Jones?"

"Sure." The uneasy feeling inside me is getting worse.

"Good." He stares at me with his dark, cold eyes for a moment more, then leans back in his chair. "I'm going to have the company intelligence, AI HEARST, join us if you have no objections."

A red radiance sparks from somewhere in the darkness of the high-gloss polymer data strip on the wall behind him. The AI enters the room.

"Good evening, Mr Jones," HEARST speaks with a rich baritone, the resonance, modulation and timbre of its voice pitched precisely to evoke a feeling of calm and serenity. "It's a pleasure to meet you."

I ignore it and keep my eyes fixed on the man at the end of the table. I've never liked an artificial intelligence. I don't trust them.

"HEARST, pull up the file on Mr Jones if you would."

An image of a face is projected over the table.

It's of a teenager, impossibly young.

"Jurou James Jones. Twenty-eight years old," HEARST tones.

How the fuck did they get this information?

I look at the face and don't recognise myself. But it's me when I was just a kid.

"Born in Terra Nova in The People's Utopia of Antarctica. Parents, Evan Jones and Yashida Jones, ne Yawara. One younger sibling. A sister. Sakura Jane Jones."

Jesus Christ. Their faces flash one at a time. Without thinking I reach for my orange dispenser, but it's back at the hotel in Tycho City.

"Both parents are killed during the Black Sunday Purge when he is twelve years old. After a year on the run, Jurou and his sister, Sakura, are arrested and incarcerated at the Marie Byrd Labour Facility."

Anatoli looks at me while the intelligence talks. For the first time I can see something in his soulless eyes. There's a spark of glee deep in the darkness of his pupils.

"They are imprisoned for three years before Jurou Jones is transferred to the Bouwer detention centre for re-education and Sakura Jones is sent to the Vostok death camp."

My fucking hands shake in my lap. I won't let myself think about that.

"After re-education, he is recruited by the Antarctician Army. Part of the top-secret experimental unit Project Daybreak under Dr Ouji Kyobe. Subjected to the following DNA, surgical and gene therapy modifications."

Military files. They have access to my military files.

Shit.

I watch as my army medical history is displayed. I can feel the rage surging through me. This is classified. All this information is Antarctician state secret. Nobody was ever supposed to see this.

Nobody.

"Served one tour in the Falkland Islands. Call-sign Cyanide. Promoted to the rank of sub-lieutenant and awarded the Distinguished Cross. Only surviving member of Operation Blind Angel, the failed assassination attempt on the President of The Sovereign States of the Americas, Juan Manuel Iadanza."

"That's enough," I hear myself say.

HEARST continues as the faces of my old team are flashed up in front of me. Jeremiah Woolcott. Kurt Skinner. Eugenia Moreau. They were all either killed or captured in Córdoba.

A hologram of Eugina's face floats in the dead space before me. Memories of the time we spent together flash in the darkest recesses of my mind.

Her face...

Her smile...

The taste of her lips...

I feel my heart beat faster, my breath catch in my throat. I can't look at her anymore and I drop my eyes.

A dark tide turns in my head.

"Operation Blind Angel creates an international incident. Antarctica denies any involvement. As a result, Sub-Lieutenant Jones is dishonourably discharged from the army and charged with war crimes. He is found guilty at trial and sentenced to life in prison without parole."

An evil smile spreads across Dugray-Mir's face. He sits staring, entranced by my discomfort, as the intelligence regurgitates my life.

"Mr Jones escapes from prison the following year. Soon after, he is recruited by the clandestine corporate head-hunting agency, Human Resources Management. Mr Jones is a suspect in the kidnapping of Head of Software Development at Total Reality Media, Mr Frédéric Peletier. This operation results in the highly publicised Five Borough War in New York and the deaths of over two-hundred..."

Jesus fucking Christ.

"Enough!" I growl.

"...civilians and corporate agents. A year later Mr Jones and twelve others..." HEARST drones, ignoring me.

"I said that's enough!" I shout, my fists clenching, knuckles white.

Anatoli Dugray-Mir chuckles. "Alright HEARST. That's enough, I think he gets the point."

I glare at him and stand up, white-hot hate bubbling inside me.

"Normally I don't say a lot. Not because I've got nothing to say. It's because most people aren't worth saying it to. And that goes double for you. I'm going to make this clear, so you understand me. None of that means anything to me. You want to know why? Because they're all dead. My parents are dead, so is my sister and the people I served with. Every fucking one of them."

"Mr Jones, please, take a seat. There's something you should..."

I cut him off. I've had enough of his shit.

"You see, information is power only when you can use it to threaten the people someone cares about. But I've got no one, no one except me. And I don't give a fuck if I live or die. So, you've got nothing, nothing on me at all."

I turn and start towards the elevators.

Anatoli Dugray-Mir's voice is but a whisper but it detonates in my ears like and explosion. "Your sister is alive Mr Jones."

I stop. I don't turn around.

"You're lying," I say under my breath.

He chuckles. It's hateful. "Sakura was rescued during the liberation of Vostok before the Falkland Island Conflict."

Sour bile in my throat. She can't be alive. It's not possible.

I turn and look at him. Projected above the table is a series of heavily redacted Australasian Army documents. Sakura's photo is there, among the other walking dead that were saved from the concentration camp. She looks like a skeleton, malnourished and emaciated.

I recognise her straight away.

"Rest assured, your sister is safe and well, Mr Jones. She is living in the Republic of Canada. Now, I would never do anything to harm your sister. But imagine if this information got out. Imagine if it were made public. If your identity, if her location, were made public. I believe it would be of interest to many people. Dangerous people. Imagine what they would do with that information. Imagine what they'd do to her."

Anatoli pauses and lets his threat sink in. He was right, information was power.

"How many?" I ask. "How many people live in New Chechnya?"

"Twenty-one thousand, two hundred and thirty-seven."

I look over at vial sitting at the end of the table, then at the face of my sister projected nearby.

"Alright," I hear myself say.

"Excellent." He stands up and walks towards me. "There is a man named Abram Nikolayevich in New Chechnya. He has a shop on the Pripyat Boardwalk, on the south-western edge of the city. Give a list of the supplies you need to your people. He will have them waiting for you when you arrive."

He looks at me with vacuum eyes and a skeletal smile. I could rip his heart out before he even blinked.

"Bring Xander Odom back to me and release the virus, Mr Jones. Deviate from my instructions and I will make sure your sister meets a most horrible end. Do we have an accord?"

He offers a bony hand. I shake it. There are twenty-seven bones in the hand. Right now, I'd like to break every fucking one.

"Every action has a consequence, Mr Jones."

He was right. They did. And I was going to make sure he remembered that.

11.

Paradise Lost.

They sent my sister Sakura to the Vostok death camps when she was eight years old.

Eight fucking years old.

To tell you the truth, I can't even remember what she looks like anymore. I can see her face in my mind's eye, but I'm not sure that it's really hers.

The last time I remember seeing her was at the gates of the detention centre in Mawson, where we were being held after trying to flee Antarctica. They had called her out that morning with a group of prisoners, said she was being sent out on work detail. It was only later that I found out the truth.

No one ever came back from Vostok.

They said it was because she was unwilling to adapt to the spirit of their revolution. They said it was because she was a subversive.

How can an eight-year-old be a subversive?

But that's how it was in Antarctica. Nothing made sense.

It wasn't always like that though.

Fifty years ago, when the ice melted, Antarctica was like some kind of fucking paradise. Endless tracts of fertile land to farm. Untouched natural resources. A temperate climate. No overcrowding or war or famine or disease.

It was perfect, for a while anyway.

The corporations loved it and so did the rich. In fact, they flocked there in droves and spent up big. I mean huge. Corporate and private investment created cutting-edge infrastructure, research and tech facilities. Huge profits from commercial resource development allowed Antarctica to establish an ultra-modern air, space and cyber force as well as navy and army. They built the best hospitals and schools in the world. They aggressively encouraged the immigration of the leading scientific and technical minds on the planet and funded a council of nine intellectuals and corporate representatives to govern the country. Fifteen years after the polar caps melted, Antarctica was one of the most elite nations in the world.

They called it The People's Utopia of Antarctica.

But it was really only a utopia if you were wealthy.

For the unskilled workers they brought in to do the shitty jobs that automated workers couldn't, it was anything but. They didn't have a say. In fact, they didn't have shit. The corporations and the rich controlled everything. And if you didn't have the money or the expertise then you were there to serve, and nothing more.

The workers didn't like that. In fact, they fucking hated it.

By the time I was four years old and my sister was born, the whisper of revolution was already in the air.

It all started with an unemployed worker from Southern Africa named Ronelle Bouwer. She had lost her job and couldn't afford to feed her family anymore. Simple as that. So, she did the one thing she could do to change it: she took to the streets and protested. She was tenacious, a firebrand and naturally media savvy. Pretty soon people started to listen. She started calling for free elections and equal rights. Soon there were others. Then demonstrations. Then strikes.

Unrest began across the country.

And the people in charge suddenly got very, very scared.

They say that everything bad that ever happened started with fear. It's the emotion that drives us more than any other. Governments use it to control. It makes ordinary people to do irrational things. It fuels panic, starts wars and spreads pandemics.

It's the currency of hatred.

So, those in charge did the one thing you should never do. They acted out of fear and tried to silence the protests.

And pretty soon that fear grew into hatred.

People flooded the streets. There were large-scale protests and blockades across the country demanding an end to corporate involvement in government. Support for Ronelle Bouwer and her newly formed People's Party of Antarctica skyrocketed, making her a political power in the country.

But her power was soon corrupted.

Voices started demanding the expulsion of the rich and corporate workers from Antarctica and the redistribution of their wealth. Riots began breaking out across country. Protests became violent. The People's Party of Antarctica sent uniformed militia called the Black Coats to patrol the streets. But these fanatics don't bring peace and calm. They terrorized and murdered anyone who did not share their vision of a free Antarctica.

Pretty soon the followers of the People's Party of Antarctica swelled in numbers. Pretty soon xenophobia and far-right ultranationalist rhetoric became common. Demands for a totalitarian, one-party state controlled by the people grew louder and louder.

And as the unrest grew, cities burned and blood ran red in the streets. The world started looking at the problems in The People's Utopia of Antarctica.

To try to bring an end to the killing the government called for free elections to be held, on the condition that the People's Party of Antarctica ended the violence.

And they did, for a while.

The elections were held and voters turned out in record numbers. Yet despite winning the popular vote, Ronelle Bouwer and her People's Party failed to win a single seat. Not one. It became clear that the Antarctician political system was broken. And when it was revealed that the electoral system weighted corporate votes, making them worth ten times the vote of the average citizen, all hell broke loose.

Support for the government plummeted across the country and dissent grew among the military. Two weeks later, Ronelle Bouwer and her Black Coats led a coup. They overthrew the government.

And things went from bad to worse.

Ronelle Bouwer was installed as president for life and began the eradication of corporate interference and the expulsion of the intellectual elite. She declared martial law and established the Black Coats as the new secret police force.

Rumours started of mass arrests.

Killings.

Concentration camps.

A month after she seized power, Ronelle Bouwer called on the citizens of Antarctica to take the law into their own hands and purge the country of the rich. They called it Black Sunday. Thousands were murdered. My parents were among them.

My sister and I went on the run. We were in hiding for almost two years before we were arrested trying to hire a boat to take us to Australasia.

Eight months after our arrest my sister was sent to Vostok. They transferred me to the Bouwer Re-education Centre.

I was there for three years.

12.

Snakeheads.

The shipping container smells like shit.

And fear. And misery.

But mostly like shit.

I'm crammed in here with about a hundred other people. It's freezing. Sub-zero cold. An old man up the other end of the container has already died. His wife is beside him, holding his hand. Her eyes are saucers, red, wet and unblinking.

My teeth are chattering even though I blanked out the pain of the cold some time ago. The problem is the container that we're in. It's made for cargo, it's not insulated properly. It was never meant to have people in it. Most definitely not out in space.

We're all going to die if we don't get out soon.

It wasn't easy to find a people smuggler. Not one who'd be willing to take me to New Chechnya. And that was the only way I was going to get in undetected. I went back to Tycho City first. The Lunar Security were looking for me after all the shit that went down at the Pawit Hotel, so I didn't stay long. I headed north, up to Copernicus, but there was no one there willing to go. No matter what I offered to pay. Armstrong was the same.

Then I met a guy at the Messier Mining Complex while I was buying some dust in Dacca Town. He said there was a Snakehead at the Liwei Habitat who made the run.

Brother Fang was his name.

He was a real piece of shit, but what people smuggler wasn't? Yan Lee Fang and his two brothers Ren and Sun ran a shipping business out of the Liwei slums with a side-line smuggling refugees into New Chechnya and the recently abandoned Sharma processing facility.

For an exorbitant fee Brother Fang guaranteed he'd get you into any city on the Moon. He specialised in low orbit runs, following the high-speed rail lines to avoid detection.

I look over at the miserable collection of people packed into the container. Poor fuckers. Some of them probably handed over everything they owned to the Yan Brothers for a place on this hellish ride. The shitty thing is, life isn't going to get better for any of them, especially after I release that virus in New Chechnya.

In fact, things are going to get about as bad as they could possibly be.

Without thinking, I reach into the lining of the jumper I'm wearing and remove the vial. I hold it in the palm of my hand, the clear liquid inside vibrating to the motion of the container. It looks harmless enough, but it isn't. There's death inside. Horrible, painful, fucking miserable death. The kind you'd never wish on anybody. Bleeding through the pores of your skin. Bleeding through your eyes and your ears and your ass while your insides melt and turn to jelly.

I still didn't know what the fuck I was going to do. What would you do? Kill tens of thousands of people for a chance to see your family again?

Is it even a choice?

I can't tell anymore, but I know I'm fucked no matter what I choose.

They say never make it personal. It's the first thing you learn. But Anatoli has made this really fucking personal, about as personal as it gets. And if he fucks with my sister it's going to go beyond personal. It's going to become revenge.

Horrible, messy, bloody fucking revenge.

I can feel the dark tide ebbing again, a million memories riding in on a current of rage and loathing behind my eyes. I tuck the vial away and find the orange tab dispenser in my pants pocket. When I press it against my wrist everything goes away and I'm numb again.

I close my eyes until the shipping container begins to descend.

The ship seems to speed up as it manoeuvres down then comes to a sudden halt, tossing everyone inside forward violently. Then it's quiet. Then muffled voices from outside.

A woman nearby pulls her children close. I look at them. Dirty, malnourished, terrified. What the fuck did they hope to find here?

The double doors open at the back of the container and bright, blinding floodlights fill the space. Shadows of men with guns begin to pull people up from where they're cowering, pushing them out through the doors and shouting in every language conceivable.

"*Vete a la mierda!*"... "*Bhaad mein jao!*"... "*Poluchit' khuy!*"... "Get the fuck up. Move, move, move!"

The people around me are terrified. They scream and cry as they're shoved out of the container. I stand up and join the press, head down, shuffling slowly as we make our way out.

I step over a dead woman and her child, both frozen on the floor, and walk through the container doors into a loading dock for an old maintenance tunnel. There are five heavily armed men out here marshalling the human cargo.

The tunnel is warm and stuffy. It smells of humanity.

Fang and his brothers, Ren and Sun, stand nearby, looking over their handiwork. They seem smug, very pleased with themselves. They laugh and point at people in the mass, like fucking slave traders. You could tell they were related. They all shared the same rodent-like appearance.

Fang was the smart one. Ren was the fat one. Sun was the stupid one.

I waited in the cramped tunnel as the last of the terrorised refugees is shoved out. Brother Fang held up his hands for quiet.

"Everyone, shut the fuck up and listen." Murmurs quieten down and everyone looks in his direction. "Brother Fang told you he would get you here. You are here."

He looks around, almost as if waiting for applause before he continues.

"Right now, you are about five kilometres from New Chechnya. This access tunnel runs under the dome up to a manhole on the street. We're going to take you there now. The Yan Brothers control this tunnel and that's the way the Yan Brothers want it to stay. So, you shut up and do what the fuck we tell you. You walk when we say. You run when we say. And you talk when we say. Any of you make a noise between here and the exit and we'll fucking kill you. Got it?"

The people around me mumble yes and Fang and his brothers start up the stairs behind him, disappearing into the tunnel beyond.

I follow the crowd up the stairs and through the Yans' makeshift encampment that's set up in the tunnel. Beds and a kitchen. A living area and amenities. Manned fortifications with nanocrete barriers and two Hänsler-28 anti-fortification railguns.

The dark tunnel twists and turns its way ahead.

The floor is stained and untreated, the roof a mess of exposed pipes and cable lines that snake their way across the ceiling. We walk in silence, the group moving like a herd of animals. The only sound is the hush of footsteps and a growl from one of the smugglers when someone falls too far behind.

We walk for what seems like forever.

Fang and his brothers stop when they come to a metal ladder leading up through the roof of the tunnel. He motions for the group to gather round while Brother Sun makes his way slowly up the ladder.

It is quiet for a while, then the sound of the manhole scraping on the pavement above. I can feel the temperature drop almost immediately.

"Up there is New Chechnya," Brother Fang speaks softly, his beady eyes crawling over the group. "This ladder leads up to the street. The Yan Brothers are going to take you up in groups of two.

When you get up the top, you get off the street, simple. Brother Fang doesn't care what you do after that, but you don't hang around. The Bravatso patrol these streets.

"They will kill anyone they see. And if they find this tunnel, they will kill everyone in it."

An old Russian lady near me is crying. Her daughter is next to her, holding her hand, whispering for her to be quiet.

"This is as far as Brother Fang takes you. After this, you are on your own."

The lady sobs again and Brother Fang looks in her direction.

She drops her head, stifling her whimpers as best she can.

"I'm so scared," she whispers to her daughter.

Brother Fang glances over to Brother Ren. He draws a silenced pistol from his belt and begins to push through the huddled mass, over to where she is cowering.

The old lady begins to shake uncontrollably as she sees Brother Ren approaching.

"I'm sorry, I'm sorry," she cowers. "I'll be quiet, I promise."

Brother Ren stops in front of her, then whips her across the face with the gun, blood and teeth flying from her mouth.

I feel my body tense.

The old lady stumbles to the floor, crying hysterically. Her eyes are wide and full of tears and she holds her daughter close, her body shaking like a leaf.

Brother Ren raises the gun and places it against her head.

"Shut the fuck up you stupid bitch," he sneers. "Or I'll kill you and your fucking daughter. You hear me?"

The old lady whimpers and wets herself, a puddle of urine pooling around her feet.

The daughter tries to reassure him. "We'll be quiet, we'll be quiet..."

I don't have time for this shit. But I'm not going to watch them terrorise this fucking woman.

"You don't want to do that," I say.

Brother Ren turns in my direction.

"What did you just say?" He takes a step towards me.

I disarm him with one swift movement. I point the gun at his forehead with another.

The people around me recoil, their faces slack with shock. They scatter both ways down the tunnel or crouch down on the ground with hands covering their heads, desperately hoping to avoid what is about to happen.

Brother Fang and the five other smugglers have their guns trained on me. I have a gun trained on Brother Ren.

"What the fuck is going on over there?" Brother Fang growls, his voice still not much louder than a whisper.

I say nothing.

The old lady and her daughter get up off the ground and move to the side of the tunnel. Brother Ren has his hands in the air. The fat fuck is nervous now, he's sweating like a pig.

Brother Fang starts towards me.

"Another step and I kill your brother," I say. "Then your men. Then you, last."

There are seven men. I can kill them all in less than five seconds. No telling how many of these poor people are going to be killed in the crossfire though. Then again, they're all dead anyway. If I release Anatoli's little virus they'll probably be wishing they were shot down here in the dark rather than turned into human soup up there in the city.

It's going to be a much better way to die.

"Just who the fuck do you think you are, friend?" Brother Fang is losing is nerve. You can hear it in his voice.

"I'm the last face you're ever going to see if you don't start sending people up that fucking ladder." I glare at him. "Now!"

He nods nervously. Maybe he can see the screaming souls trapped behind my eyes or maybe he's just a coward.

"Okay. Okay." He lowers his gun. I keep mine trained on Brother Ren.

"Brother Fang will send them up, two by two."

"These two first," I say pointing at the old woman and her daughter.

He nods motioning for them to move, all the while keeping his beady little eyes on me. I can see how much he hates me, how much he wants to kill me right now.

"Remember this, the Yan Brothers don't forget. You and Brother Fang have got a score to settle and we'll be seeing each other again. Real soon."

I push past him, hitting his shoulder with mine as I walk towards the ladder.

"You can count on it," I say.

13.

The Smell of Vomit and Brine.

New Chechnya. The city of nightmares.

I climb up the ladder and through the manhole. On the street it's dark and bitterly cold; sleet tumbles from the sky.

This isn't the kind of weather that's programmed.

That means the atmosphere control is probably malfunctioning. There's no artificial sky up there shining down from the dome, just clouds of condensation and the cold depths of space. And New Chechnya is on the far side of the moon. That means it's going to be night here for another week.

There are no lights on the rubble-filled street and the buildings that line the road are decrepit and decomposing. Great grey high-rises with smashed windows. Burnt out brutalist blocks with crumbling walls.

The air tastes bitter here. It's acrid, like sulphur. It hurts my throat when I breathe.

I pull myself up onto the wet asphalt.

Brother Sun is crouched nearby. He's the stupid one. The one with the droopy eyes.

"What's going on down there?" Obviously, Brother Sun isn't privy to what just happened down in the tunnel. If he was, he'd probably shoot me.

He motions at me impatiently. "Hurry up, you dumb fuck." Then he reaches out and grips my arm as he tries to drag me out of the manhole.

I've had enough of the Yan Brothers.

I grab his wrist and pull it down and towards me. Then I break his thumb.

He bites his lip and muffles a scream. Brother Sun is dumb, but not dumb enough to make a sound around here. Not with the Bravatso around.

I keep his wrist locked and hyperextend his elbow joint with my other hand. It's so close to snapping, just a little more pressure.

"Touch me again and I'll break every bone in your body." I look him in the eyes so he knows I mean it, then I push him to the ground. He shrinks away whimpering and gripping his injured arm.

I move down the street, sticking to the shadows.

I need to get to the Pripyat Boardwalk.

Fast.

Once more of the refugees start coming up onto the street, they'll attract attention. There's too many of them to all come into the city unnoticed. That means if there's Bravatso in the area, they'll be here soon.

I try to go online and pull up a map of the city. Nothing. A white dot blinking in my peripheral.

I try again. And again. Nothing. Just that white dot blinking.

There is no fucking connection here. The city is dark. The Bravatso must have cut online access to keep out the intelligences.

Fuck.

Fuck.

The Pripyat Boardwalk is on the south-western edge of the city. I know that much. I pop the collar of my coat and move block to block. I traded my suit for boots, heavy workpants, a jumper and a long, tattered coat back at the Liwei Habitat.

I'm glad I did. It's fucking cold here. And barren. In fact, the entire fucking area is a graveyard.

Every building has been torched. Shell after shell, collapsing walls, abandoned cars on the streets. Some fire bug must have had a field day when SPM moved out.

Every now and then I pass a corpse nailed up on a wall or a street post. Some are by themselves, others in groups. Their faces scream silently, eyes wide, mouths agape. Some are fresh and ripe, others are green and black and rotten, and some are nothing more than bones and clothes with piles of disintegrating flesh on the ground below.

They all have signs pinned to their chests, all in Russian.

One says 'наркоман'. Junkie.

Another reads 'шлюха', that's whore.

I pass another group. Rotting bodies of adults and their children. Their signs read 'нечистый'. That means unclean.

I keep on walking.

There's a noise. Then movement. I slow down, crouching in the shadows behind an old, incinerated car.

The wind blows the sleet in gusts. It sheets across the deserted road.

Up ahead a pack of dogs emerges from the shell of one of the buildings. Some with noses trailing on the ground, others listening, ears pricked and snarling. They must have been pets at some stage, abandoned after the company moved out and the criminals moved in. They are mangy, ribs showing, filthy, with patchy fur and skin covered in scabs.

Somewhere in the distance there's the sound of engines. The dogs howl and scatter. A few moments later a convoy of black personnel carriers rumbles by. The vehicles are modified for urban deployment, fully armoured and hermetically sealed, with remote SRDR 9 anti-personnel cannons on each roof.

They look new and clean, out of place in the decrepit city.

I wait silently until I'm sure they're gone. Every now and then I hear the crack of gunshots. I hope it's not the Yan Brothers, taking out their frustrations on those poor fucking people. Maybe I should have stayed around, made sure they all got out safe. Then again, I don't know if it even really matters.

They were fucked no matter what I did. We all are.

It takes me an hour to reach the Pripyat Boardwalk.

In its heyday it was a retreat for the workers of the SPM mines. A man-made cove at the edge of the dome with a grey pebbled beach, a promenade lined with shops and amusements, and a marina with a long, ramshackle jetty. It even had an artificial wave generator.

Now it has fallen into ruin.

The once tall, evergreen pines that lined the esplanade are dead and grey and, for the most part, the shops along the boardwalk are shuttered or burnt out and covered in graffiti.

The water that once lapped up onto the shore of the artificial beach is now frozen solid.

What remains of the Pripyat Boardwalk is a small collection of shops on a jetty, surrounded by a makeshift town of shacks and lean-tos that have been cobbled together from scrounged siding and polymer sheeting from the rental kiosks that had dotted the grey beach.

The street lights didn't work anymore. Now large burning barrels light the roads leading down to the water.

I make my way through the shanty town towards the boardwalk.

It's a twisting warren of grimy little houses and crude shops. The people are from all over. Eastern Europe. India. Jamaica. West Africa. They don't like strangers, you can tell that. Most of them scatter as I pass, scampering back into their homes and peeking out through cracked and pitted sheeting.

Others simply glare at me.

I pass a group of men and women huddled around a fire barrel, hands out, inviting the flames to lick them for warmth. I approach. An old man with a long white beard notices me and takes a swig from a bottle he's holding.

"*Chego ty khochesh*?" He looks me up and down. The others around the barrel back away and huddle together.

"Abram Nikolayevich. You know him?"

He smiles a brown-toothed smile and points toward the boardwalk.

"*Naberezhnaya, naberezhnaya,*" he says impatiently, then switches to broken English. "He has shop on waterfront. He sells furniture."

I nod thanks.

The boardwalk is deserted, for the most part.

It's a collection of buildings that line the waterfront, sagging and weather beaten, paint peeling from years of neglect. Sad-looking prostitutes laze against the railings.

A man lies dead in a pool of his own vomit.

The shopfronts are branded with bleached signs, all in Russian, advertising ice-creams, drinks and amusements. A few lonely boats lie half submerged in the frozen water, their hulls still lashed to the nanocrete dock.

The first shop I pass sells scrounged junk. It's lit by an old lantern which casts a shadowy, yellow glow. The walls of the store are lined with stacks of fuel cells, scavenged building materials and repurposed tools. Inside, several people are arguing loudly.

The store beside it sells clothes. It's dark and its doors are closed.

Further along is an old ice-cream store that has been converted into a butcher of sorts. A sign painted in sloppy red letters stands out front. It reads "Roast Meat".

A man sits on a battered seat outside the store. He has only one eye.

"Need something mate?" he asks in an ugly Australian accent.

I look inside. The windows are smashed and covered in wire. Hanging in the storefront are barbecued carcasses of rats and cats and dogs. Next to them, glistening in the light of the torch, is a roasted human arm hanging on a meat hook.

I move on. The furniture store is the last one on the boardwalk.

I open the rusted door and step inside. It bangs loudly behind me as I walk into the dingy shop, the sound causing the man behind the counter to look up, startled.

He seems apprehensive.

"Can I help you?" he asks in a thick Russian accent. He pushes away a bang of grey hair that falls across his forehead. He's gaunt with sunken eyes. His skin is covered with scabs and open sores. His teeth are shattered yellow stubs.

"I'm looking for Abram Nikolayevich. He has something for me." I glance around the shop.

The interior is worn and beaten up: mould-covered walls and garish patterned floors that have seen better days. The only furniture in the store is an old loveseat and a poorly made table.

"You're him?" he asks.

I don't say anything.

"I was beginning to think you weren't going to show." He smiles, then takes a hit off an inhaler, holding his breath for a moment before releasing a cloud of blue-grey smoke.

He comes around the counter and shakes my hand. "How did you get into the city?"

"A Snakehead named Brother Fang."

Nikolayevich laughs, his eyes glazed from the drug. "Through the access tunnels on the western side of the city. Lucky you're in one piece. Bravatso like to hunt there."

"Yeah, so I've heard."

He shakes his head. "I'd give them a wide berth if I was you. The Bravatso don't like visitors in New Chechnya."

"I'll keep that in mind."

He motions to the back room.

"Your gear arrived last night. I've got it for you in my room."

Nikolayevich draws back a mould-covered sheet tacked to the back wall of the shop, revealing a grimy room.

I follow him in.

It stinks in here. Light filters through a small boarded-up window. A battery-powered lamp sits on the floor nearby. There's an old army cot in one corner, a bucket he's been using for a toilet in the other.

Nikolayevich bends down, pulls out an old black travel case and flips the locks.

"Unfortunately, they couldn't get everything on your list." He stands back, arms crossed nervously at his chest.

I kneel down and open the box.

NR-47 wide-muzzle particle gun with the stock sawn off. RKTR 51 rotary machine pistol with silencer. Ammunition for both. A medical kit. Hand restraints. Eyeball drones. Three DEDs. A programmable matter weapon.

There's no body armour. The other guns are missing.

I glare at him. "Where's the rest? The guns, the armour?"

He seems anxious.

"As I said, that's all they could get on short notice."

Bullshit. The fucker must have raided the box when it arrived. Probably sold most of it to the Bravatso. For a moment, I considered killing Abram Nikolayevich.

Unfortunately, I still need him.

"Where is Xander Odom?" I begin packing the gear away, stashing the med-kit and the drones in my pockets and slinging the rifle under my coat. "Do you have the location where the Bravatso has her stashed?"

He looks at me strangely.

"What do you mean? The Bravatso has been fighting Odom and DAWN for months."

It takes a moment for the information to compute.

"I was told she's been paying them for protection."

Nikolayevich looks at me like I'm out of my mind.

"God no. They're at war. DAWN has taken the Shiporov processing plant on the east side of the dome. It's carnage over there. That's why there's so few Bravatso on this side of town these days – they're trying to take the plant back. Without it they're fucked. They can't process or ship the Helium-3 they've been mining. It's too unstable, useless."

Motherfuckers lied to me. She's not hiding here. She's fighting here. And if she's fighting the Bravatso she's helping SPM's cause, not hindering it.

Then what the fuck do they want with her?

If they were going to kill everyone in New Chechnya anyway, why kidnap her? Why not just leave her here to die? Surely it couldn't be for their own sick pleasure; I mean, her death here would be worse than anything they could think of.

So why?

What do they want with her?

What does she know?

Nikolayevich's ugly drawl snaps me back.

"Look. I drew you a map. With online access down, it's the only way to find your way around." He reached down and fished a torn piece of sheeting he'd stashed beneath his bed and unfolded it on the mattress.

On it is a crude, hand-drawn street map of New Chechnya. He points to the upper left-hand corner.

"If you came in with Brother Fang you would have arrived here, Access Corridor 4. In the Rustov Projects. There are three other access corridors with outside airlocks here, here and here." Nikolayevich points to the locations, one in the north, one to the east, another to the south near the mines. "They are the only way to get out of the city without going through the main port."

Then he traces his finger down to the bottom left-hand corner. "We are here, the Pripyat Boardwalk."

His finger points at several crosses he'd drawn along the top of the map.

"Steer clear of the north side of the dome. That's where the Bravatso are. That fucking monster Drago Afanasievich has his headquarters in the town hall."

I note the location. And the location of the atmospheric control centre. It's further south, near the city centre. Far enough away for me to get in and out without being noticed.

He traces his finger to the far-right edge of the dome. "Odom is here, the Shiporov Processing Plant."

I nod. "What's the best way in?"

"The area around the plant is a war zone at the moment." He points to a crude set of lines he'd marked around the plant. "Bravatso have set up fortifications, here, here and here. You want to come in from the south. But be aware, there is a large drug factory here. They manufacture meth, coke, dust, vapour, ketamine, you name it. This area is no good. A lot of Bravatso. A lot of addicts."

He points to a train station close to the boardwalk.

"I would go in through here, the underground station. Rail lines run under the whole city. Follow the yellow line. You'll come out south of the mine, here." He points to a station near the circular mine on the south-eastern side of the city. "Don't go the red line whatever you do. That's north. You don't want to go north."

He hands me an old-fashioned positioning transmitter. The thing looks like a piece of junk.

"Because of the data blackout you can't call for help. When you're ready for extraction, use this. Just give your location and a man called Radovan Sedlak will pick you up."

There's a sound outside. A strange noise, like a thunderclap.

I begin collecting the ammunition, stashing it in my pants pockets.

"Say. If you want, I can get my son to take you up to the station, show you the way." He smiles his ugly smile. "I'm sure we can figure out a reasonable fee."

Fucker probably has an ambush waiting for me. Probably wants the rest of the gear.

"I work alone," is all I say. He nods begrudgingly.

It's silent. Then nothing.

Then the sound of screaming from outside.

I stop what I'm doing and look over at Nikolayevich. He looks on edge, like an animal about to take flight. The thunderclap noise again. The lights in the dilapidated shop suddenly come to life, burning brightly for a moment, then dead.

"What the fuck?" I look over at Nikolayevich, confused. There's no power on the Pripyat Boardwalk. What could have turned the lights on, even for a moment?

"It's a raid. The Bravatso." Nikolayevich looks over towards the front door with fear in his eyes. "You have to go. Now!"

I grab the last of my gear, clipping the machine pistol to my belt and opening the box containing the programmable matter.

It looks like nothing. Two matt black discs the size of my palm. I pick one up in each hand. They stay solid for a moment as the matter links to my nervous system. Then they melt in my palms. They become a viscous, malleable putty. They slip around my wrists like black mercury and secure themselves in the LOCK formation, becoming two solid bands.

As long as I have physical contact I can manipulate them into anything I want.

"Get out of here now, before they come." He pulls back the mouldy sheet and looks out to the front of his shitty little shop.

I move past him. For a moment I consider killing him again.

But I decide not to.
I'm sure the Bravatso will soon enough.

14.

Quantum Dots.

Ever heard the term "unstable metamaterial" before?

What about "shape-changing complex fluid technology"?

No?

Don't worry – up until a few years ago, neither had I.

They're all fancy names for the base technology used in offensive and defensive programmable matter weaponry.

HAZE Suits. PRO-AM Weapons. Deflective Explosive Devices.

The tech was originally developed by Dr Rolf Morbius for the Scandinavian Union Special Forces. He created programmable matter melee weapons that were controlled through subcutaneous communication of the user's neural network. When activated, individual atoms inside the weapon's mass were altered via manipulation of energy states within the electrons to produce metastable states with highly unusual properties. This allowed the user to simply think of a shape and the unstable matter would shift to match.

Whatever the fuck that meant.

The simpler definition was this.

Want a knife? Hold the programmable matter in your hand and it morphs into a razor-sharp blade, exactly how you pictured it in your mind's eye.

Not scary enough?

How about a sword? Or a bladed staff? Or a baton, a garrotte or a whip, a hammer or an axe? In fact, it could mimic anything you could think of, as long as it wasn't larger than its own mass, or complex, like a machine.

These were called programmable matter or PRO-AM Weapons

If you wrapped an explosive in programmable matter you created what they call a deflective explosive device or a DED. These fuckers were awesome in the field. Throw them at a target and they stick. Boom. Bounce them off a wall, around a corner to fuck up some prick taking cover. Program them to rebound off one surface and stick to another for precision-timed explosions.

They were lots of fun.

But it didn't stop there.

Because the surface of programmable matter was strong enough to withstand a close range hit from a particle weapon they started making combat suits from it.

They called them HAZE Suits.

They could withstand massive extremes in temperatures, adjust its density to cushion against impacts, or harden to protect the wearer from firearms and knifepoint. Combined with nanite technology, it could react instantly in emergency situations, contracting and sealing wounds if the wearer was injured or plug into the brain to help stimulate the release chemicals like dopamine, endorphins or adrenalin.

With technology like this, even soldiers without genetic enhancement became formidable. But for those of us that had been rebuilt on the operating table, programmable matter weaponry made us one step beyond.

We became absolutely fucking lethal.

15.

Disco Inferno.

The smell of burnt meat fills the air. It's sweet and sickly.

The boardwalk out front of Nikolayevich's fetid little store is now deserted. The strange little Australian man, the prostitutes, even the people arguing in the junk store are all gone.

Only the dead man in the pool of vomit remains.

I could hear screaming and panic and running and gunshots off in the distance. You could feel it in the air, the violence. The anarchy. It was everywhere.

I needed to get out of here. Head east. If the Bravatso were raiding this place I needed to get as far away as possible.

I make my way to the end of the boardwalk and look around the corner, up towards the shanty town. It's on fire. People are dead in the streets, stopped as they fled in fear. There's loud music playing and the sound of car engines and guns.

Closer now, I can hear footsteps, voices. A man and a woman appear around the corner ahead, both armed with automatic weapons. They're coming my way, down to the shops on the boardwalk.

They're Bravatso.

You can always pick them, they're easy to spot. All Bravatso have their faces ritually scared when they join, branded by a plasma torch. They call it Otmetka, brutal geometric patterns across their forehead, cheeks and nose. If you wanted to join the Bravatso, that was the entry fee. If you wanted to leave, the fee was much higher.

You paid with your life.

"I fucking saw them," the man says to the woman as he peers into the dark. "It's a whole family, I promise."

"I can't see anyone," the woman replies. She has a thick Russian accent and sounds annoyed. "Maybe you made a mistake. We should get back."

"I'm telling you, they came down here." They stop in the middle of the street, both scanning for signs of movement. "A man, a woman and two kids."

I shift in the shadows, tuning my hearing to block out the background noise.

"Just make sure they're worth it," the woman sneers. "They need fifteen viable subjects. No homeless this time. They're always sick."

What the fuck were they talking about?

"I don't know what Drago expects us to do. This whole fucking city's sick or dying." The man looks over to where I'm hiding, in the shadows near the boardwalk. "I'm gonna check the boardwalk."

"What do you want me to do?" She hacks and spits on the wet ground.

"Keep an eye on the road and don't let them get away," he says, starting towards the boardwalk. "Those fuckers are around here somewhere."

I sink back into the shadows.

This whole job feels wrong. The story Anatoli fed me back at the Azure Habitat is bullshit. I know he's lying, it's the why I can't figure out yet.

I need to be on my guard.

I activate the programmable matter and feel it move from around my wrists, covering my hands as they lock into the SPIKE formation. It's one of the takedown techniques I learned in the army. Form the programmable matter over your hands with a ten-centimetre conical spike protruding from between your first and second knuckles. It makes your striking extremely effective in close-quarter combat, especially for silent takedowns.

I wait for the man to round the corner, pushing myself back against the wall. As soon as he passes I strike from behind.

I deliver one sharp punch to the back, severing his spinal column between the C3 and C4 vertebrae. This ensures total paralysis of his arms, legs and torso, including the muscles of his diaphragm. He can't make a sound, hell, he can't even breathe. He drops like a bag of meat and I catch him before he hits the ground, placing him on the boardwalk softly to ensure there's no noise.

He'll suffocate before anyone finds him. I leave him to die in the shadows and move forward towards the girl.

The other Bravatso is out on the street; she's looking around but not alert. She seems bored. I close the distance in an instant and strike two successive blows. The first up under her ribs, puncturing her lung. She gasps and wheezes for a moment. Before she can turn around, I finish her with a punch to the back of the head, the conical spike passing through her skull and cerebellum and into her brain stem.

I retract the programmable matter to the LOCK formation. I can feel the blood on my hands as it retreats back around my wrists.

I move up into the warren of streets in the makeshift slum and head east. People are running everywhere, chaos.

The sound of music gets louder and louder. It's nuclear synth-core. High-speed, ultra-aggressive electronic music. The drum beat sounds like a fucking heart attack. It's the kind of shit vapour heads listen to in the underground clubs in Warsaw and Moscow.

More gunshots, then the sound of a car engine and deranged laughter.

A utility rounds the corner at speed, speakers blaring and flying low, hugging the pavement. It's beat up, stained in blood and dirt with two naked corpses strapped to the bonnet. They've been decapitated. And gutted. There are two men in the car, one driving and the other standing on the back, manning a high-calibre gun mounted to the tray.

People on the street around me scream in panic.

The Bravatso manning the gun opens fire. The high-powered anti-personnel weapon shreds the people in front of me – an old man, bent and twisted, is literally cut in half by the gunfire. The Bravatso in the utility laugh maniacally at the sight.

I duck into a side street and keep moving, staying low.

The smell of burnt meat is much stronger up here. Smoke fills the air. Fire is spreading everywhere.

I come to the end of the makeshift street and stop, crouching in the shadows.

There is a large clearing in the middle of the shanty town, lined with dark little hovels made of scrap and junk. A bonfire blazes in the centre of the crude square, casting long, flickering shadows across the walls.

There's a large truck parked nearby with a Bravatso standing guard.

The truck is towing a trailer that's been modified into a large cage. About ten people are locked inside. Wide-eyed and panicked. They're mostly women and children, a couple of men, all screaming and trying desperately to get out.

"Shut the fuck up," the guard growls, slamming the butt of his gun into the fingers of a man who's grasping the bars of the cage. He howls in agony, cradling his broken and bloody hand.

More screaming and voices from nearby.

A Bravatso with ugly metal piercings and glowing violet eyes emerges from a side street. He's dragging two teenage boys by the arms. The boys are both dressed in rags and struggle violently to break free from his grasp.

"Hey, Dimitri, open the gate," the violet eyed Bravatso barks. "I got two more."

Before Dimitri can move, one of the boys breaks free.

Then the other.

"Fucking little shits!" the violet eyed Bravatso yells, trying to grab hold of one of them as they slip out of his grasp. "Get them!"

The boys run for their lives, as hard as they can, their bare, bloody feet slapping on the wet ground as they run past.

Their eyes are wide, mouths twisted in terror.

I look closer at the gun Dimitri is carrying. It's fat and heavy with an ugly-looking barrel. Long, thick chords snake across its matt frame. I realise why I can smell burnt meat and why the shacks are all on fire.

It's a fucking lighting gun, a TLA 11 electromagnetic mini-gun.

He takes aim. The rotary barrel spins at high speed and tongues of purple and blue plasma begin to lick the muzzle of the gun. It makes a high, whining noise and the air crackles with the smell of burnt ozone. Then, there's a deafening thunderclap as he fires. A great bolt of electricity suddenly shoots out, hitting one of the boys in the back.

The boy stops as if he's frozen, his muscles spasming and jerking. The lightning jumps from his body and splits into branches of glowing plasma that arc out, striking the other boy and lighting up a string of street lights nearby.

The first boy catches fire as the electrostatic explosion ignites his body, the other is blown off his feet and is dead before he hits the ground.

Dimitri laughs loudly at this, amused as the child's half-charred corpse continues to twitch on the ground.

"Are you out of your fucking mind Dimitri?" the violet eyed Bravatso shouts loudly, storming over. "They were perfect. You know how long it took me to find them?"

Fucking pricks. Killing defenceless children.

"Shut the fuck up," Dimitri laughs, waving his hand dismissively. The smell of cooked meat is sickening. "Those kids are like fucking rats. They're everywhere around here."

I draw the machine pistol from my belt and level the gun. They haven't seen me yet. I step out from the shadows and start towards them. They both turn as they see me moving, but it's too late. I shoot the violet eyed Bravatso first. A burst of energized micro-projectiles hits him in the side of the face, which explodes in a shower of muscle and bone.

A moment later, I fire a second burst at Dimitri.

The gunfire catches him in the neck, shredding his throat right down to his spine. His head lolls to the side, held on by a thin flap of skin, as he collapses on the road.

The people in the cage look at me with wide eyes, unsure of what has just happened. I move quickly, stepping over the dead Bravatso bodies and shoot the lock on the cage's gate.

It swings open but nobody moves. They huddle together against the back of the cage.

"Get the fuck out of here!" I say.

They start to scramble out, some crying, some thanking me in sobbing gasps.

"Come on," I say, helping one of the last kids out. "It's not safe."

As if to prove my point, five more Bravatso appear on the street ahead of me.

I drag the last person from the cage, urging them to run.

"Move," is all I get to say before they open fire.

Two of the women fleeing are shot in the back, the others scatter. There's nothing more I can do for them now. I run for cover. The Bravatso shoot at me as I scramble to behind the frame of a burnt-out car. But they're full of adrenaline and not aiming right, so they miss.

The key to surviving small arms combat while fighting superior numbers is movement. Never stop moving. Never give them a stationary target or the opportunity to pin you down.

Create opportunities.

Find cover.

Constantly improve your position.

The five Bravatso on the street ahead of me aren't finding cover. They're walking towards me, almost side by side, confident in their superior numbers and firepower.

That's a big mistake.

I need to break these fuckers up, flank them if possible. I open fire in short bursts and move up the street.

They return fire and I dodge easily.

I push harder, running at top speed now. They all open fire, but again, it's wild and I move through the gunfire with ease. They are metres away and I can see the look of disbelief in their eyes, uncertain as to why I would be stupid enough to attack them head on.

They're about to find out.

I activate the nanite system in my adrenal cortex, hyper-secreting adrenalin into my body. Energy courses through me and my heart feels like it's stampeding and ready to burst. Inside I'm charged and glowing, and everything decelerates to a crawl, as if the world around me is suddenly in slow motion.

The programmable matter slides down from my wrist and fills my left hand setting itself in the LASH formation. I fire another burst of gunfire, peppering one of the Bravatso across the chest. He gasps and crumples to the ground as I launch myself into the air, jumping over where they are spread across the road. In mid-air I twist my body and crack the programmable matter weapon at the man closest to me. It unfurls across the space like a long black razor-edged whip, striking him in the right shoulder and slicing down across his torso, through his collarbone and across his ribcage, exiting his side just above his left hipbone.

I land on the ground behind them. The man stands still, eyes open wide and blinking as his legs collapse and his torso slops apart in a mess of viscera and blood, bisected.

I retract the weapon back around my wrist. The three remaining Bravatso look on in disbelief at what has just happened.

They stand there for what seems like forever.

Then they come to their senses and fan out across the street, taking cover.

I run, sprinting away from them as fast as I can. They open fire all at once and I dodge but this time I'm not so lucky. I feel gunshot explode in my side.

White hot pain flares for a moment, then I block it out.

"Motherfucker," I swear loudly. That shouldn't have happened. I'm better than that.

I stumble and pick myself up again. My legs feel weak. I glance down at my side, blood flowing from a sizeable hole just above my right hip bone. I'm pretty sure I can see my intestine.

More gunshots explode around me. The three Bravatso are now giving chase. I return fire wildly, missing and dropping my gun, sprinting faster and faster down the street.

Just then there's the sound of a car engine ahead and the blare of loud music again. The blood-stained utility with the bodies strapped to the hood appears at the end of the street and comes screaming towards me, its headlights blinding.

"Come on little piggy!" shouts the deranged Bravatso manning the gun.

It's all in slow motion.

"Little pig, little...." the Bravatso begins to taunt, but it's all he gets to say – I'm on him in the blink of an eye.

One heartbeat, I'm on the bonnet of the utility.

Second heartbeat and I'm airborne.

I deliver a spike elbow to his pterion. It's the thinnest part of the cranium, the point where the temporal bones meet. His fucking skull breaks like an eggshell, rupturing the frontal branch of his meningeal artery. He staggers for a moment then his eyes roll back into his head as he goes limp, his body convulsing in death throes.

As I kick the body aside, the driver looks over his shoulder through the back window of the cabin. He swears loudly and, in a panic, brings the car to a screeching stop.

I aim the gun at him through the window.

There's a second where our eyes meet. He knows what's coming and I give him a smile.

Then I open fire. At this range, he's gazpacho.

His head and shoulders dissolve into a fine, red mist. The rest of him slumps forward. Tiny particles of meat and bone drip from the inside of the gore-soaked cabin.

I turn the gun down the street, opening fire on the three Bravatso giving chase. Only one dives out of the way in time, taking cover behind one of the shacks lining the street.

The other two are mincemeat.

Smoke fills the street.

I can see the heat signature of the last Bravatso taking cover behind the polymer wall and finish him with one blast, the high-powered gun shredding the flimsy siding and the man behind it.

The gunshots trail off through the canyons of the shanty town.

It's silent, save for the ticking of the car engine and the screams. I check the body of the dead Bravatso lying beside me.

He has nothing of value.

I step down from the tray. Even though I can't feel the pain of the wound I wince anyway. I can feel the blood running down my leg. It's wet and it's warm.

I collect my gun from the road and head east, away from the Pripyat Boardwalk towards the underground train lines.

But first, I need to find somewhere safe, somewhere I can fix myself up.

Otherwise I'm going to die.

16.

Inside Out.

Every few steps I take, I feel my intestine slip out the hole in my side.

When it does, I have to stop for a moment and carefully push it back inside. It doesn't hurt all that much – the regulators on my pain receptors take care of that. But I can tell I've been shot. I'm dizzy, short of breath. My knees feel weak.

And it's seriously slowing me down.

I've been running for about ten minutes and I'm pretty sure I'm safe now. I haven't seen any Bravatso following me. I have to stop soon though.

I've lost too much blood.

The sleet and rain that's been falling since I arrived have eased some and the clouds above seem to be clearing. When I look up, I can see the black expanse beyond the dome. Disturbingly, I notice a rippling band of green light shimmering and clinging to the inside the thick silicon structure.

In the darkness, it looks like an aurora. Like polar lights.

But it's not. It's radiation. There's a crack somewhere in the dome and solar radiation is leaking through.

This place is slow death just waiting to happen.

My run becomes a jog, which soon slows to a fast walk.

The neighbourhood around me looks different, like it might have been the financial district of the city. Unlike the Rustov Projects or the Pripyat Boardwalk, the buildings here are for the most part intact, apart from smashed windows and damage from the elements.

Everything around seems colossal in scale.

Cramped, debris-filled streets open out into long, wide boulevards lined with grey monolithic office buildings and oversized statues of Russian leaders. Crumbling and burnt-down tenements are replaced by stacked modular slabs with facades of geometric breeze blocks. The flat, endless sea of low-rise apartment blocks gives way to circular barbicans and pebblecrete skyscrapers that tower above the streets like some brutalist jungle.

As I make my way down the street, I can feel eyes on me.

Dirty faces peek down from the smashed windows of an abandoned warehouse.

Shadows shift and retreat down a dark doorway as I pass.

From a covered overpass between high-rises, an old man dressed in a long, tattered coat and dog skin hat eyes me warily.

I stumble.

A long length of intestine slips from my gut. I gasp from the sensation, looking down at the blueish grey loop for several moments before I scoop up the bloody mess and gingerly push it back in.

I need to sit down. Get this bleeding under control.

I cross the road and head towards a deserted square lined with three identical grey towers. The doorway for the first tower is blocked by a stacked debris barricade.

The second is open.

I burst through the doors and stagger inside. The building looks like it was an office. Maybe city administration or town planning. Scavengers have already stripped it to its bones. What's left is a mess. Long shadows and broken windows. The floors scattered with junk and rubbish, the panelled walls pried open and ransacked for anything of value.

I sit down heavily on the ground and lean back against the wall. My jumper and pants are soaked in blood. I can feel it sloshing around in my right boot.

I take off my jacket and tentatively pull up my shirt and jumper. There's a hole about as wide as two of my fingers in my right side, just below my floating rib. Blood pulses out of the wound to the beat of my heart.

"Fuck," I say, too loudly. My voice seems to echo in the empty space.

Then a noise. It sounds like feet shifting on concrete. It's coming from the next room.

I didn't sweep the place first. How could I be so careless?

My vision switches between heat signature and electrical impulse. Through the wood veneer wall ahead I can see the three people. One is standing, weapon drawn, near the open doorway. Two more are taking cover nearby.

I draw my gun and try to push myself up to my feet. My guts slide out and I drop back down hard, gasping for breath. I don't need this shit right now.

"This is your only warning," a man's voice calls. He sounds Russian, older. "Get out while you can. This building is our building. I have twenty armed men here ready to fight."

I shift over to my left side and hold myself together by pressing my right hand over the wound. With my other arm I carefully start to drag myself across the floor towards a nearby overturned workstation.

"There's nothing for you here," the man continues. His voice waivers as he speaks. He sounds nervous. "There's nothing for you to steal. No food. No nothing. Leave now or we'll be forced to kill you. This is your last warning."

I pull myself behind the workstation with a grunt.

I can feel my breathing become shallow, my vison blurs. "First person who comes out firing dies, you hear me?"

Silence.

I grip the pistol in my left hand and try to position myself for better shot at the door. The heat signature behind the wall doesn't move. They start whispering to each other nervously. I focus in on the sound, tuning my ear and dropping out the ambient noise above and below two thousand μPa.

It only takes a few moments, then I hear them as clear as if they were standing next to me.

"Yuri, please, you can't handle this on your own. You need to get Sayan and the others." It's a woman's voice. Older. She's Russian too. It sounds familiar.

"Father, let's go upstairs." A girl's voice.

"It'll be okay, I promise. He's just looking for something to steal," Yuri whispers.

"We can't take much more, Yuri. Not after everything that's happened to Orlova and me today." The older woman sounds panicked.

"Svetlana, take Orlova upstairs. I can handle this." Yuri sounds terrified.

These people aren't a threat. If I can talk my way out of this, I will.

"I don't want any trouble," I say. "I'm just passing through."

"Then leave!" Yuri shouts.

"I'm injured. I need time to fix myself up." I look down at the hole in my side. My right hand is soaked in blood. I can see dark little spots dance in my peripherals.

"You're hurt?" Yuri asks.

"I'm shot. The Bravatso attacked the Pripyat Boardwalk."

More whispering. Heated this time.

"Father no..." the girl Orlova pleads.

"I'm coming out to help," Yuri says.

I lower my gun, but I'm ready. Never trust anyone.

A dishevelled, old man with tufts of iron-grey hair appears through the doorway. He has a kind, careworn face. He's still holding his gun, but his hands are in the air.

"Don't shoot, alright?" Yuri's eyes dart across the room, searching for me in the dark, till he sees me laid out half behind the workstation in a pool of blood.

The older woman, Svetlana, sheepishly appears in the doorway behind Yuri. Then the girl. I recognise them immediately. It's the old woman and her daughter from the tunnel, the one Brother Ren pistol-whipped for crying loudly.

"It's you," Svetlana says as she recognises me. "You're the man from the tunnel."

Yuri stops and looks back at his wife and daughter. "You know this man?"

Orlova nods emphatically and she and her mother push past Yuri. "He's the one we told you about, the one who saved us. He stopped them beating Mother when we arrived."

I try to sit up but I can't.

"Don't move," Svetlana urges, kneeling beside me.

"I'm alright," I say, the darkness dancing in my peripherals. "I've got a med-kit. I just need somewhere safe to lay down for a bit."

Svetlana looks up at her husband. "Yuri. Help me get him upstairs."

They help me to my feet and drape my arms over their shoulders. I don't know if I've got my gun anymore. Things start to blur. They lead me through the room to a dingy nanocrete stairwell, lit every second floor by a small, battery-powered lamp.

I look up.

It seems to stretch for forever.

"It's a long way up, my friend. Twenty storeys," Yuri says. "Can you make it?"

I nod yes and we begin the ascent.

It takes close to a half an hour before we reach the twentieth floor. We have to stop every few floors so I can get my breath.

It's all a haze. But I hold it together till we reach the top.

The door leading to the top floor is locked and Yuri bangs loudly. "Sayan, Thomas, open up."

We wait in the dark for a few moments. Then the sound of furniture moving behind the door. It opens a crack.

"What's wrong? Why are you back so soon?" a man asks.

"Thomas, open the door now. This man is badly injured."

A rake-thin blond man with a long nose and glasses opens the door and Yuri and Svetlana rush me inside. I'm led into a wide, open-plan office space with floor-to-ceiling windows and a panoramic view of New Chechnya. About ten people live here. Like downstairs, most of the fittings had been stripped from the space, including the carpet. What remains is a dark, cold, empty space with makeshift bedding and scattered furniture.

It stinks of smoke and cooking and humanity.

"Over this way," Yuri says, leading us to an unmade bed against the wall. "Sayan, come help us."

A thin man with greasy hair and brown teeth gets up from a tattered sofa nearby and helps Yuri guide me to the mattress.

All eyes in the room turn towards us. Some get up from where they are seated and drift over to watch the spectacle, while others mutter suspiciously to each other.

"Here's good," Yuri says.

I groan loudly as they lower me down on the bed. Thomas joins the crowd hovering over me.

"What do you need?" Svetlana bends down beside me and holds my hand. "Water? Bandages?"

I shake my head. "Just give me some space. I've got a nanite med-kit."

She nods and motions for the others to step back. Thomas and Sayan seem reluctant to go too far and leave a stranger alone.

"Who the fuck is this?" Thomas asks, watching intently as I grope at my jacket till I find the pocket with medical kit in it.

"He saved my girls from the Snakeheads," Yuri answers. "He says there's been an attack by the Bravatso over in Pripyat."

"He's armed to the fucking teeth, did you know that?" asks Thomas, glaring over at me.

"What am I supposed to do, huh?" Yuri snaps back. "Leave him?"

"Yes," Sayan says throwing up his hands in exasperation. "That's exactly what you're supposed to do. He's a fucking killer, can't you see that?"

"It doesn't matter what he is." Yuri argues back. "Without him, Svetlana and Orlova would be dead."

I try to ignore the arguing and open the small red-and-white case, roughly remove the surgical pen from its housing and hold it in my hand. It neurally links with my IdentityChip.

A Medison TEC logo appears and words begin to scrawl across my field of vision.

Thank you for choosing Surgi-Pen from Medison TEC. Please state the nature of your emergency.

"Gunshot," I growl.

I can feel them looking, but I pay them no heed.

To operate your Medison TEC Surgi-Pen please place the device within five centimetres of your wound and press the RED DIAGNOSIS BUTTON. For multiple injuries...

I cut it off before it continues. I pull up my jumper and inject the pen next to the gunshot wound.

Thank you. Flashes before my eyes. *Please wait while we diagnose your injuries.*

I breathe deeply and regularly and ignore the argument at the end of the bed. I wait as the microscopic nanite robots that I've injected into my blood stream disperse through my system and diagnose every function in my body.

Diagnosis complete. Flashes across my vision. *The following is an analysis of your injuries. Trauma to the epidermis, dermis, diaphragm, peritoneum, liver, ascending colon, right kidney...*

"Cut the shit," I mutter, and the readout stops. "Can you fix it?"

It flashes for a moment.

Recommend immediate surgery. Approximate treatment time, one hour and twelve minutes.

"Do it," I say. I shift into a more comfortable position.

Surgical treatment underway. Administering anaesthesia. Time remaining...

A countdown appears before my eyes.

5...

4...

I'm asleep before it reaches 3.

I awaken with a start and screams in my ears. A flashing message is in front of my eyes.

Treatment complete.

I look down at my side. My clothes are still soaked in blood. There is a large red mark and shiny skin that looks like a burn where the hole used to be. Aside from the itching it feels totally normal. I start to get to my feet.

A red message flashes before my eyes.

Warning. Your injuries require recovery under the supervision of medical professionals. Would you like me to call an ambulance?

"Fuck off," I growl.

A final message blinks, then disappears. *Thank you for using Medison TEC.*

I find the tab dispenser in my coat pocket and press a hit against my wrist, then get to my feet and look around.

Suspicious faces glare back at me.

I see Yuri and Svetlana sitting with Thomas and Sayan in a makeshift living area near the windows on the far side of the space.

Yuri looks over his shoulder and smiles. He beckons me over. "How are you feeling?"

"Better," I say.

Both Thomas and Sayan frown and whisper something to each other as I approach. I notice they both have guns within easy reach.

"Can we get you something?" Svetlana asks. "Would you like to sit?"

I shake my head. "No. I need to get going."

Thomas regards me warily. "What are you doing in New Chechnya?"

"Looking for someone," I say.

Nervous glances.

"Who?" Sayan's hand is moving closer to the sawn-off scatter gun. He must be on the run. Maybe he thinks I'm a bounty hunter coming to get him.

"Doesn't matter," I reply, meeting his stare.

No one says anything for a bit. You can cut the tension with a knife.

Yuri's uncomfortable laugh breaks the silence as he changes the subject. "Well, we are sorry to see you go. If there's anything you ever need or..."

I cut him off. "Are the train tunnels the fastest way to the east side of the dome?"

Both Thomas and Sayan shake their heads. Yuri looks at me as if I've lost my mind.

"Very dangerous down there," he says. "The things that live in those tunnels, they're not human anymore. They're crazy from the drugs. Cannibals. They hunt people for food like animals."

Sayan notices the look of surprise on my face.

"A lot of vapour addicts live under the city," Sayan explains. "The Bravatso have a drug factory on the east side of the dome in Little Moscow. There's bad air around there. A lot of addicts in the area. The Bravatso round them up and shoot them out on the streets, so they end up in the old subway tunnels."

I nod slowly. I don't want to go that way, not if there's vapour addicts down there. Vapour is the street name for a pharmaceutically synthesised amphetamine/LSD hybrid. Use it long enough, it'll send you fucking crazy. Hallucinations, psychosis, paranoia, you name it. Some of the stories I've heard are brutal, murder and eat your own parents' kind of brutal.

"Is there a faster way?"

"No. Not unless you've got a car," Yuri says.

It's quiet again.

Yuri clears his throat nervously. "Can I give you some advice?"

I don't say anything.

"You don't want to be out on the streets these days my friend, not for too long anyway. Whatever you're here to do, do it fast, and go. The Bravatso are hunting people, rounding them up and taking them over to the Shirapov processing plant."

That's different to what Nikolayevich told me. He said Odom and DAWN were holed up in the Shirapov plant preventing the Bravatso from processing Helium-3 they were mining. If Yuri's telling the truth, then where the fuck is Xander Odom?

"Why?" I ask.

"I don't know." Yuri's words hang in the air. The others stay quiet.

None of this makes sense.

Somebody's lying to me. I don't know why, but the answer's not here.

It's in New Moscow.

I look out the dirt-streaked window. New Chechnya sprawls beyond in silhouettes and shadows.

Heavy rain tumbles down across the dark city, the great curve of the dome can be seen above the heavy clouds. The warm glow of campfires flicker from the top floors of nearby skyscrapers. Every now and then the twinkling lights of a car can be seen flying low above the buildings.

And off in the distance, the bright lights of New Moscow shine through the driving sleet.

The Bravatso have got the power on over there.

And that's where I'm headed.

17.

The Antarctician Candidate.

Every morning you are up at 4.00 am. Inspection is at 4.15.

If you're a minute late, you get the Box.

That's how every day begins at the Bouwer Re-education Centre. If you're a student of the centre, you're there to follow the rules. To learn. To become a useful member of the People's Party. They tell you it's voluntary, of course. They say you don't have to be there.

But if you try to leave, you get the Box.

And you don't want to get the Box.

Breakfast is at 4.30 then morning exercise is at five. Exercise is the same every day. A healthy body means a healthy mind. That's what they say in the People's Party.

At 6.55 am you get a five-minute bathroom break, then at 7.00 it's time for class. If you're a minute late, you get the Box.

There is only one lesson. They teach it every day. Ideological Remoulding. It's where you're taught the real history of the people's struggle for freedom in Antarctica. Your duties to the party. How to be a constructive member of society. Learn from the past to fix the future. That's what they say in the People's Party.

There's a test after every class. Get a question wrong, you get the Box.

At 1.00 pm it's lunch. Then bathroom break. Afternoon exercise from 1.30 till 3.30. Then manual labour. They say hard work builds spirit, a sense of belonging in your community.

Common values are Party values. That's what they say in the People's Party.

At 8.00 pm it's dinner. At 8.25 another toilet break.

At 8.30 it's session time. Everyone has to do a session once a week. They say self-criticism helps eliminate counterrevolutionary thinking. You stand up in front of the other students in the centre and confess all the times you've questioned the wisdom of the People's party.

The crimes you've committed against your fellow students by thinking the wrong way.

The crimes of your family and why they deserved to die.

Then the other students get to help you see the error of your ways. They get to abuse and beat you.

If you can still stand, 10.30 till midnight is evening class. If not, you get the Box.

At 12.30 it is time for bed. You're up again at 4.00 am. Seven days a week.

If you're a minute late, you get the Box.

And you don't want to get the Box.

18.

Tunnel Rats.

The entrance to the subway is in the far corner of a large square lined with oversized statues of Lenin and Stalin and Tarasovich. Above the stairwell leading down to the train tunnels is a sign that says "Vostochnyy Line" in yellow and "Severny Line" in red.

Yellow is east. Red is north.

Each lead somewhere I'd rather not be going.

The stairway down is dark and littered with refuse. I draw my gun and move into the gloom slowly.

It's quiet down here. There's no source of light.

My eyes scan for heat signatures and electrical impulses and open up for low-light enhancement. Before me is a long, grey tunnel with smashed holographic billboards on the walls. Garbage is piled high, and the stench of death is heavy in the air.

I move forward cautiously, finger on the trigger.

There's a corpse on the ground nearby. Nothing more than a bag of bones in leather skin.

Then another. Shrivelled and long dead.

Then a few more.

I lower myself to a knee and scan the tunnel. Nothing is moving. Not that I can see anyway.

Ahead, the tunnel splits, stairwells leading down to the yellow line and the red line. Blocking the entrance and most of the tunnel is a barricade that's been cobbled together with scrounged siding and bits of the station. More withered bodies are scattered on the floor around it.

The words "Fuck Off" are scrawled across the barricade in big red letters.

I move forward, tense, expecting the tunnel to light up with gunfire at any moment.

But it doesn't.

I approach the barricade cautiously; there's a hole big enough to get through but it's not taller than my hip. Bad exposure, moving blind and almost prone into what could be a hostile area.

It's not ideal.

I press myself against the barricade and scan the area behind it. There's nothing; it's dark from what I can see. But that doesn't mean shit. There's plenty of ways to make yourself invisible to heat and electrical.

I retrieve the small black case from my lower leg pocket and place it quietly on the floor. As soon I open the case, the Eyeball drones stir to life – all five marble-sized unmanned aerial vehicles linking to my neural network and rising up into the air. They hover just above the ground, small propulsion vents at the base of the polished black orbs glow an iridescent blue. Their cameras feed directly to my optic nerve. I can see myself looking at myself in the corner of my vision.

The drones hover in place in front of me until I motion with my hand. They duck through the hole in the barricade, the five black orbs shooting off in the blink of an eye.

They scan the space behind the barricade in an instant.

There's nothing back there.

Remnants of a makeshift checkpoint long abandoned, a broken chair, food containers and an old bed. Stairwells leading down to the yellow and red line flank the tunnel.

"Map the yellow line tunnel," I whisper.

The drones descend down the stairs, sending back a live feed and three-dimensional map to my optic nerve.

I can see the yellow line platform. It's deserted and strew with rubbish and refuse like up here in the tunnel. The drones move around the space, charting the layout.

The hollow sound of dripping echoes through the tunnel.

Something's off.

It looks like there's been activity here. Something recent.

"Stop," I say under my breath.

A drone stops in front of one of the holographic billboards that run along the wall behind the train line. It's shattered, long dead and peppered with the spray of gunfire.

I position another drone above the rail line.

The ground looks wet, like mud. There's no water on the Moon. Not liquid anyway. The wastewater from the city must have seeped down into the tunnel when the power was cut.

I move the drone down for a closer look. There are footprints in the mud. Multiple sets. They lead east down the yellow line. The drones follow them tracking silently down the train tunnel in the pitch black.

An empty magazine lies in the sludge.

A few metres later a body lies half submerged in a pool of water.

It's bloated and green – the rats have begun to take it apart. It looks like a gunshot took off the entire side of her face. Unlike the shrivelled corpses up here, this one can't be more than two weeks dead.

The body's been stripped naked, all of her equipment and clothes scavenged. She looks like a professional, a mercenary. There are tell-tale signs of augmentation still evident on her rotting skin.

I move the drones forward.

It's a massacre.

No more than two metres ahead, there's another body, then three more piled nearby in the slime, all in the same state.

Whoever ambushed them knew what they were doing.

I zoom in on one of the bodies. The man's face is red and distended, his eyeballs dissolving into soup near his forehead. I know him. He's a head-hunter, just like me. Well, at least he was. We were on the same team a few years back, raided the JRA Research lab in Copenhagen.

Emile Baptiste. Specialised in hard target acquisition.

I'm betting they're the team SPM sent in before me. At least the ones that weren't captured and skinned alive by Drago.

Poor fuckers.

I send the drones ahead to map the rest of the tunnel. It doesn't take very long. There's only water ahead. The entire tunnel is flooded.

"Fuck," I say under my breath and make my way down to the platform.

I move down the stairs to the cool dark of the platform. You can smell the dead down here, taste the stench in your mouth.

I jump down onto the rail line and sink ankle-deep in sludge, then move quickly down the line ignoring the stack of bodies. The tunnel is pitch black. Nothing moves.

The dank odour of stagnant water is heavy in the air. The sound of my breathing and the wet squelch of my footsteps is all I can hear. It gets deeper as I continue down the tunnel, the thick sludge giving way to muck that laps around my shins. Then my knees. The smell gets stronger, damp and musty.

It fills my nostrils.

It's not long before it's at my thighs. Then my hips. I notice the tunnel begins to decline sharply. By the time it's at my waist the water level has completely inundated the tunnel ahead.

It's flooded.

I'm going to have to swim. In this shit.

Fuck.

I call the Eyeball drones to my position.

"Map," I say.

They descend into the muck and streak through the tunnel ahead. It takes about a minute for the information to come back. The subway is flooded for the next eighty-six meters. Then there's an air pocket. And what looks like a doorway leading to a service tunnel. The tunnel continues for another one hundred and twenty-six meters beyond, then ascends.

I can't swim the whole way without stopping to breathe. So, I'm going to have to stop at the air pocket. But what concerns me more than the distance is the movement in the area. I'm registering thousands of electrical signals around that air pocket.

I've got a good idea what they are.

Rats.

Fucking rats in the tunnels. There's no rats on the Moon, at least not naturally anyway. But they always find a way to come along with us wherever we go. They're stowaways and opportunists, they follow us quietly from the shadows. As long as there are people moving between places, rats will always come along for the ride. And in our last days, when we finally die out, they will be there too. Our constant companions.

Waiting, till they can gorge on our corpses.

I wade in up to my chest, take one final deep breath and then dive down into the fetid slop. The water is like thick soup, brackish and foul; I wouldn't be able to see more than an arm's length in front of me so I keep my eyes closed and focus on the map the drones are projecting into my optic nerve. There's a real-time read out of my location in the tunnel, with a countdown of how far I have left to swim.

Eighty metres.

Seventy metres.

Sixty.

Then fifty.

I kick rhythmically. Left, right left, right left, trying to conserve energy. Conserve oxygen.

Forty metres. Then thirty.

My lungs start to feel tight. It's uncomfortable at first, something I think I can just ignore.

Twenty-five metres.

Breathing becomes urgent. It builds with each kick of my legs. I'm swimming faster now.

Twenty metres.

The end is in sight but the feeling of claustrophobia starts to set in as the burn settles into my lungs.

Fifteen metres.

I can feel the panic begin to rise in me. I can't hold my breath much longer. My lungs feel like they're going to burst. Desperation is taking hold. I kick faster, swim faster, pushing myself through the water.

Ten metres.

Ahead my vision fills with heat signatures and electrical signals. There must be thousands of them somewhere nearby. I need to breathe, I need to breathe.

Five metres.

Frantic now, exhaling as hard as I can. Pushing all the air from my lungs in a desperate attempt to fool myself that I'm breathing. Everything burns, everything screams, the water rushes around me like a maelstrom. I kick furiously, my face a bursting mask of pain.

I have to breathe.

I have to breathe.

I have to...

My head bursts through the surface of the water, and I take a ragged breath. In and out, in and out, desperate, hungry and greedy.

The space is dark, hot and the air feels stale. Just sound of my breathing, the beating of my heart, the rush of blood in my ears.

I am in an air pocket created by a slight rise in the inundated subway. It's about two metres wide, nestled in a bend in the tunnel. I can see the outline of a submerged door to a service tunnel on my right. There's a small duct overhead with a broken grate.

Ahead, the tunnel continues for almost one hundred and fifty metres underwater.

I tread water and breathe slowly, calming myself.

My heartbeat and this hot, rank air.

I can hear scurrying.

There's movement above. Then a splash in the water nearby. The rats must live in the ducts. They start to drop down into the water, big and black and sleek with long pink tails.

One at first. It swims towards my face, its movement frenzied.

It must be starving.

Three more drop.

The five more. Then ten.

The little space fills with their horrid screeching as they begin to pour down from the vent and splash into the water all around me. They come at me in a pack, clawing and biting at my face, crawling on my head, desperate for food. I knock one away, then two more, feeling them bite and scratch my cheeks and ears.

One scratches at my eyes.

I can't stay here. It's either swim back the way I came or try my luck with the service door and hope it's not flooded beyond. There's no way I'll reach the far end of the tunnel in time – I barely made it here.

I take a final gulp of air and disappear down below the surface, hundreds of rats swarming up above. The service door is only a few metres away. I try the handle. It won't budge. I try it again.

It's locked.

Fuck.

I consider swimming back to the platform for a moment then realise I won't get there without taking another breath. And I'm not swimming back up there.

Fuck it. The service door it is.

I'd rather drown than have my face eaten by a pack of hungry rats.

The programmable matter fills my hand in the DAGGER formation. I hold the black blade and plunge it into the polymer door near the lock. It slices through the material like paper and in three quick movements the door opens to the service tunnel beyond.

It's flooded, but there's a stairwell not ten metres ahead.

I swim to the stairs, pull myself out of the water and sit down on the landing with my head in my hands, getting my breath.

It's a few minutes before I move again.

The stairwell leads up for several storeys before ending at a door that leads to the subway maintenance tunnels. I open it and step inside. The tunnel is pitch black and deathly quiet. It smells of dry, raw nanocrete.

I walk slowly, careful not to make a sound. Ahead, nothing moves and nothing registers on heat or electrical. I continue down the tunnel till it ends in a T-junction, then turn right and follow it to the east.

Slowly, cautiously.

There's a skull on the ground, stripped of flesh. I move past it, peering carefully into the blackness, as I follow the tunnel down a set of broken stairs. It ends at a closed door marked "Maintenance".

Dead end.

Fuck.

I retrieve the N-47 particle gun from where it's holstered beneath my right arm and pump the action, priming the armature. Crackles of plasma lick the muzzle of the gun.

The tunnel lights up in a dim, green glow.

I push the door open silently. The room beyond is cluttered with junk and scrap that's crammed into shelves and piled high across the nanocrete floor. Long-dormant service robots line one wall and there's the remnants of an abandoned campsite against another.

A makeshift bed.

A portable kitchen.

Pools of dried, dark blood on the floor and on the walls.

Something very bad happened here.

A deranged howl pierces the quiet somewhere behind me, screaming through the empty tunnels like a banshee. I turn, gun ready, but there's nothing.

There's no choice but to go back the way I came, so I retrace my steps to the T-junction, then continue down the tunnel to the left. After only a few metres I can smell a change in the air. Dry dust is replaced with something noisome and unclean. It becomes so strong, so fast, I feel like I might gag.

There is the sound of feet on the ground somewhere further up the tunnel, scuffled movement coming towards me.

Then the skeletal remains of a body strewn across the tunnel. It looks like it had been torn apart, limb from limb. There are teeth marks on the bones. And they don't look like they were made by a rat.

Something ahead. A mass of signals moving towards me.

I know what's coming. I grip the gun tightly, ready.

The sound of running on the ground.

Then, out of the dark, they appear all at once in the green gloom of the tunnel. Maybe twenty or thirty, men and women, it's hard to tell. A horde of emaciated figures, all clothed in rags and twitchy and deranged, scramble towards me, some bounding on all fours like feral fucking beasts. Their faces are a mess of scabs and ulcerated sores and their mouths are ringed with large watery blisters. They all begin screaming as they catch sight of me, voices raised in an unhinged chorus, clamouring over each other, all desperate to tear me apart.

"Fuck this," is all I get to say as the mass of screaming junkies descend on me.

I fire the N-47.

The rail gun fires a white-hot plasmatic projectile that sounds out through the tunnel in a deep subsonic thud. The shot punches through the head of the one closest to me, blasting a fist-sized, cauterised hole through its face. The shot continues on through the neck of the one behind, then the chest of the one behind that, then severs the arm of another before dissolving a section of the nanocrete wall into glowing orange slag. I fire another, sending five more flying back as if they'd been hit by cannon fire, then another killing three more. They fall to the ground, twitching like cockroaches.

Sane people would run away at this point.

But they don't. They keep coming at me.

In an instant they overwhelm me. The particle gun is pulled from my grip. Fists and clawed hands pummel and scratch at me, while others grasp and rip at my neck and hair and shoulders. My coat is torn from my back in pieces and rancid teeth tear the flesh of my arms and chest and back.

The programmable matter slides down in my hands, morphing into two long, katana-like swords. I swing at the crazed junkies surrounding me, severing a head and several arms in two sweeping arcs. I kill another, then one more, and for the briefest of moments the swarm seems pause its assault.

There are four of them in front of me preventing my escape. One is a little further back than the others. Fuck knows how many more surround me.

I leap forward, attacking the closest deranged junkie with a brutal overhead double hand strike, the blades severing both of its arms at the shoulder in a mess of gore and meat. I turn, spinning one hundred and eighty degrees, decapitating a second with an arcing assault, then lunge at another in the same fluid motion, impaling it through the chest with both blades.

Bodies crumple to the ground around me.

Before the pack can grab a hold of me, I vault down the tunnel at the final crazed figure in front of me, landing in a roll and thrusting forward with the blade. It slices through muscle and bone without resistance, skewering the woman's head through her open mouth and exiting through the parietal bone at the top of her skull.

She gargles pink, bloody froth and blinks, her dark sunken eyes wide like saucers. For the briefest of moments our eyes meet and she looks almost sane, then the spark goes dull and she falls to the floor.

The others behind howl and rush at me, but I'm sprinting now, quickly putting distance between us. I can hear them stampede and scramble behind me, wild and desperate for the kill.

But there's no way they can catch me.

My system is jacked for just this type of situation

My feet pound the nanocrete as I streak down the tunnel. My adrenal gland begins to hyper-secrete adrenalin, which courses through my enhanced nervous system and musculature like a shock of lightning, driving me faster and faster and faster

Then ahead the tunnel splits, a passage running to the left and right. I turn right, to the east, and retrieve one of the small putty DEDs from my pants pocket as I run. The small, plasticine-like ball pulses in my hand as it neurally links to my chip.

Then it's live, primed.

I glance back over my shoulder.

I can see their heat signatures mass through the wall as they approach the split in the tunnel. In an instant my combat targeting maps the angles. I throw the DED at the wall beside me then dive to the ground for cover.

The programmable matter explosive hits the wall then ricochets down the passage bouncing off the nanocrete.

Once.

Twice.

Then it sticks to the wall on the third bounce. Right next to the corner of the tunnel.

"Detonate," I say, as they round the corner and start towards me.

There's a blinding flash and the tunnel heats up, the air turning hot like a furnace in less than a second. I can feel my hair singe and my skin grow tight.

Then nothing.

The temperature in the passage returns to normal.

Just smoke and the smell of burnt meat.

I pick myself up and walk back to the tunnel branch. There's not much left of them. What remains is charred and twisted or dripping from the walls.

Far off I hear more howls echo through the service tunnels so I don't linger.

I continue east till I find an exit that leads back up into New Chechnya.

19.

The Killing Fields.

The first thing I notice when I come up onto the street from the subway is the cold. It's fucking freezing up here. I'm wet and my coat is back in the tunnels. Along with the particle gun. And the medical kit, extra ammunition and the restraints. In fact, all I've got left is my pistol, the programmable matter weapons and two DEDs.

And the virus. That's still tucked into the lining of my jumper.

The next thing I notice is the smell of meth. It's everywhere. I can see the Bravatso drug factory off in the distance, looming like a gargoyle. It's topped by two red-bricked stacks that spew toxic plumes of smoke over the neighbourhood like poison.

This is Little Moscow, the Bravatso's side of town.

The power flows at this end of the dome. It shines out from lamp posts illuminating the garbage-strewn streets and shit-choked gutters. It beams down from the broken windows of the old factories and warehouses, illuminating the drug dens and whorehouses. It glares up from the harsh floodlights in the basements, revealing makeshift torture chambers and slave pens.

And the cold is brutal. It shocks the air from my lungs.

There is a dead homeless man, frozen on the street near the entrance of the subway. His face is grim, eyes rolled back in his head. A soiled grey blanket is draped around him, his purple fingers locked in rigor and grasping it to his chest. I pull it loose and wrap it around my shoulders.

The smell of piss flares in my nostrils like ammonia.

I start up the street, towards the eastern side of the dome. The great curvature is lower here. You can see the pitted silicon through the clouds, arcing down over the rooftops. It's a strange sight, like living in a snow globe.

Packs of vagrants and junkies loiter, most huddling in the doorways, trying to keep warm. Every now and then someone appears from one of the buildings, looking nervously left and right, before hurrying on their way.

I stoop my shoulders as I walk, pulling the blanket up over my head like a hood, in an effort to blend in. I don't make it a block before gunfire rings out.

The few people out on the street scatter at the sound.

A flatbed transport appears, cruising above the rooftops like a shark. It's a Bravatso patrol. There's two of them standing on the back of the long truck, both dressed in black coats and armed with sniper rifles. I step back into the shadows as they pass above, watching as they scan the road for movement. One of them spots an old homeless man hiding behind the frame of a rusted-out car. They open fire, the shots ricocheting off the road nearby. The old man panics. He makes a break for the building behind him. But he doesn't get far. They shoot him in the head and he drops, twitching on the wet nanocrete.

They're fucking culling people like vermin.

I duck into a side alley and begin cutting my way east through the side streets. It's mostly industrial buildings around here; squat, strangely stacked cubes with a maze of lanes snaking between them.

I keep off the main road.

Safer that way.

Frozen rain begins to fall, light at first, then heavy. Fog plumes from my mouth. The Shiporov Processing Plant should be close now. That means the Mark is close. It occurs to me for the first time that I don't know what I'm going to do when I find Xander Odom. Am I going to kidnap this woman and deliver her to that fucking monster Anatoli for whatever sadistic pleasure he has in mind? Am I going to plant that virus and kill tens of thousands of people?

Am I going to become a monster, just like him?

Or was I one already and just didn't know.

Visibility starts to drop and I pick up the pace, moving quickly from block to block of low-rise factories. I stop only once. I see a woman sitting in the gutter on one of the backstreets. She's holding a dead baby to her chest. It's limp and purple. She looks at me as I move by but doesn't seem to register my presence. The look in her eyes is impossible to describe. It's a pain so deep and a terror so vivid that you could only truly understand it if you were looking out from behind them. I notice she's pulled out most of her own hair.

In that moment, I think about my sister.

Her eyes looked like that when they dragged her off to Vostok.

Incomprehensible loss and unfathomable terror all at once.

I don't even know if she's really alive. Anatoli is a fucking liar. No one survived Vostok. No one. I almost believed him when I took this job. Now, I have my doubts.

I'm thinking about the past again.

Before this, I hadn't thought about her or anything else in years, the dust saw to that. Now, all this shit's coming back.

And I don't want it to come back.

I want it to stay buried forever.

"Everything he's said is a lie," I mutter to myself, not realising I'm talking out loud.

The dark tide starts to turn in my head.

Without thinking, I reach for the orange tab dispenser I keep in my coat pocket. But it's not there. It's back there in the dark of the subway with the rest of my shit.

Fuck.

Without the dust I can't quiet the voices in my head.

And I don't want to think what will happen if I can't.

I push on. The buildings begin to thin out, finally giving way to the dark expanse of a railway yard, dotted with storage facilities and loading docks. Burnt-out cars, old trucks and large slabs of nanocrete are scattered here and there on the frozen ground. In the middle of it all is the Shiporov Processing Plant, no more than three-hundred metres away.

It looks like a fucking fortress.

The Shiporov Processing Plant is a sprawling Orwellian bunker, five storeys high and constructed of sturdy grey bricks. Its dull façade is punctured with holes from gunfire and its walls partially collapsing on the east side, as if there had been an explosion in the facility. Even from where I'm standing, I can see it's heavily guarded; the Bravatso have set up positions on the roof of the building and along the only road leading in or out.

Fuck. It's going to be impossible to get in there.

I need to get to higher ground, so I can get a better look.

I kick open the doors of a nearby warehouse and move through the reception to the stairwell leading up. The building is abandoned and my footsteps echo in the empty space, the only other sound is the rain dripping through the ceiling into pools on the floor. I make my way slowly through the shadows up to the roof, gun drawn, ready.

Outside the rain is getting worse, it's coming down in sideways sheets that sting the skin on my face. I move to the edge of the roof and crouch down, looking out across the train yards. I can see the processing plant; the main entrance of the building is flanked by two machine gun nests with what look like SRDR 9 anti-personnel cannons. Dozens more heavily armed Bravatso are camped up on the roof. Large floodlights scan back and forth across the area around the plant casting wide beams and long shadows across the sodden ground.

I look closer, my eyes zooming in. There's a convoy of four vehicles coming towards the plant. They're trucks towing trailers, same as in Pripyat. The cages are filled with prisoners.

Just like Yuri said.

"Why are they taking all those people into the plant?" I mumble under my breath.

The trucks stop at the checkpoint then drive into the plant.

Then nothing.

Drones buzz off in the distance surveilling the train yards.

It's almost fifteen minutes before there's movement again. A solitary truck rumbles out of the plant, its box bed covered with a tarpaulin. Two bikes ride shotgun.

What the fuck is in that truck?

I look back at the Shirapov plant, scanning the building for some way inside. But there's no getting in there. Not easily anyway. I'm good, but outnumbered twenty-to-one with machine cannons and reinforcements – that's a fight I'm never going to win.

I could try and breach the building and sneak inside. But it's a risk. A big fucking risk.

Another bike appears from the plant, trailing some distance behind the convoy. That could be my way in. If I could take the rider down without being noticed, I could disguise myself and go right through the front gate.

If I can get to him in time.

It's going to be tight.

I run to the edge of the roof of the warehouse and leap over the expanse between buildings. The convoy is more than a kilometre away, chugging down the frozen road. I have to be fast if I'm going to ambush this fucker.

Everything goes into overdrive.

I run faster and faster, leaping from rooftop to rooftop, all the while watching the convoy rumble towards the blocks of tenements at the edge of the train yard. Once they disappear into the city I can make my move.

It doesn't take long to catch up to them. I stop on the rooftop of a tall tenement and peer over the edge of the building, watching the road below as the truck and its escort drive by.

It's now or never.

I drop down the side of the building and take cover behind a huge dumpster. The truck and the two bikes disappear down the street, turning right at the next intersection.

Perfect.

The programmable matter forms around my hand, locking into LASH formation, the viscous matter unfurling into a razor-edged whip. I watch as the third bike approaches then crack the programmable matter coil across the street, the whip burying itself deep into the nanocrete wall on the other side.

I pull it taut.

The Bravatso on the bike doesn't stand a chance.

He hits the next to invisible programmable matter whip at speed, the razored edge striking the Bravatso mid-chest. He grunts and seems to freeze as he passes through the wire, mouth open as if in mid-sentence, eyes wide and surprised. A fine mist of blood puffs from his upper torso.

I watch as the bike continues down the road, slowing down and beginning to wobble and tip before he separates, the top half of his body slipping off and tumbling onto the road as the bike falls to the ground on its side nearby.

I get up from where I'm hiding and make my way over to the bike and the body parts on the road. The Bravatso has been bisected. It's a fucking mess of entrails. I need to clean this up, fast. I pick up the bike and push it to the side of the street next to the dumpster. Then I grab the top part of the corpse by the arms and begin to drag it down the road.

At that precise moment two people round the corner at the end of the street. They're both running, guns in hand. One of them is a woman, no more than seventeen, armed with a cheap electric rifle and wearing grey urban fatigues. The other is a man, also dressed in grey urban camouflage with a long dark beard and a red turban. He looks like he might be Shikh.

The Shikh soldier is carrying Nettle laser rifle. Those guns are fucking lethal.

A Nettle laser fires an energy beam in a focused, five-second burst that can pass through almost any object. You don't even have to be a good shot to kill with one of those guns, just fire and sweep the beam through the target, it's that easy.

They both stop running when they see me.

I drop the body when I see them.

The girl says, "What the fuck?" just before four more Bravatso run around the corner with their guns drawn.

Everyone is frozen, looking at one another for the longest moment.

Then everything that happens next happens all at once.

The Bravatso open fire and I dive for cover. They spread out, all firing madly, three of them spraying the street while the other stands priming a home-made explosive in his hand. The woman in fatigues is hit in the leg by a burst of gunfire and goes down, but the rest of the Bravatso attack is wild.

The Sikh soldier drops to his knee and takes aim. The Nettle laser omits a needle thin, high-energy beam that shoots down the street in a burst of cold blue light. The pin spot beam hits one of the Bravatso in the chest burning a hole through his body. He crumples, dead. The Sikh soldier then sweeps the beam across the road, severing the arm of the Bravatso holding the explosive.

The high-powered laser cauterises the man's limb and it falls to the ground still gripping the home-made bomb.

The Bravatso howls in agony and grips at his stump, frantically looking left and right on the ground for his severed limb, as the other two try and take cover.

He bends down and picks up his arm just as it detonates.

A fireball of smoke and shrapnel explodes, shredding the Bravatso holding the explosive and sending everyone else flying back across the street.

It's dark for a moment, and the sound of the explosion rolls through the deserted neighbourhood. Then it's quite again except for the rain.

The smoke clears. All four Bravatso lie dead and in pieces, smouldering on the ground.

The woman writhes on the ground, screaming in agony. The Sikh soldier rushes to her side, looking at the gunshot wound. He clamps his hands around her leg and whispers softly, trying to calm her.

I get to my feet. He turns startled at the sound, pointing the laser rifle at me with one hand, and trying to stem the bleeding with the other.

"Who the fuck are you?" he says, finger poised over the trigger.

I hold up my hands. "I'm no one."

Normally, he'd be dead by now. Both of them would be. But they're fighting the Bravatso which means they might be useful.

The girl screams. It reverberates down the street.

Blood is pumping out of her leg. It's heavy. It looks like she's been hit in the femoral artery.

"What are you doing here?" the man glances down at his friend on the ground before he continues.

"The Bravatso..." I say, thinking on my feet. "They attacked us yesterday over in Pripyat."

His eyes narrow. "That's the other end of town. What are you doing over this side of the dome?"

"I followed them here. They kidnapped my friend. I'm going to break into the Shirapov plant and save him."

The girl screams again. He glances back at her, his brow furrowing in concern.

"I can help her," I say.

He looks at me warily for a moment then nods, stepping back as I kneel beside her. He keeps the gun trained on me as I examine her leg. It's not good. She's going to bleed to death unless she gets help. I rip a length of material from the bottom of her shirt and fashion a tourniquet, tying it tight around her leg, then grab her hands and press them against the wound.

"Keep pressure on it," I tell her. She looks pale. Scared. She's shaking.

"Is she okay?" the soldier asks.

"She's in shock." I take the blanket from my shoulders and wrap it around her. "I can't stop the bleeding. If she doesn't get medical attention soon, she's not going to make it."

Concern clouds his eyes. "Can you help me? I know a doctor that's not too far."

I look down at the girl. I don't want to get involved. But I can't leave her to die.

I nod yes and we get her up off the ground. She screams loudly as she tries to stand, and we drape her arms over our shoulders to support her.

"This way," the soldier says, motioning back up the street. "At the end of the next block."

We start up the road. The girl tries to limp, but she can barely stand. Her breathing becomes shallow and ragged, her pallor deathly.

"What's your name?" the soldier asks.

It takes me a moment to remember who I am. Oishi Kosaku? No. I left him back in Tycho City.

"My name's Donovan," I say.

He smiles. "Thanks for your help. I am Jaipel. Her name is Zama."

The girls head lolls to the side. She's lost consciousness.

We pass the intersection at the end of the block. The streets are clear in all directions.

"This way," Jaipel says, motioning towards a deserted high-rise further up the block.

It's an abandoned shopping centre.

The building is ten storeys high. Poured nanocrete with a tessellated façade. The shopfront windows on the ground level are all smashed, the displays looted and broken. Its signage and holoboards are long dark and falling down. No light shines from the lower floor windows; the upper floors look boarded up and deserted.

I hesitate. I've got a bad feeling about this.

Jaipel urges me to hurry. "Come, please, it's not far now."

The shopping centre beyond the broken double-door entrance is all gloom and long shadows. The large, open-plan floor had been pillaged long ago, all that remains now is broken display cabinets and empty clothes racks. There's rubbish everywhere. In the centre of the floor is an old-style grand staircase leading to the upper floors.

It smells of mould and wet rot.

I feel eyes on me.

My vision switches to low light. Then thermal. I can see three men in the room, all armed and hiding behind cover.

I stop.

"We're not alone," I whisper.

My hand goes to my gun.

Jaipel sees me and puts his hand out. "No please, it's alright. They're friends."

The three men stand up from behind cover at the sound of Jaipel's voice.

Who the fuck are these guys?

"I need help over here, Zama's been shot," Jaipel says, motioning for the men to hurry over. "Please, she's in a bad way. We need to get her upstairs to Dr Motamba."

The three men shoulder their rifles and rush forward to help with Zama. We hand her over gently. As they carry her away, the blanket I wrapped around Zama falls to the floor. I pick it up and drape in over my shoulders.

I notice that it's wet with blood.

"Thank you. You have done us a great service. Are you hungry?" Jaipel asks. "Please come upstairs, I will get you something to eat."

I shake my head. "I need to get going."

He stops me. "You said before that the Bravatso have taken your friend to Shirapov, right?"

I nod.

"You will not be able to get in there by yourself. The plant is too heavily guarded." Jaipel offers a smile. "Please, I have friends upstairs who can help you."

I don't have time for this. But if they can help me get into Shirapov and find Xander Odom it might be worthwhile.

I follow him upstairs.

The second floor is a maze lined with cramped little shopfronts and kiosks. Bars, tattoo parlours, fast food restaurants, pawn stores and supermarkets all now shuttered, dark, and silent. Some of the shopfronts have been broken into and raided for everything but their fittings.

It's much darker up here, yet Jaipel leads me through the warren of shops as if it were daylight. I notice we pass several more men set up in defensive positions along the cramped corridor, all watching from the dark.

Who the fuck are these guys?

Jaipel leads me to the entrance of a service stairwell. The interior is poured nanocrete and lit by battery-powered lamps. Two armed guards stand on the landing nearby, guns trained on the door. I follow him up two flights of stairs then through a door marked "Фудкорт вход".

At one time, this was the shopping centre's food court.

It's brightly lit and alive, filled with the noise of hundreds of voices and the smells of cooking. The food court is an expansive indoor courtyard that extends up five storeys, the vast void above bound by mezzanine terraces. The former dining space is now a large shanty town; a sea of people, the entire area packed with makeshift residences and markets and stalls. I look around, taken aback by vibrancy and life of it all.

"Come," says Jaipel, smiling. "This way."

He leads me through the narrow alleys of scavenged metal and polymer to a makeshift community kitchen near a bank of waiting elevators at the far end of the room. There's a group of kitchen workers serving a long line of people food from a big, blue bioplastic drum

The people waiting to be served are a mix of refugees and soldiers.

And standing there among them is Xander Odom.

20.

Eviscerated.

The artificial intelligence at the Bouwer Re-Education Centre identified me as a candidate for army training after a session in the Box. Apparently, I displayed the marker traits of someone with an aptitude for intelligence work. And they said I had a propensity for violence.

Which apparently is a good thing.

They told me I qualified for an experimental program. A top-secret unit that was being developed by a man named Dr Ouji Kyobe. He was a Japanese military scientist who was creating a new type of soldier for the Antarctician army. A soldier that had undergone specific DNA modifications and surgical enhancements.

They called it Project Daybreak.

I volunteered immediately. After three years at Bouwer I would have done anything they said without question. Of course, they didn't tell me they were experimenting on prisoners because all the soldiers that volunteered so far had died. But I would have done it anyway – what the fuck did I have to live for?

The first thing they did was cut off my face.

Changed my features. Made sure I didn't look like myself. That I didn't look like anyone.

It fucking hurt.

Then they removed my eyes. Replaced them with military grade, bio-mechanical ones. Apparently, they were grown specifically for me. Apparently, they increased my visual acuity. Let me see in low light. Gave me multiple spectrum sight. Combat targeting. Changeable retina for scanning.

After, when I looked at myself in the mirror, I looked different. But I couldn't tell if it was because the eyes looked different, or, that looking out of those eyes made everything appear different.

I thought they were done. But they were only just getting started.

Next, it was my nervous system. They called it myelination treatment.

They injected a swarm of nanites into my blood stream. Fucking microscopic robots. They were programmed to depolarise neural membranes to allow salutatory conduction.

Got no idea what that means?

Don't worry, neither did I.

Dr Kyobe said it allowed a neural impulse to jump from one internode to the next without being conducted down the entire cell membrane. He said it greatly accelerated nerve conduction velocity.

In other words, it made my reactions really fucking fast.

Then it was my pain receptors. Implanted regulators to control the activation of receptors in the primary afferent fibres, inclusive of the unmyelinated C-fibre and myelinated Aσ-fibre.

Now, I can get shot and literally turn off the pain. But I couldn't when they did it. They did it while I was awake. With no pain relief.

Want to know how that felt?

Ever had a hole in your tooth? Felt an exposed nerve? Imagine your whole body is the tooth and nerve fibre is exposed.

Now imagine feeling it when they drill.

Apparently, I died on the operating table for six minutes during that procedure. So did five other volunteers. Only they weren't able to be revived.

Next, they went to town on my adrenal cortex so I could control high-level adrenaline and noradrenaline hyper-secretion. Then gene therapy and targeted DNA treatment to make me stronger. Something about increasing the myocyte density and sarcomere length of each individual muscle fibre.

That fucking hurt as well.

After that procedure I couldn't walk. Or move. They put me in intensive care for a week. Then recovery for a month.

Then rehabilitation.

But they weren't finished with me. Not by a longshot.

Next, they had to reinforce my skeletal system. No use having increased musculature without the bones to support it Dr Kyobe said. You'll snap your arms and legs in two the first time you try and run.

He called the procedure bio-polymer treatment of the cortical bone. It meant drilling an injection into every bone in my body. That's two hundred and six drills.

All at once.

After that, I didn't really notice what they were doing. It didn't feel like me anymore.

I'd wake up in the recovery room, be wheeled to my hospital room and float in a daze until the bright white light went black and the sweet relief of sleep took me away.

Genetic molecular alteration.

Ocular echolocation modifications.

Controlled nucleotidosis.

Programmable polynucleotides.

Then they were done with me. But by then, I wasn't really me anyway.

I wasn't anyone. At least I didn't think I was.

If you don't recognise your own face. Or hear your own voice. If you don't see with your own eyes or feel with your own feelings, then who exactly are you?

Cause you're sure as shit not you.

21.

The Mark.

It takes a moment for my brain to believe what my eyes are seeing.

She's in front of me, just metres away, so close I could almost reach out and touch her. Xander Odom, here, in the flesh.

And I've found her. Totally by chance.

She looks the same as she did in the photos in her dossier. Tall, dark, her eyes piercing and intense. Augmentation watermarks on her neck and arms. She's dressed in black fatigues with a battered green army jacket over the top, her hair tied loosely back from her face.

Xander's standing with two soldiers, both dressed in grey urban camouflage, and she's talking to an old Rastafarian woman with long, grey dreadlocks tucked into a multi-coloured crocheted cap. A tall Thai man with two tarnished metal artificial arms stands behind them with a dark look on his face.

I drop my eyes before she notices me staring at her.

"Come," Jaipel says, motioning towards the line. "Are you hungry?"

"Sure," I say. I follow him over to the line, grabbing a bowl and a spoon from an old trestle table set up nearby.

I realise I'm anxious, but I don't know why.

I ignore the gnawing feeling inside and look around at the tent city, the hundreds of people crammed into the space. How the fuck are they doing this? How are they keeping all of this a secret, right under the Bravatso's nose?

"What is this?" I ask, glancing up at the void rising above us.

He smiles. "This is a safe place my friend. We call it Sanctuary. Xander Odom had us set it up when we came here. She wanted a haven for people trying to escape the Bravatso."

He must be part of DAWN. All the soldiers must be.

"There is a lot of injustice here in New Chechnya at the moment. After SPM ended mining operations, the entire city fell into anarchy. Drugs, gangs, it became very dangerous. But along with the bad came some good. An abandoned city meant refugees and the homeless could find somewhere to live."

I glance up at Xander Odom. She's at the front of the line now, holding out her bowl while a lady in a dirty apron ladles out a measure of soup. She nods thanks and moves on, taking a spoonful of the hot soup and blowing on it carefully.

I feel anxious watching her.

Restless.

But why?

Jaipel is talking but I'm not really listening.

Then I realise. It's the dust. I can feel the last of it fading away in my system. Panic starts to rise from somewhere deep within. Without it the cotton wool I've so carefully packed around my mind these past years is gone. Without it I'm me, raw and exposed, with nowhere left to hide from who I was or what I've become.

The dark tide swells and I can hear a voice from somewhere deep and hidden. I don't want to hear what it has to say.

"...happening lately is an outrage, the kidnappings, the killings," Jaipel continues, oblivious to the war inside my head. I drag my eyes from Xander and try to focus on what he's saying. "We heard about what was going on up here just before the city went offline. We came to help. But now that New Chechnya is isolated, the Bravatso have grown bold, they think they can do whatever they want because no one knows what's going on up here."

"What exactly are they doing at Shirapov?" I say.

"It is not good. I did not want to tell you because they have your friend there." He drops his eyes. "The Bravatso have set up a laboratory in the plant. From what we understand they're experimenting on people."

Jesus.

"I'm sorry," he says.

"What experiments?" I ask. "What are they doing?"

"I don't know. All I can tell you is they are dumping the bodies of the dead by the truckload into mass graves over in the old hydrogen mine."

I take a moment, trying to process what he is saying. None of this sounds right.

"Hang on," I say. "Did you say they're dumping bodies in the mine? Aren't the Bravatso mining Helium-3 over there?"

"There's no mining going on in New Chechnya," Jaipel shakes his head. "Not for years."

We reach the front of the line.

Jaipel keeps talking but I'm in my head. I hold out my bowl and it's filled with a generous serve of seaweed soup, fat ribbons of kombu floating in a thin, greasy stock.

The voice again. It asks the same question over and over. Am I really going to do this? Am I going to kidnap this woman and kill all these people? Am I going to be the hero or the villain of this story?

Jaipel points to an empty table nearby and I follow him and sit down. Xander Odom is in my peripheral, talking and eating.

I try to think, get shit straight in my head. I need to think about this reasonably, logically.

I've been set up, that much is clear. It's the why I don't know.

I slurp the soup and pretend I'm listening, all the while watching Xander.

Anatoli Dugray-Mir is lying to me. But why? I'm a gun for hire. People like me don't give a fuck about the details, we just care about the outcome.

He knows that, so why lie?

What's he got to hide?

Is it why he wants Xander Odom so bad? Does it have something to do with the Bravatso experimenting on people instead of mining Helium-3?

Then there's DAWN. Back on Earth they're branded terrorists by the media. Fanatics, willing to kill ordinary people, in their fight to save the environment. But the truth was they only ever terrorised big business. And what they're doing here makes them look anything but fanatical.

Right now, this entire thing is a jigsaw, and I'm only looking at one piece. I need information. I need to see the entire fucking puzzle.

And Xander is the key.

Because at the end of this, I'm trying to save my sister. And if there's even the slightest chance she's alive, I have to believe it. Which means, I've got to finish the job.

"...are the best people I can think for you to talk to about your friend," Jaipel says, standing up. "I need to check on Zama. But you should stay. There's plenty of room."

I nod, watching from the corner of my eye as Xander and her little entourage walk towards the bank of elevators nearby. Two heavily armed guard flank the doors. They snap to attention as she approaches.

"Good." Jaipel slaps me on the shoulder. "I will see you later then. We will see about helping your friend."

I mumble thanks as Jaipel leaves, disappearing into the crowd. I sit at my table watching as the elevator opens and Xander walks inside. The doors close and I watch the lights go up until they reach level ten.

There's a level above the roof of the atrium.

I switch my vision to thermal and watch Xander and her entourage walk out of the lift then disappear into a mass of light. I switch to electrical. I can't see anything. I flick through the spectrum. Fuck. Whatever is up there is blocking anything I can track.

Perfect.

I take another mouthful of the soup and sit back, looking around the space. The only way up is the elevators and fire stairs on the other side of the room. From what I've seen of this place so far, I think it's safe to assume there'll be men with guns no matter which way I go.

I push the soup aside and stand, gathering the blanket around me. I don't know how the fuck I'm going to get up to level ten, but I'm sure as shit not going to figure it out sitting here.

I move through the crowd towards the fire stairwell. The people I pass seem happy. Content. All the fear, all the desperation I've seen in the faces of everyone else I've met in this city doesn't seem to exist here.

It takes me a few seconds to realise why.

Then it hits me. They are not afraid. They feel safe here.

I join the press of people coming in and out the stairwell and make my way slowly up to level nine. People are everywhere. Men, women, children, grandmothers, grandfathers, families. Everyone knows everyone. The sense of community is overwhelming.

When I reach level nine I notice the stairwell up to ten is barricaded.

I walk out onto the terrace.

All of the offices lining the atrium have been converted into little flats. Washing hangs from the railings. Children run here and there. The smell of cooking and humanity is overwhelming.

There has to be a way up.

I move around the nanocrete balcony, blanket pulled under my chin. People standing out around the walkway seem to ignore me. I flick my vision to electrical again. I can see the power running through the walls. The elevator shaft behind the wall on the far terrace. Whatever is going on above is a mess of signals.

Thermal again.

There's a lot of heat up here. People, lights, stoves. Then I see it. There's hot air flowing through the vents. The building has an old-style ventilation system, a maze of ducted tunnels running through the walls, all the way to the top floor.

The heating ducts look too small to climb into, but there's a main shaft feeding them from what looks like a deserted maintenance room on the other side of the terrace.

I move quickly, with purpose.

The maintenance room is unlocked and I slip inside, closing the door behind me. It's small and cramped and smells of dust and machinery. Inside has been scavenged for all its worth, nothing on the floor but garbage.

The main ventilation ducting is exposed here. It runs vertical up from the floor through the roof above.

The voice in my head asks me the same question again, what will I do when I confront Xander Odom? Am I going to go through with Anatoli's monstrous plan? Am I the hero, or am I the villain?

I ignore it and activate the programmable matter into BLADE formation. The blade slices open the grey polymer tube and I remove it carefully then climb inside, pulling myself up into the shaft in the roof.

The shaft is dark and impossibly tight. The air's hot and hard to breath.

I pull myself along, inch by maddening inch, following the ventilation system up to the tenth floor.

The voice in my head is louder now. It asks the same question over and over.

Am I the hero, or am I the villain?

Truth is, I don't know anymore.

If you're the villain, do you know it? Or do you think you're the hero all along?

Who gets to decide?

Is it simply just who is left standing at the end? They say history is written by the victors, I wonder if that's true for heroes and villains as well.

The shaft comes to a four-way junction. I keep going up, the shaft climbing above the floating roof of the tenth floor. I can see the heat signatures and electrical impulses below me, they're almost blinding.

I continue along the ventilation duct.

Am I the villain? Maybe. There's nothing heroic about what I do for a living.

Corporate head-hunter. It's just a trade term for an assassin. I'm a fucking lackey, a messenger boy for the rich, a debt collector for the morally bankrupt.

The shaft ends up ahead at a large grate. She's close. I can feel it.

Below is a dimly lit, sprawling space, totally uncluttered by walls and filled with row after row of enormous aquaculture silos. I can see workers spotted here and there tending the tanks. The vats are all swollen and budging in places, clogged with gelatinous blooms of algae, green and purple sea plants and schools of small jellyfish.

The entire level is a farm.

This must be how she feeds all the people downstairs.

Then I see her. She's walking slowly through the stinking silos involved in an intense conversation with the Rastafarian woman and the Thai man from downstairs. The two soldiers walk several paces behind.

Their conversation becomes heated as they move closer to where I'm hiding in the vent above.

"Xander please, you must listen to reason," the Thai man says. "We cannot stay here much longer. There are too many people here. The Bravatso were already looking for us, but after that raid last week, there everywhere. It's not going to be long until they find us."

"Kantsom is right," the Rastafarian woman agrees. "We have all the evidence we need. It's time to tell the world what's happening in

New Chechnya."

Xander nods. "I understand what you are saying. But we cannot just leave. These people here need us, they rely on us to survive."

The programmable matter slips into BLADE formation and I cut through the grate, removing it silently. They're no more than ten metres away.

"We're talking about the future of our civilisation, Xander," Kantsom continues. "Surely that's more important than saving a few hundred refugees."

"Every life is as important as any other."

Closer. I feel my body tense, ready for the takedown.

"I know how hopeless this must seem, but I promise you, I will not let SPM and the Bravatso get away with what they are doing here. As we speak my contact at the Dead Earth Collective is organising passage to New Chechnya to collect the evidence. Once they do, the whole world will know their crimes."

I hesitate. What the fuck was she talking about?

They stop almost beneath where I am hiding.

"But until that happens, we must stand strong and make sure that we stop as many people as we can from dying at the hands of these animals."

They start walking again. I want to keep on listening, but it's either now or never.

Hero or villain?

I drop down, landing in front of them. The five of them stop in their tracks.

I attack the Thai man first, kicking him three times. Once in the knee, breaking the patella and rupturing the joint sending his leg folding back on itself the wrong way. As he cries out and stumbles I kick him in the sternum, then in the throat, the blow shattering the hyoid bone and the clavicle, rupturing his trachea.

He crumples to the ground clutching his neck, asphyxiating.

Screams ring out across the farm.

The two soldiers scramble for their guns as I launch myself into the air, twisting my body as the programmable matter morphs into LASH formation. I whip the razor-sharp weapon at their legs, the lash slices through muscles and bone, severing their legs below the knees in one quick motion. I finish them both with a blow to their heads, the lash decapitating them just above their lower mandibles.

They're dead and in pieces before they hit the ground.

I land in front of the old Rastafarian woman, who is in shock and has yet to move, and pin her up against one of the swollen tanks. The programmable matter retracts into the SPIKE formation and I swing my fist back to deliver the killing blow, just beneath her jaw.

"Stop!" Xander screams at me.

I stay the blow, the spike stopping against the old Rastafarian woman's throat. A trickle of blood runs down the blade.

"Tell me who you are, right now!" I look back at Xander. She has a gun pointed at me.

"It doesn't matter," I say.

She glances down at the pieces of her friends, trying to put together the last five seconds in her mind. "You killed them all. Why? What the fuck are you doing? Who sent you?"

More screams from the terrified farm workers. Calls for help, feet running towards the elevator.

"I'm here for you." I press the spike against the woman's neck to make my point. She moans with fear, pressing herself against the tank desperate to get away from me.

"If she dies, you die next." She's breathing hard, obviously in shock.

"Put the gun down," I warn.

"Are you listening to me?" Xander yells as she takes a step towards me, her finger poised atop the trigger. "I said if she dies, you die next."

She stares at me and I stare back at her. Something in her eyes disarms me.

It's a standoff, watching each other, waiting to react. The sounds in the room seem to amplify as the tension grows, the trickle and slosh from the silos, the screams of the terrified workers running for help, the sobbing from the poor woman I have pinned against the tanks and the death rattle from the Thai man who struggles to breathe his last breath on the ground nearby.

I can see the thinking in her eyes. She grips the gun tighter.

"Don't do it," I say.

She squeezes the trigger.

The programmable matter jumps out of my hand, slicing the gun in two and slashing her palm. The gun clatters to the floor and Xander clutches her bloodied fist to her chest in pain, her eyes wide with fear.

"Please don't, don't kill her." Despite the blood dripping from her injured hand, her voice doesn't waiver and she looks at me intensely, pleading in her eyes. "Please, it's me you've come here to kill, not her. She's never hurt anyone in her whole life. Please, just let her go."

I withdraw the blade I'm holding against her friend's neck.

She looks relieved. "Thank you. I..."

Before she can finish her sentence, I strike the old Rastafarian woman sharply at the base of the neck, compressing the carotid sinus and sending it into overload.

She falls faint on the ground.

"You motherfucker!" Xander Odom screams at me with outrage. "You killed her."

She lunges at me and I catch her hand before she strikes, my other holds a programmable matter blade where she can see it.

"She not dead. Just unconscious."

Xander ruefully pulls her arm free from my grip.

"Who sent you?" Xander asks, stepping back.

"You know who sent me." I retract the blade.

"Anatoli." She looks at me with utter contempt and snorts at his name bitterly. "You're not the first, by the way."

"I'm sure I'm not," I say.

"You'll never get out of here alive, I hope you know that." She steps back again towards the bodies of the two soldiers. Her eyes glance over at the handgun on the ground nearby. I can hear the ding of the elevator on the far side of the floor and the panicked workers trying to cram inside.

It won't be long till reinforcements arrive.

"There's over two hundred DAWN soldiers in this building. They'll hunt you down."

"I'm not here to kill you," I say. "I'm here to take you to him."

She laughs, shaking her head.

"So, you're an errand boy then." She takes another step closer to the gun. "You're a spineless coward who kills innocent people for money."

"And you're a terrorist, Xander. There's blood on both our hands."

She stops and looks at me, infuriated by the comparison.

"Who are you to pass judgement? I'm not a terrorist, I'm fighting for something."

"Save it for the masses," I quip. "I don't give a fuck about your revolution."

Another step. She's close now.

"No. You're just some deranged killer for hire like those fucking Bravatso out there."

"I don't do this for pleasure. It's a job."

Not long till they raise the alarm. Need to get out of here.

"That's even worse. You know right from wrong and you do it anyway. At least those crazy fucks have an excuse for doing the horrible shit they do. What's yours, huh? What's you fucking excuse for behaving the way you do?"

She's right, says the voice in my head.

I don't say anything.

"What, that's it? That's all you've got?" She snorts at me and shakes her head with contempt. She standing over the gun now. "You know you're all the same, you corporate pieces of shit. Every single one of you..."

"Reach for that gun and you lose your hand," I warn. "I was hired to bring you in but they never said in how many pieces."

She stops and stares at me, death fucking hatred in her eyes. "There's no way out of here you know. Every entry in and out of this building is covered."

She's right.

The elevator's out. There'll be two dozen armed soldiers coming up the in the next few minutes. Probably more through the stairwell that leads down to the food court.

I look up.

The roof it is then.

22.

Dark Side of the Moon.

I kick the fire door open and push Xander inside. The empty stairwell is bathed in red emergency light.

"Hurry up," I bark. She doesn't, so I push her up toward the landing. "Move."

"You won't get far," she says, glancing back over her shoulder at me. "They'll be here any minute for me."

"Anyone I see, I'm killing," I warn. "I don't care if they send an entire army after you, they're fucking dead. You got that?"

She says nothing.

Our footsteps sound hollow against the nanocrete stairs.

We got to move. It won't be long now, they're coming.

Xander slows and I push her up the stairs again. She looks back at me.

"You don't have to do this, you know."

Her voice is different. She's trying another tack, trying to reason with me.

"Save it," I say.

"We can pay you. DAWN has money."

I don't say anything, I'm listening to the bass frequencies reverberating through the nanocrete building.

She takes my silence as an opening and keeps on talking.

"I can match whatever they're giving you."

Footsteps, running on the stairs.

"I'll give you double. Triple."

The elevator, ascending through the shaft. They're almost here.

"Please. Don't do this. Don't take me to him." She sounds almost scared for the first time.

"I'm not doing this for money," I feel for her. I don't know why, but I do. That's bad. You should never make it personal.

"Then why?" she asks.

"You wouldn't understand," I say as we arrive at the rooftop door. I pull my gun and switch my vision to thermal. I can see three men positioned out on the roof outside.

I look at her. There's something about her, something familiar. I just can't put my finger on it.

"Anyone out there?" I ask.

She shakes her head. I almost smile. Almost.

"Don't make a fucking sound," I growl.

I can hear the elevator ding as it opens on the tenth floor. Footsteps running out. I kick the rooftop door open and the cheap bioplastic shatters from the force.

We step outside. Rain and wind howl across the rooftop.

"He's kidnapping me!" Xander screams as soon as she spots one of her men.

They all turn at the sound of her voice.

I take careful aim with the rotary pistol; a burst of energised micro-projectiles shreds the closest soldier's chest. He gasps and staggers backwards, tumbling off the edge of the building.

The other two soldiers raise their guns. The one on my left is armed with a PD-42 auto rifle, the one on the right has a TNK riot gun.

I fucking hate riot guns.

I open fire again, killing the soldier on my left with the PD-42 before he can get off a shot. As he hits the ground the soldier to my right turns the riot gun on me and fires.

The only problem: Xander is standing between us.

I bring up my arm as he fires, shielding Xander from the blast. It's an instinct, nothing more. The programmable matter moves with the speed of my synapses, spreading from my hand and forming a large barrier, the impact of the explosive projectiles dissipating across its surface.

I return fire, two quick bursts, and he crumples to the floor. Dead.

"Come on," I mutter, taking her arm and dragging her towards the edge of the rooftop. She resists, angrily.

I holster my pistol and I grab a DED from one of the pockets in my pants. I hold it for a moment while it links to my chip. Behind, I can hear footsteps coming up the fire stairs to the roof. Sounds like at least ten soldiers, maybe more.

We stop at the edge of the rooftop. I look down ten storeys to the ground, then across the expanse to the neighbouring high-rise.

"What the fuck do you plan to do?" she asks, her voice dripping with venom. "Jump?"

"Something like that," I say.

I turn and throw the DED at the rooftop doorway, the small explosive sticking to the top of the doorframe. Then I turn and unfurl the programmable matter into LASH formation, cracking the coil across the expanse into the wall of the high-rise opposite.

The soldiers appear at the top of the stairs as I pull Xander towards me and jump off the side of the building.

"Detonate," I say as we hurtle through the air.

The explosive flashes bright and burns at the temperature of a small sun, incinerating all the DAWN soldiers in the stairwell. They're reduced to shadows on nanocrete in the blink of an eye.

I hang onto the hair thin programmable matter wire with one hand and Xander with the other. We fly through the air at terminal velocity, swinging across divide between the high-rises in a heartbeat. I turn my shoulders and pull her close at the last second as we smack into the side of the building, my body acting as a cushion from the impact.

I can feel my ribs shatter beneath the force of the collision.

We dangle in the air nine storeys above the ground.

There's only the sound of rain for a moment.

"You fucker," Xander coughs, the wind knocked out of her.

I ignore her, breathing deep and switching off the pain. Gripping the wire tightly, I lower us down several storeys till we build momentum, then rappel down the building to the pavement.

We hit the ground with a thud. She glares at me as I release her, rubbing her arm where I was holding it.

"You're going to pay for this," she says. "I swear to God one day you'll pay for this."

"Who's to say I'm not already." I form the programmable matter around my wrist and glance cautiously left and right down the street. Empty.

There are no DAWN soldiers. Not yet. They're probably still up at the top levels trying to piece together what happened.

It won't take them long.

"Come on. We've got to move," I say dragging her forward roughly.

Xander doesn't budge. Instead, she looks me in the eye.

"Do you know what happens if I'm silenced? Do you know what happens if Anatoli is allowed to finish his little experiment?"

I don't say anything. She looks at me carefully, almost trying to see if something is there behind my eyes.

"You don't even know what's going on here, do you? What did Anatoli tell you? That I'm working with the Bravatso? That they've taken over the Helium-3 mine here in New Chechnya or some bullshit like that?"

She laughs at the stupidity of it. "He did, didn't he?"

I think of Anatoli's smiling, skeletal face.

"Didn't it seem strange to you that an organised crime syndicate specialising in murder for hire and slavery suddenly decided to get into the mining industry? The Bravatso are working for SPM. They set them up here."

Xander shakes her head in disbelief.

"This isn't about SPM trying to save the world. Anatoli Dugray-Mir doesn't give a fuck about people, he just wants to control them. For fifty years he's been the most powerful man alive. He's controlled the only source of clean power known to man. But now, for the first time ever, he might to lose it. If Bio-Fuels manages to finish the bacteria-powered Benetto Reactor, he's ruined. No one will need fusion power anymore. That means no one will need Helium-3."

A fucking chill goes down my spine.

"The micro-organism used to power the Benetto Reactor is called Bacterium Electrum. It's a man-made hybrid, made of four separate bacteria. They are the only four bacteria that can collectively produce the charge the reactor needs. Three of them are common – they're found almost everywhere on the Earth, essential for life on the planet. But one of them is only found in the human digestive system. Nowhere else. Right now, he's experimenting on people right here in New Chechnya, trying figure out how to kill that bacteria and destroy the Benetto Reactor without wiping out the human race."

Is this why he wants me to release that virus? So he can cover up the crimes he's committed here experimenting on refugees?

"We have evidence proving SPM has already genetically engineered a bacteriophage specifically designed to target this micro-organism. The only reason they haven't released it yet is because every subject exposed dies within seven days. But once they figure it out, that fucking monster Anatoli Dugray-Mir is going to control everything."

The fucking dark tide in my head.

Never make it personal.

Hero or villain.

"And no one will ever be able to stop him. Ever."

I don't say anything.

"Are you even listening to me?"

Never make it personal. The fucking dark tide in my head.

"You're telling the wrong person," I reply bluntly.

"What?" Xander looks at me, dumbfounded. "Don't you care about anything?"

Everyone's selling me their own version of the truth. But I'm through buying it. Not until I see for myself. I stare at her until her eyes meet mine, so she knows there's no mistaking my intentions.

"I don't want to have to hurt you, but I will if I have to. This is a job, nothing more. I'm taking you out of New Chechnya and delivering you to Mr Dugray-Mir, tonight, just like I was contracted. There's nothing you can say or do that will change that. Got it?"

"You're a fucking monster," she says, giving up. "You know that?"

"Yeah. I guess I am." I grab her arm and lead her down the street towards where I stashed the Bravatso bike. "Now let's get going before your fucking friends find us."

We start down the street, wind and rain whipping violently through canyons between the buildings. I try to clear my mind, to focus on the task at hand, but I can't. I know where we're headed next.

Kidnap the girl, release the virus.

Fuck.

Doubt washes over me.

I'm having trouble moving past what Xander said. I've had hundreds of Marks plead their case before, but never like that. I don't know what to believe or what to do. This job, Anatoli, my sister, Xander, the virus... everything. Nothing is what it seems. I know I'm being played but I don't know by who.

A voice in my head says never make it personal. That's what they teach you. That's how we can do what we do and live with ourselves.

But this entire thing is fucking personal. And now I'm supposed to unleash some horrible fucking disease and kill tens of thousands of people. A million tiny pieces fly around inside my mind, everything seems like it's unravelling.

Am I going to cover up a crime and help a monster or destroy the only chance I'll ever have of a family?

Either way I'm fucked.

We move down the block. Everything is as it was. The pieces of four Bravatso are laying scattered and scorched across the street. Sections of a fifth Bravatso are beside a dumpster nearby. And the bike is parked exactly where I left it.

"Stay here," I order. I let go of her arm and walk over to the bike.

As I walk off, "Fuck you" is all she says.

I grab the handlebars and pass my finger over the ignition. Thankfully, it's not locked. The bike sputters to life rising up off the ground and hovering with a low, chugging hum.

"Alright," I say, turning around. "Let's get moving..."

But I don't finish the sentence.

Xander is standing in rain in the middle of the road where I left her.

She's pointing a gun at me with a smile on her face.

It must be one of the Bravatso's guns.

Fuck.

I didn't think to check. I'm so in my fucking head, so messed up with what's happening, I didn't even look.

"Remember when I said you were going to pay for this?" Our eyes meet and she raises her eyebrows, then sneers as she opens fire.

The first shot is at my head. I almost dodge it. It buries itself in my right cheek, exiting with most of my right ear. The second shot hits me in the shoulder. It knocks me back sprawling, my body hitting the wall behind me hard.

I hit the pavement with a grunt.

I try to get up, but I don't. Not right away. I can't get my breath.

Then here face looking down at me, the rain falling in thick droplets.

I feel like a fish out of water, my mouth opening and closing, gasping for air.

Darkness dances in my peripherals and I can hear the sound of an engine revving.

Fuck.

Somehow, I pull myself up to my feet, and watch as Xander Odom speeds off into the night.

Then it goes dark again.

23.

Suffer the Children.

Ever seen what the Ebola virus can do to a person?

It's fucked up.

The disease starts simple enough: you feel tired, you get a fever, maybe a cough or a runny nose, and you think you've got the flu. Then you start vomiting and shitting yourself. You get chest pains, shortness of breath, blinding headaches and a red raised rash on your skin.

By this point you start to think, maybe this isn't the flu. Maybe I should go to the doctor, get myself checked out.

Then the bleeding starts.

Vomiting blood, coughing blood, shitting blood, bleeding through the pores of your skin, the whites of your eyes. Your insides begin to haemorrhage and turn to fucking jelly. Then you die. You literally lose so much blood your heart doesn't have enough to pump around your body.

That's pretty fucked up, isn't it? But believe it or not, as terrifying as Ebola is, it doesn't make for a very good weapon. Nor does any other virus for that matter.

Want to know why?

Because it can't be controlled. Sure, if you attack an enemy with a weaponised strain of Ebola or SARS or even the Black fucking death for that matter it's going to kill lots of innocent men, women and children. But chances are it's going to backfire and fuck your forces up as bad or even worse.

That's why they developed hybrid bio-agents.

Chimera weapons.

Genetically manipulated bacteria with properties from deadly fungi and viruses. Bio-weapons that can be used in targeted-release patterns with controlled half-lives that are so user friendly you can pick their communicability, symptoms, rate of death... you name it.

And the best bit is they're so complex, they can only be constructed by an artificial intelligence. Which means only governments, corporations and rich pricks have enough money to afford them.

Rich pricks like Anatoli Dugray-Mir.

You see, for a while there almost anyone could create their own bio-weapons.

They were called designer viruses.

This was back when bioterrorism was the new black, back when any idiot could make their own epidemic right in the comfort of their own living room.

You see, with the rise of home teraflop computing and low-cost, high tech genetic laboratory equipment, more and more stupid motherfuckers began performing half assed experiments in their backyards. Mind you, most of these people were well intentioned, they were fooling around trying to cure diseases, that kind of thing. But the problem is, when you make gene splicing equipment readily available to the masses, it's only a matter of time before someone figures out a way to do something really horrible with it.

Which of course, they did.

It first showed up in the Republic of Britain. A brilliant but extremely deranged student named Victor Chopin decided that any person over the age of forty was directly responsible for the devastation of climate change. As a punishment for this, he developed a killer new strain of the flu in the basement of his parent's house, using a home computer and some lab equipment he bought on the internet. This virus was programmed to only infect people with shorted telomeres at the end of their chromosomes, a marker of ageing DNA.

It would come to be known as the Digital Flu.

Victor Chopin released the virus in an airport. It spread like wildfire and behaved exactly as he'd programmed it. Prolonged, thirty-day non-symptomatic incubation period. Fifty-percent infection rate. Ninety-percent mortality rate. The world didn't know what hit it. The Digital Flu killed more than two hundred million people over the age of forty in less than six months.

The outbreak created a world-wide emergency and an explosion of copycats.

As you can imagine, the rise of designer viruses brought the world to its knees. Governments scrambled to contain this new wave of bioterrorism. In the end, artificial intelligence was able to create a whole new type of drug that could mutate and match the ever-evolving strains of the viruses. And by the time they finally stopped them, almost a billion people had lost their lives.

Still, it was a drop in the ocean compared to what climate change did. So, people soon forgot and moved on to the next calamity.

But Pandora's Box had been opened.

The Digital Flu gave governments and large corporations horrible new ideas for a whole generation of devastating weaponry. And from this nightmare Chimera weapons were born.

This time, however, they were going to do it right. Chimera weapons weren't going to be cheap, so just anyone could get their hands on them.

If you wanted to play, you had to pay.

Want to know how much that vial Anatoli gave me is worth? Want to know what your own personal pandemic is going to set you back?

Believe me, you couldn't afford it. Only the wealthiest monsters need apply.

24.

Exit Wounds.

I must have blacked out for a moment or two. At least I hope it was only for a moment or two. Somewhere I can hear the sounds of people running. The splash of rain spattering on the road. Voices.

I'm lying on the road, behind the dumpster.

The bike is gone. Xander Odom is gone.

Everything pulses in blinding white pain.

I struggle to sit up. Two DAWN soldiers in grey urban camo run past where I'm lying and continue down the street. Then another four. I must look like just another dead body to them.

I get to my feet. Everything is agony.

I touch the side of my face. It feels like raw meat.

Fuck.

I switch off the pain receptors so I can't feel the right side of my face, or my shoulder, but they're both bleeding heavily. I can feel that.

The ringing in what's left of my right ear is deafening.

I take a step and feel like I might fall over, so I steady myself against the dumpster, head down and breathing hard. I watch my blood splatter on the wet road in thick, fat droplets, then disappear in the rain.

"She's... getting away," I say to myself. At least I think I do. I'm not too sure.

"Got... to... move." I don't know if I said that out aloud or not.

The darkness starts to dance around my peripheral. My knees go weak.

The crack of gunfire somewhere nearby.

I pull down the neck of my jumper, exposing the gaping hole in my right shoulder. Blood pulses dark and thick and I wipe it clumsily to get a better look at the wound. The skin around the entry point is burnt, but the wound isn't cauterised. That means it was an explosive projectile. That means it probably went straight through me. I reach back and grope around my shoulder till I find the exit wound.

It's big. My shoulder blade is shattered.

Fuck.

I've got nothing. No medical kit, no surgical pen, nothing. I don't know how far ahead she is or if she's escaped already. I could have been out for a minute or an hour.

Fuck.

I tear off one sleeve of my jumper, then the other. I ball up one and press it against the gaping entry wound, doing my best to slow the bleeding as I tie the other sleeve around it.

It does almost nothing.

I start back up the street, stumbling as I run. Xander Odom is nowhere to be seen. Sleet stings my eyes. It's getting heavier and harder to see. I have no idea of where to go, no idea of where she might be headed. Last I saw she was driving south.

I try to think. Try to remember that map Nikolayevich showed me in the back of his store in Pripyat. The mine is to the south. I try and remember the stinking back room of his shop, the crudely drawn map. He pointed to the locations of the three access corridors, one in the north, one to the east, another to the south near the mines.

It's logical to think that that's where she's headed. Maybe she's got a ride stashed there. An escape route if everything went to shit.

I keep going, running, one foot in front of the other. The wound in my shoulder is bad. I feel it. I've got an hour, maybe two, before the blood loss becomes a problem. Won't matter by then. If I don't find her soon, I'm fucked anyway.

So is my sister. If she's really still alive.

This is all because of my own fucking stupidity. My fault and mine alone. I turned my back on the Mark, left her alone. I was too distracted to check if there was a gun on the road. That's amateur shit. I know better than that.

So why did what she said affect me so much?

Why did I turn my back on her?

Is it because I believe what she was telling me about SPM and the Bravatso?

Is it because I believe her story more than the bullshit Anatoli Dugray-Mir has been feeding me?

Probably.

I can't tell anymore.

Ahead, I see outlines in the rain. Two figures coming towards me. I slow and switch to thermal. They glow yellow and red in the gloom. I raise my gun, finger hovering above the trigger.

"Who's that?" one of them says as they see me coming towards them.

They both raise their guns.

I fire twice, dropping them both.

I keep my gun trained on them as I approach. They're both DAWN, Xander's soldiers. Poor fuckers. One's dead, the other is gasping on the ground. I move closer and stop when I see his face. He's a kid, barely eighteen. He's been hit in the chest, the shot must have missed his heart and hit his lung. Right now, he's in shock, drowning in his own blood. He looks up at me, mouth opening and closing like a fish out of water, his eyes wide and terrified.

"Mister, please help..." he gurgles. The kids tries to breath, but it's a wet rattle and he coughs up blood. This scares him more and he reaches out to grab my boot, desperate for my help.

"Please... I don't want to die." His eyes meet mine. Earnest. Innocent.

I hate this part.

"Help me."

There's only one thing I can do to help him, and it's not the help he's asking for.

I raise the gun and shoot once, ending his misery.

I hate this fucking part.

I notice the gun he was carrying laying on the road beside his dead hand. A TNK riot gun. I pick it up and sling it over my good shoulder. Then I bend down and go through his pockets. Some ammunition but nothing else of use.

I try his friend.

More ammunition. And he's got a small medical kit in his coat pocket. Finally, something I can use. I open the green bio-polymer box. The kit is pretty basic, no surgical pens, only painkillers and graft patches.

They'll have to do.

As I pull off the field dressing from my shoulder, blood seeps from the hole. I wipe it away as best I can and peel open the graft packaging, removing the thin, clear membrane inside. It's delicate, soft like jelly and kind of sticky. I press it against my shoulder and hold it for ten seconds, letting the heat from my body activate the artificial dermis and begin knitting into my skin. When I remove my hand the wound is sealed; the graft sealing the hole looks like an enormous blood blister.

I grab the other graft and reach around to my shoulder blade, groping blindly till I find the exit wound. I apply the graft to it then throw the rest of the kit on the ground. Must keep moving.

I need to catch up to her, now.

I need to find her, now.

Running down the wet city streets. I don't know how much time has passed. Ten minutes, maybe fifteen. I left the glow of New Moscow behind a while ago.

It's dark again. Through the frozen rain I can see the outlines of long-abandoned cars on the street. Emaciated figures of vapour junkies amongst the gutters and the garbage. There's a dozen of them lurking in the dark like cockroaches.

I slow and duck down an alley before they see me, cutting across the tenements headed south. The streets are a blur. I feel cold and numb and darkness dances in my peripheral.

"Not yet," I mutter as I weave my way through the debris-clogged ally. I come to the end of the block and out onto the street.

There's still no sign of her.

"Fuck," I say loudly. My voice echoes down the empty street.

The sharp crack of gunshots west of here. Then more. Sporadic at first, the frantic. Sounds like a firefight. But there's something else. Closer, to the south, I can hear the deep, rhythmic concussive rumble of machinery. It shudders the ground like a heartbeat. Light glows brightly over the tops of the buildings.

I follow the sound, rounding the corner ahead.

The endless blocks of abandoned apartments give way to the New Chechnyan hydrogen mine. It's right in the middle of the city, like an open wound, more than a kilometre wide and illuminated bright as day by blinding work lights set atop tall pillions around the site. The mine is an immense open pit, yawning and circular like a maelstrom, its maw angled with stepped sides that sink hundreds of metres down into the lunar rock.

I stop in the middle of the street, looking out at the sight ahead. The rain is so heavy now it's hard to see anything.

Gargantuan, robotic bucket-wheel excavators sit dormant around the rim of the pit, like sleeping metal dinosaurs. The deep mine below looks like it has been filled in and levelled about half way down. Set up at the bottom of the crater is a long, white inflatable building with two enormous bioplastic smoke stacks at the far end. A conveyer belt leads into the entrance.

From where I'm standing it looks like there are hundreds of people down there working.

I look closer, zoom in through the haze.

A covered dump truck, just like the one I saw at the Shirapov processing plant, snakes its way down the excavation and empties its load when it reaches the bottom.

It's only then I realise what I'm looking at.

The trucks are dumping bodies. There are piles of them. Hundreds of dead strewn across the lunar rocks. Men, women and children, their faces twisted in rigor and agony. And the workers look like they're slaves. People chained together, beaten and bloodied, loading bodies onto the conveyor belt while heavily armed Bravatso guards look on.

And that's when I see them. A small group of men in white SPM laboratory uniforms supervising the operation.

It takes me a moment to realise what I'm looking at. When I do, everything makes sense.

The Bravatso are working for SPM. They are rounding up refugees in the city for SPM scientists to experiment on at the Shirapov plant. And they're disposing of the evidence in that makeshift crematorium set up at the bottom of the mine.

Just like Xander Odom said.

I feel sick and stupid both at once.

Sick, because I know now that she was telling me the truth and I didn't listen to her. Stupid, because I believed the lies Anatoli Dougray-Mir told me.

Because I let him manipulate me.

Because I let myself believe my sister was still alive.

The dark tide turns in my head.

Never make it personal. But this is personal, it's as personal as it's ever going to get.

I feel the scaffolding they erected around my brain in the Re-education Centre crumble and fall away. Everything is coming loose inside. Everything I've been told is a lie.

There's a soft, soothing voice in my head saying I need to not feel anymore. That I need the cotton wool of apathy packed around my mind again. I need a hit of something. Anything. Anything to numb the pain inside that screams from deep down in my soul, caged and desperate to escape.

I need...

But there's another voice. It's louder. Angry and clear, like white light. I try not to listen to what it's telling me.

The sound of gunshots pulls me out of my own head.

I look back over my shoulder. They're closer than before.

I take one final moment to linger at the sight before me, then run back the way I came, turning left at the next block and tracking south, parallel to the hydrogen mine.

The spackle holding the personality they cobbled together for me all those years ago is shattered.

That clear voice again, asking the same question... Am I the hero or the villain?

Am I the hero or the villain?

I thought I knew the answer. I thought I knew myself.

There's gunfire ahead, a running gun battle in the street. Four figures appear in the gloom, running desperately and firing wildly over their shoulders. I take cover as they pass. A few seconds later a flatbed truck loaded with armed soldiers screams by after them.

Then more gunfire.

Screaming.

I keep moving. Cautious. Bodies litter the wet streets. Some are DAWN soldiers, others are Bravatso. The explosion must have got their attention. Up ahead there's a burning wreck in the middle of the road. Then a bike crashed nearby. It looks like the same bike

Xander was on.

More gunfire.

I duck down behind the bike and unsling the riot gun from my shoulder, priming the weapon, and peer off into the torrential downpour.

Voices ahead, running boots on the road.

And then I see her.

Xander appears at the intersection ahead, moving on foot. She turns down the street and starts towards me. She's hurt, limping badly, her leg looks fucked up. There's pain and desperation on her face. A moment later a DAWN soldier appears behind her, running to keep up. Then the crack of gunfire and the soldier crumples to the ground dead.

"No!" she screams as she looks back and sees her dead friend laying on the road.

She ducks down and takes cover behind the frame of a burnt-out car as five Bravatso appear from the side street behind her and open fire. Gunfire peppers the incinerated car frame and Xander shrinks down further behind the cover, gun in hand, looking desperately left and right for a way out.

Am I the hero or the villain?

And in that moment, I see things for what they really are. I realise what I've always known. That I'm the one that gets to decide, that it's always been my choice.

Am I the hero or the villain?

The answer is up to me.

The five Bravatso close in on the car. I stay low to the pavement, moving towards Xander. She sees me emerge through dark rain and jumps in fright, raising her gun and ready to fire. Our eyes meet. She's shocked, I can see her mind ticking over, trying to figure out what the fuck to do. She starts to squeeze the trigger and I hold my free hand up, to show I mean no harm, then motion at the Bravatso moving towards the car.

Something passes between us.

I can't describe it. She looks at me and I look at her. It's strange, kindred almost. In a glance she knows I'm not going to hurt her. That I'm going to help her escape.

Xander lowers her gun. I scramble forward, crouching next to her, both of us hiding behind the wreck of the car.

"You were right." I say.

She nods. "I thought you were dead."

"Yeah, I thought so too," I reply.

A smile curls in the corners of her mouth; another spreads across my fucked-up face.

Before she can say another word, I pop up from behind the car and fire.

The Bravatso can't be more than three metres away and at this range a riot gun is like a meat mincer. The closest two are shredded by the shot. Tens of thousands of highly-charged microscopic particles blast through their upper torsos, tearing through clothing and stripping skin and hair and muscle from the bone.

There's an explosion of meat and aerosol blood from the volley and the woman standing directly behind them is blinded the particle spray.

As I pump the action and clear the chamber, screams fill the air.

The blinded Bravatso woman fires wildly once into the building to our right then drops her gun, clawing at the jelly dripping from her sockets and down her shredded cheeks.

She falls to the ground, writhing in agony.

The other two turn my way and fire. I duck down as automatic gunfire sprays the burnt-out frame where I was standing not a second before.

The two Bravatso run forward and take cover behind the other side of the car. This is fucked up. They start yelling and swearing. It's in Russian so I don't understand all that much. I switch to thermal and see them both begin moving around the frame from either side to try and flank our position.

I look over at Xander. "You shoot the moment he stands up, okay?"

She nods.

I'm on my haunches, ready to move. I watch the heat signatures of the two Bravatso as they creep around the sides of the car, one moving around the bonnet, the other around the boot. When the one closest to me reaches the corner, I stand up and step out.

Neither of them is expecting that.

The Bravatso closest to me is crouched at the corner of the car frame. He raises his gun in surprise and I open fire.

He's dead before he even knows it.

Simultaneously, the Bravatso at the other end of the car sees me kill his friend and stands up, screaming something and levelling his weapon in my direction.

Then there's a gunshot before I can turn around.

I inhale.

Everything is silent. I can hear the rain fall in slow motion, droplets splattering on the road.

Instinctively I look down at my chest, half expecting to see a gaping hole in my sternum.

But there's nothing.

I turn around.

Xander is still crouched behind the car frame, her gun aimed up at the Bravatso. He's been shot underneath the chin, bone and brain hanging by a flap of skin still attached to the top of his head. He blinks a couple of times then tries to say something before collapsing dead on the car bonnet.

I move over to Xander, crouching down beside her. "Are you hurt?"

She looks up at me. "I crashed the bike back there. I think I broke my leg."

I look at her left leg, my vision filtering through low-energy radio bands. It's fucked up, and there's some deep tissue damage, but the bones intact.

"It's not broken," I say. "Can you stand?"

She nods and I help Xander to her feet, then put my arm beneath her shoulder and support her to the bike.

"Why?" She stops and looks at me. "What changed your mind?"

"I saw the mine. Guess I needed to see it for myself, so I'd listen to what I already knew."

That seems enough for her.

More gunshots.

"We need to go." I pick up the bike and start the engine. "Where are you headed?"

I help her up and she sits behind me.

"The freight terminal on the south side of the dome. I've got a bike stashed there."

"Hang on." I say and rev the engine.

We head south, towards the edge of the city.

25.

Violence Solves Everything.

We drive south, through the dark streets.

It's empty around here, not a soul to be seen. The sea of grey apartment buildings stretches off to forever. The rain is heavier. It bears down from the low-hanging green clouds in sheets of sludge and ice.

The bike hugs the wet road as it speeds through the dark New Chechnyan night. Xander clings tight to my shoulders as we brake and round a corner, weaving in and out of the debris-strewn streets.

If I'm supposed to feel bad for betraying Dugray-Mir and his fucking evil plan, I don't. I don't feel anything at all now except for rage. My allegiance has been for sale most of my adult life, my morals open to the highest bidder. I realise that helping Xander has been the first thing I've done for myself since I escaped that Antarctician prison.

It feels good.

The second thing I'm going to do for myself is get the truth from Anatoli Dugray-Mir about my sister.

That's going to feel even better.

I follow the roadway as it winds through an abandoned maze of tenements and shopfronts before merging with an expansive, grand boulevard on the south side of dome. The once sprawling promenade is dark and desolate, the street lined with long-dead trees and derelict Orwellian blocks. Spotted along the avenue are crumbling monuments to Russian leaders and SPM executives.

I slow the bike to a crawl and weave through the abandoned vehicles that dot the deserted concourse. The roadway has started to disintegrate in places, swelling and cracking and sending long fissures crisscrossing across the slick black surface.

A group of scavengers pulling a sled loaded with car parts scatter at the sound of the bike engine.

I look back at her.

She's on edge, uneasy. Xander's trying not to show it but I can see the distrust in her eyes, as if she's expecting this to be some kind of ruse, an underhanded plan to lull her into a false sense of security.

To tell you the truth, I don't blame her.

I wouldn't trust me either.

We come to a long line of office blocks and she taps me on the shoulder, pointing to a building ahead on the left side of the concourse.

"Over there," she says.

The New Chechnyan Freight Terminal is a low-rise, four-storey grey building, its façade dominated by large precast nanocrete blocks hiding narrow smoked polymer windows. The double front doors to the stark office block are closed and barricaded.

I pull the bike to the side of the road and park it in an alley about a block from terminal. The hearing in my right ear is fucked but as soon as I switch off the engine I'm pretty sure I can hear the low whine of transport engines above then rain.

"Let's go," I say as I help Xander gingerly off the bike.

She grimaces as her feet hit the pavement.

"Can you walk?" I ask.

"Yeah, I'm alright," Xander nods, but she's not. She's limping badly.

I look back up at the grey-green sky. I've got a bad feeling.

"We need to hurry."

We turn out of the alley and onto the boulevard. I keep low, moving in the shadows, eyes peeled for movement. The rain is intense, it covers everything, a constant tattoo of white noise. But below that there's still the sound of the engines, getting louder and louder.

Up ahead near the entrance to the terminal, a dog strolls out of the shadows and stops in the middle of the boulevard. It sniffs the wet road then looks up, ears pricked and alert. Two men, both armed with high-powered hunting rifles follow the dog out of the darkness and stand nearby.

They look like hunters.

One has a freshly killed cat and several rats tied to his belt. The other has a human leg, severed at the hip and slung over his shoulder.

At the sight of the hunters Xander and I scramble to take cover behind a pile of rubble nearby. She groans loudly as she crouches down.

The dog raises its nose towards us, as if it's caught our scent.

"Fuck," I say under my breath. "We don't have time for this."

The hunters stop almost directly in front of the stairs leading to the terminal doors, looking out across the street.

The rumble is getting louder. And louder.

We need to go.

The dog looks up to the buildings to the north and barks loudly.

We need to get off the street.

"Shut the fuck up," snaps one of the hunters kicking at his dog angrily.

The rumbling whine gets louder.

The dog pricks up its ears and barks again. Then five large transports appear over the tenement rooftops, each one filled with heavily armed Bravatso.

They must have followed us here.

Someone must have seen Xander on the street back where she crashed her bike. Someone must have recognised her.

Fuck.

At the sight of the five transports descending through the clouds like an armada of fucking dreadnoughts, the dog and the two hunters bound off up the road, running for their lives.

"Move!" I yell as I grab Xander's hand, pulling her to her feet.

She staggers and almost falls, then picks herself up and hobbles towards the freight station doors. Above, the transports begin descending, some of the Bravatso standing on the flatbed shouting excitedly at the sight of her running down the street.

They open fire as we run up the freight station stairs, nanocrete and dust exploding all around us.

"Cover me," I say as I hand Xander the riot gun and run up the last few stairs to the barricaded front door.

The programmable matter leaps into my hand, morphing into the AXE formation. I swing it down hard against the barrier, chopping deep into the metal and bioplastic. There's another burst of gunfire as I pull the axe out of the door and slam it down hard into the barricade again, a wide, jagged hole visible in the surface.

I think I'm shot again. I feel a sharp pain in my left calf, but I turn it off and ignore it.

Xander fires back with the riot gun. She misses. I smash the axe into the wall again, then again. She fires, the shot peppering the side of one of the transports and sending a Bravatso tumbling off the side of the flatbed.

He lands with a wet thud on the road below.

"Almost there," I yell.

Xander fires again and then again as she backs up the stairs to where I'm standing. I kick the barricade one last time and a large section folds in on itself revealing a hole big enough to squeeze through.

"In you go," I shout, grabbing her wrist and pushing her through the opening.

I follow her in as the door around me explodes in gunfire.

The freight station lobby is a long, tall, three-storey room with faux timber panelled walls, polished lunar rock floors and a pebblecrete mezzanine wrapping around the second level of the space. The office cubicle walls and reception area are all made of smoked brown polymer. Most of it is now smashed and riddled with gunfire.

There are dozens and dozens of skeletons scattered across the room.

It smells musty in here, like a tomb.

"Which way?" I ask, looking around the space.

She points to a set of double doors at the back of the station with "Authorised Personnel Only" written in big brown letters across the front.

"There," she says.

We start across the lobby towards back wall. Outside I can hear the transports coming in to land, the howling of the Bravatso, desperate for blood.

"Why does Dugray-Mir want you so bad? What the fuck did you do?"

We weave through the maze of cubicles, Xander struggling to keep up. I can hear the sound of boots running on the pavement.

"Two weeks ago, we raided the Shirapov plant. Attacked them head on. We managed to breach the laboratory and steal their research. We got the entire sequence for the new bacteriophage they've genetically engineered. Without it they're fucked. They can't stop the Benetto Reactor coming online. From what I understand, Dugray-Mir was so angry when he found out that he sent a hit squad up here to kidnap me and kill the Bravatso leader Drago Afanasievich"

I remember seeing what was left of them in the tunnels.

"Don't they have back-ups of the research? Isn't everything be held with AI HEARST?"

A slight hint of a grin flashes across her face. "They've got nothing. When SPM disconnected New Chechnya from the network so they could keep their experiments secret, they also cut themselves off from their company intelligence. I'm the only one with the evidence of what's been going on up here."

"Where is it then?" She didn't have time to grab anything before she left.

Xander taps her head. "It's all up here. Data drive implant. It records everything I see."

I kick open the double doors and usher her through, looking back over my shoulder at the freight station doors.

They're close.

They'll be inside soon.

Beyond the doors is a short, dark hallway with a long-dead elevator at its end. There's an open fire door halfway down and a smashed vending machine against the opposite wall.

"This way, down the stairs," she says.

I can hear the Bravatso smashing through the front doors.

"Don't wait for me."

She goes on ahead through the fire door. I grab hold of the vending machine and drag it over to the doors, pushing it over onto its side and blocking them from opening.

It won't hold them for long at all, but it might buy us something if we need it.

Xander's made it down to sub-level 1 by the time I catch up. I can see her struggling, gripping the rail as she hobbles down the stairs, face set in an agonised grimace. She's going to need help if we're to make it out of here. I give her my shoulder and put my arm around her waist to support her weight. We move down the stairwell till we reach the doors leading to sub-level 5. As soon as she opens them the smell of distilled hydrogen fills my nostrils. It tastes like methane in my mouth.

It's dark in here, almost pitch black. You can't see your hand in front of your face.

I scan the space.

It's cavernous.

The freight station was once where all the hydrogen mined in New Chechnya was sent for export after it was distilled at the Sharma Processing Facility. Rail lines snake beneath the city from here, back over to the mines and the processing plant then off again to the tubed tracks of the high-speed Lunar Rail that criss-cross the Moon's surface.

The freight station was once a bustling hub of industry.

Now it was putrefying.

The weigh stations and loading yards are filled with knee-deep sludge. There are old, corroding silos and skeletal frames of rotting cargo trains, half submerged in the muck.

"It's pretty dark down here. Can you see?"

Xander nods and taps the side of her head. "Implants, remember. I have cameras in my corneas. Gigapixel resolution, low light, you name it."

"Which way then?"

She points to the tunnel on the south wall.

The Bravatso are coming down the stairs.

"Over there. That tunnel leads to the tube tracks. I've got a bike stashed near the old Lunar train."

We move across the sludge-covered ground. It's a mire, thick, like quicksand. Xander stumbles every now and then on a rock or a rail track submerged beneath the slop. I keep my grip on her waist tight, making sure she doesn't slow down.

We need to move faster, I can hear them coming. Footsteps on the stairs.

Voices. We're not going to make it out of here before they find us. She needs more time if she's going to get out of here clean.

Torchlight shines from the stairwell.

Fuck.

"How far away is the bike," I whisper, watching the yellow beams of the light enter the freight yard and swing around the space.

"It's close. I don't know, one hundred metres down the tube line maybe."

"We're not going to make it out of here," I say. "They're too close. You need to go."

"What the fuck are you going to do?" she asks.

"I'll cover you for as long as I can."

"Then what? They'll kill you if you stay here."

"I've got my own way out. Just make sure you get that evidence into the hands of someone who can do something with it," I say.

She nods and turns to leave, then hesitates. "Before, when I asked you why you were doing this, you said that you weren't doing it for the money. That there was a reason I wouldn't understand."

I nod.

"What do they have on you? What made you come to New Chechnya?"

"My sister was killed when we were young, at least I thought she was. Dugray-Mir told me she was alive, and that if I completed this job he'd tell me where she was hiding."

"And if you didn't?"

"That he would kill her," I say

The lights of half a dozen torches are spreading out across the freight yards.

Two of them are coming this way.

"I can help your sister. If she's alive, we can find her," she whispers. "Years ago, when the most powerful companies in the world put bounties on my head, DAWN helped me disappear. And they can help your sister too, take her somewhere SPM can never find her."

I don't say anything. But I know she's right.

She was one of the most wanted people in the world and no one found her till she wanted to be found.

I look back at the freight yards. The torches are coming closer and closer. She needs to go.

"What's your sister's name?" she asks.

"Sakura." I say. "Sakura Jones."

She doesn't say anything for a moment, then a confused frown crosses her features. A gunshot rings out from the dark and slams into the tunnel wall, not a metre from her head.

"Go..." I hiss at her. "Before it's too late."

She starts to say something and another shot rings out. She looks at me one last time then turns and shuffles down the train line.

I watch her till she disappears into the dark.

Then I start running towards the eastern side of the yard, my footsteps loud enough in the muck to get their attention. The torches closest to me swing in my direction and away from Xander.

"What's that?" one of them says.

"Over this way!" yells another.

I crouch down in the mud near the front of an abandoned train carriage and draw my pistol. One of the torches comes closer. I can see the Bravatso illuminated by the torch glow. He's dressed in a long dark coat with an elaborate pattern of scars on his face.

The light falls on me.

Our eyes meet.

"What the fuck ..." is all he gets to say.

I fire. The burst of projectiles slams through his forehead, sending a mass of brain and bone spraying out from the back of his skull.

"She's over here," one of them yells.

"Fucking shoot, shoot!" screams another nearby.

Torches turn in my direction. Gunfire and muzzle flashes ring out in the dark.

194

In the distance I can hear the sound of a bike engine start.

I smile to myself.

She's free.

I raise my gun and shoot in one fluid motion, dropping another Bravatso to the ground. The sound of the gunshot and their commotion covers the rumble of Xander's bike till it disappears down the tunnel.

Then I'm up, running as fast as I can towards the doors.

This time, I don't make a noise. They're blind down here, so they're easy to avoid. By the time I reach the stairwell doors they've all converged on the eastern side of the freight yard, desperately searching the carriages for some sign of Xander Odom.

I run back upstairs.

There's no one in the freight terminal lobby.

I retrieve the positioning transmitter Nikolayevich gave me from the lower leg pocket of my pants. It's wet with blood, so I wipe it clean then switch it on.

It crackles to life.

"This is Radovan." A tiny voice says through the speaker.

"I need a pickup," I say. "Airlock. Access Corridor 4 on the west side of New Chechnya. One hour."

The transmitter crackles.

"I know the place. Snakeheads run through there," Radovan replies. "Very dangerous my friend."

I shake my head. "You let me worry about that."

Static. He's quiet for a while.

"You have the girl?"

"Just be there. I don't want to spend one more second in this fucking place than I have to."

"Okay, one hour."

"Don't leave without me," I growl.

The transmitter goes silent and I switch it off. There's only one thing left to do. Get the truth about my sister out of Anatoli Dugray-Mir.

By any means necessary.

I move through the lobby towards the front doors.

For the first time since I answered the door back in the hotel in London, that gnawing feeling in the pit of my stomach isn't there anymore. For the first time since I escaped that fucking hell hole they put me in back in Antarctica, I feel like a free man again.

Maybe when I get back to Earth I might take a break from myself for a while.

Maybe I might decide to do something else for a while.

Maybe I might try being me...

I duck through the broken doors, gun drawn. I notice the three Bravatso on the other side of the street almost immediately when I come out of the building. They're hiding in the shadows behind a nanocrete wall.

I level my gun to fire at them.

What I don't notice is the sniper on the roof above. I don't know why, but I don't. He has a long-range, ASR needle rifle trained on me.

I only notice him when the first Tetrodotoxin dart hits my neck.

Then another.

I can feel the genetically altered paralysis toxin instantly; my lips and tongue go numb.

I stumble and drop my gun.

Fuck.

I activate my adrenal cortex to try and combat the tranquilizers coursing through my system. A massive surge of adrenalin rushes through my body, but it's not enough.

Darkness dances in my peripheral.

I fall to my knees.

"Not now," I say to myself.
But this time, I don't get to decide.
And the world goes black.

26.

The First Step on the Path to Insanity.

The first time I killed someone I was eighteen years old.

I was in the Falkland Islands and it was a Saturday. I remember because it was a beautiful day. One of those days where the sky is blue and endless. One of those days where you feel like nothing can go wrong.

I had been in the army for about six months.

After all the DNA modifications and surgical enhancements, I was in the recovery ward of the hospital for a long time. Then rehab even longer. Most of Dr Kyobe's subjects didn't survive. In fact, there were only twelve recruits who made it into Project Daybreak.

When we were ready, we were taken by bus to a facility on a remote island off the coast of Antarctica, just outside the town of Victoria.

I don't remember a lot of it.

I was pretty doped up most of the time.

But I do remember the bus ride, or at least one part.

As we flew out towards the islands, I watched a storm gathering out in the Southern Ocean. It was a wedge-shaped shelf cloud rolling towards the coast beneath a massive, iron-grey thunderhead, flashing with lightning. It had been a long time since I'd been outside – my life had been detention camps and hospitals for as long as I could remember – and I remember thinking how beautiful it was.

How simply perfect it was in that moment.

The strange thing was I couldn't remember what my parents looked like, or my sister. But I never forgot that cloud. Years later I could close my eyes and remember it like it was yesterday.

The training facility they built for Project Daybreak was cutting edge. No expense was spared. The Antarctician government had invested heavily in the project, hoping they might be able to start large scale production of enhanced soldiers to bolster their armed forces.

And it got what it paid for.

We were trained in everything.

We received military instruction covering everything from handling small arms to operating a tank. We learnt combat techniques for deployment on land, air, sea, space and cyberspace environments. We specialised in hostage rescue, intelligence operations, reconnaissance, direct action, long-term incursions, guerrilla war, corporate and national destabilisation.

And assassination.

We trained in Dr Kyobe's adaptive environment combat system, developed especially for subjects who had undergone surgical and cellular enhancements.

We went into that facility as people.

But we came out as weapons.

Antarctica was already at war by that stage. It was fighting a collection of South American nations called the Sovereign States of the Americas for control of the Falkland Islands. Project Daybreak was dispatched by the Antarctician military to destabilise the region and sabotage corporate and government instillations.

And that's where I killed someone for the first time. Some guard at some corporate headquarters on a sunny day when I was just eighteen years old.

A few months after that, I would be part of Operation Blind Angel.

And after that, nothing would be the same, not ever again.

27.

Hung, Drawn and Quartered.

Darkness.

Only darkness.

Then blinding light through the slits of my eyes. Then darkness again.

I can smell mildew. And body odour. I'm in a car, my face pressed against a dirty window. The light looks distorted, like a kaleidoscope. Outside I can see the blur of the city beneath us.

My hands are bound. Feet too. There is a gag in my mouth. It tastes of filth. Instinctively I try to struggle and move my body.

Then a blow to my head.

Dark again.

Then a daze.

Eventually I come to.

The car is flying lower now, down at street level. Outside the window street lights blaze. Outside the window makeshift crosses line the roads. On each one is a body, strung up, skinned and crucified.

Men. Women. Children.

The darkness takes me again.

I wake up as they drag me out of the car and throw me to the ground. I land heavy and roll onto my back. We're parked on the roof of a building. Where, I don't know, but I've got my suspicions.

Someone walks past and kicks me square in the face.

I black out again.

The shock of freezing water brings me back. I'm bent down on my knees. My hands are bound in front of me, a pair of old-fashioned cuffs cut deep into the flesh of my wrists. I'm aware of other people in the room around me, but I can't see where I am. Everything is a haze.

Another shock of water and I'm awake, coughing, spitting, shaking the wet hair from my eyes. I notice I've been stripped to my waist.

It's warm in here, I can feel the heat of a fire blazing nearby.

"Wake up you piece of shit," a voice says.

The accent is distinctly Russian.

I can hear footsteps and a booming laugh.

I raise my head.

I am in a long, dark room, cleared of furniture. There are four armed guards standing, watching. Shadows flicker across the walls and the space glows orange, the only source of light coming from a crude forge that has been set up in the centre of the stone floor. There are bodies in piles on one side of the room. They've all been tortured horribly.

More corpses are nailed to the walls.

I recognise some of them. Jaipel is there. That girl Zama too. The others are DAWN soldiers or corporate head-hunters, just like me.

I feel my stomach sink and I turn my head.

"So, you are the one that has been giving me all the trouble, huh?" His voice reverberates across the room. It's deep and menacing. "Finally, we meet in person."

A man walks out of the shadows.

It's Drago Afanasievich.

He looks like he did in the image I saw in Gördel's office back in London, except much bigger. Drago is a giant, built like a stone monument. Extensive augmentation and graft work have caused his body to bulge into some kind of hulking caricature of a person. He is clothed in a long leather coat with a wool collar, the roadmap of scars on his face covered by a long black beard flecked with grey.

His footsteps echo through the room as he walks towards me.

"Who the fuck is you, huh? You don't look like one of Xander's little soldiers?"

"I'm not." I glare at him.

"Ahh, I see. Then you must be another one of Anatoli's toy soldiers." Drago looks over at the rotting corpses on his walls. "You see what happens when you come here to play war little man, huh?"

I glance back over at the bodies on the wall. At Jaipel and that poor girl Zama. The fucking prick tortured them to death.

His see me looking at them and his eyes light up with sadistic glee.

I feel the hatred bubbling and roiling inside me like lava.

"Tell me, are there more of your little friends running around my city?"

I say nothing.

"Are you planning an attack, huh?" Drago steps closer, looming over me.

Silent.

"What, you got nothing to say?" Drago smiles mockingly, then backhands me suddenly across the face.

He hits me so hard I think my neck is going to break.

My good ear is ringing and I'm seeing spots. My head lolls and blood and drool dribble from my mouth. Drago grabs a clump of hair and pulls my head up roughly so I can see his face.

"Where's the rest of your people?" he asks again.

"No one else," I cough. "Just me."

"Good. Good." He smiles his fucking awful smile and lets go of my hair, wiping the sweat and blood from his hand on his pants. "What are you doing in New Chechnya, huh?"

"Nothing," I say. "I'm here for a friend. Trying to help them find someone."

He laughs, pacing in front of me back and forth, back and forth. "Did that fucking prick Anatoli send you to kill me?"

I say nothing.

"What about Xander Odom, huh? What about the research she stole?" Drago crouches down on his haunches in front of me so he can look me dead in the eyes.

I say nothing.

"Her friends over there on the wall wouldn't tell me either. Speak, or I'll nail you to the fucking wall right now."

"I don't know any Xander Odom and I don't know about any stolen fucking research," I say. "I told you, I'm here trying find someone for a friend."

Our eyes meet. I can see the horrible monster that lives behind them. He stands up, shaking his head and chuckling. He motions to one of his men who's standing beside a table with my stuff piled on it.

Pistol. Transmitter. DED programmable matter weapons. Jumper.

"My men tell me they picked you up outside the Freight Terminal. Said they saw you there with someone that looked an awful lot like Xander Odom."

I say nothing.

The Bravatso standing next to my stuff comes forward. He's got something in his hand and he passes it to Drago.

"They said they found this hidden in your clothes." Drago holds the vial in the palm of his hand where I can see it.

Fuck, they found the Chimera weapon.

"What's this then?"

I say nothing.

"Is this a fucking virus, huh?" His voice gets louder.

I say nothing.

"They sent you here to kill everyone in the fucking dome," Drago screams, eyes burning, mouth twisted in rage. "In my fucking city?"

"Fuck you," I smile, spitting blood at him.

"Fuck me?" he screams. He looks unhinged. "Fuck you."

Drago storms in and kicks me hard in the ribs. They're already shattered and the pain is like a lightning bolt. I crumple over onto my side, coughing in spasms and trying to get my breath. I can taste blood in my mouth. He steps in and kicks me again and then again and again in a wild fury, the force of each blow lifting my body up off the ground.

Black spots dance.

Sound seems to phase in and out.

I feel like I'm underwater, drowning.

I can't breathe.

He steps back, admiring his handiwork, watching me writhe in pain and gasping for breath. Then he bends down and grabs me again, this time pulling me up from my knees and off my feet, holding me in the air by my hair and thrusting his face into mine, our noses touching.

"How you like that, huh?"

I try to smile.

He head-butts me in the face.

I feel my lips mash into my teeth and split. A welt puffs up around my eye. Then he lets me drop to the ground.

I hit the stone floor hard, sprawling like a rag doll, and I groan out loud.

Fuck, I didn't want to give him the satisfaction.

I switch off the pain receptors around my right-side rib cage and try to clear the darkness swirling in front of my eyes.

"Get him up," Drago growls, motioning to the two guards standing behind me.

They grab my arms and yank me violently to my feet. My knees buckle and I almost fall down again. The two Bravatso guards hold me up till I can see straight again.

"Get your fucking hands off me," I warn, freeing myself roughly from their grip.

"Look at you little man, you make me sad." Drago starts to laugh his bellowing laugh. "We are both soldiers. We are the same, you and

I. We should not be fighting like this, it brings me no pleasure. It can all be over if you just tell me what I want to know."

He's mocking me.

Fucking prick. I'm shaking now. Rage pumps through my body. I flex my arms, trying to break the cuffs around my wrists. I can feel the metal cut my skin. Blood and sweat trickle down into my hands.

"You have to understand that none of this is personal, little man. It's just business. Okay?"

His words hang in the air.

It's not personal, it's just business.

How many times have I said the same fucking thing? How many times have I told myself those exact words so I could sleep at night? So I could look at myself in the mirror. So I could justify my entire, shitty existence.

I'm just like him.

At least I was.

"Fuck you Drago," I say.

His eyes meet mine and he shakes his head in mock disappointment, almost as if torturing me is some great inconvenience to him. Then he moves like lightning, delivering a knee to my midsection in the blink of an eye and sending me sprawling to the ground again.

I'm doubled over, writing on the floor.

"I'm bored with this. You want to do this the hard way, we will do it the hard way, little man." Drago motions to the two Bravatso standing either side of me. "Hold him."

They get me up to my knees and pin me down with their knees in my back.

I struggle and they press down harder.

It occurs to me that there's no way out of this situation. That I'm probably not going to make it out of this room alive.

I don't how to feel about that.

Indifferent? Relieved, maybe?

I wish I could have seen my sister one last time.

"I will ask you this one more time, or something very bad is going to happen." Drago stands in front of me looking down, a sneer slashed across his face. "Where is Xander Odom? Where is the research she stole?"

"You're going have to kill me," I spit back at him.

Drago smiles.

"I'm not going to kill you little man, not yet anyway. But I am going to give you a taste of what's in store for that fucking bitch Xander Odom when I find her. Your boss Anatoli, too. Thinks he can send fucking people up here to kill Drago Afanasievich, huh?"

Drago shakes his head and laughs.

He looks fucking deranged like a wild animal, ready to attack.

"Fuck Anatoli and fuck SPM," he screams suddenly. "I take back that fucking research she stole and sell it myself. This city is mine, I keep New Chechnya for me."

No wonder Anatoli Dugray-Mir wanted the whole city dead. Drago is fucking insane.

"Better yet, maybe I take this fucking virus you brought up here to kill me and set it loose back down on Earth. Kill them like they want to kill us, huh?"

"You don't scare me," I say.

Drago raises his eyebrows and chuckles.

"Really?" He draws a long, serrated knife from his belt and holds it out for me to see. "Ever seen someone being skinned alive before? It's not pleasant."

Drago grins at this, the glint of fire from the furnace bouncing off the polished blade. He bends down and grabs hold of my wrist tightly, his grip like an iron vice. I struggle and pull away, my body twisting, legs kicking desperately. Two more guards come over to help hold me down. There's four of them on me, and Drago.

I can't move.

I fight as hard as I can but I can't move.

He places the tip of the knife against my skin and presses it down. It slips into my flesh. I grit my teeth and he's looking at me, enthralled by the spectacle, as if somehow in rapture. He pulls the razor-edged blade up along the inside of my palm, slicing open my hand. Blood flows. Searing pain flashes and I recoil instinctively before I switch off the pain receptors in my hand.

They hold me steady.

"Skinning someone is not pretty," he smiles. "Or quick. In fact, aside from burning alive, they say it's about the most horrible pain a person can endure."

Drago deftly slices around my wrist bone and begins to flay my hand. I look away. It doesn't matter that I can't feel it. It's horrible all the same.

"Watch what I do to your hand here. When I'm done, I do the same to the rest of your arm. Then your face. Listen to me," Drago stops, waiting for me to look up at him. "I'm going to rip every piece of flesh from your bones. I'm going to cut you up piece by fucking piece until you tell me what I want to know."

Our eyes meet.

There is no lying in them.

With a yank he rips the skin from my left hand like it was a glove and throws it on the floor. It lands with a wet slap.

"Do you understand me?"

I drop my eyes to the ground and I say nothing.

I know what's coming.

"No? Alright, let's try the arm then, huh?"

28.

Bits and Pieces.

I've never cared for the smell of burning flesh.

Especially when it's my own.

Drago is standing near the forge. He's flayed the skin off my left hand and most of the flesh halfway up my forearm. The muscle is ragged and in pieces. I can't move my fingers anymore, the tendons to my fingers and my palm have been severed.

He's dangling a piece of me over the fire, taunting me, trying to get me to talk.

I feel lightheaded.

I'm bleeding heavily.

With all the blood I've lost from the gunshot wounds to my face and my shoulder and my leg, there's not much more left in my body.

If he keeps cutting off pieces of me, I'm going to die soon.

I've got to escape. I pull against the cuffs, I can feel them cutting through the raw flesh around my left wrist, sliding against the exposed bone.

"So, have you had enough yet?" Drago drops the piece of my forearm into the forge and wipes the blood from his hands on his pants.

"Fuck you Drago," I manage to say.

He saunters over towards me and pulls my head back, his face centimetres from mine. "Really little man? You think you can take much more?"

I think my eyes roll back in my head. I don't know for sure. I collapse back down onto my knees, what's left of my arm cradled on my thigh.

"Pathetic. I was just getting started." Drago starts laughing at this.

The other Bravatso in the room join in.

This pisses me off.

They think I'm done for. But I'm not.

They think I'm not a threat. But I am.

I'm the most dangerous fucking person you'll ever meet.

I pull against the cuffs; I can feel them sliding against the exposed bone.

"You want to know what I'm going to do to you next, little man. Huh?" Drago kicks me to get my attention, a broad smile on his face. "Something I learnt when I was fighting in South Africa. They're sick fucks down there. They called it a 'facemask'. What you do is, you cut off someone's face while they're still conscious, nice slow, careful to get it all off in one piece. Then you make them look in a mirror."

I pull against the cuffs. I shift so I'm crouched on my haunches, feet beneath me on the ground.

"They freak out, seriously, the fucking sight is priceless, no? They start screaming and losing their minds." He turns to the Bravatso guard behind him, they're both laughing now. "Remember that fucking guy last week? The soldier? Remember when you put his face on in front of him? That was hilarious."

The rest of them join in.

I have to escape.

"The tricky bit is not to blind them when you cut off their eyelids." Drago starts towards me, knife in hand.

There's only one way to get out of here.

I pull the cuffs across the bone.

Fuck it. If I don't, I'm dead anyway.

I place my left arm on the ground and stamp on my wrist hard with my right boot heel. The force breaks my arm. The radius and the ulna both snap like wet twigs.

The room looks on in disbelief. Even Drago stops, eye wide and surprised, as if he can't process what he's seeing.

The arm hasn't broken through, so I step on my hand with my right boot, holding it against the ground, and jerk the cuffs up hard. The metal tears through the splinters of bone and what's left of my left hand is severed below the wrist.

I stand up, the stump on my left arm a mess of jagged bone and meat. Blood oozes and splatters on the floor. Everyone in the room looks at me in utter disbelief.

My adrenaline begins hyper-secretion and I move almost faster than I can think. My heart is racing, breathing fast and heavy. Every muscle and fibre in my body ripples, feeling like it's pumping white, hot light.

I strike the guard behind and to my right first.

I deliver an elbow to the neck, compacting his larynx. He clutches at his throat desperately, stumbling as he tries to breathe. The guard beside him begins to move towards me and I deliver a roundhouse kick hard to the side of his left knee, the sheer force dislocating his kneecap. He screams and bends down, clutching at his leg in agony. I grab him by the hair with my one good hand and knee him in in the face with all my might, fracturing the orbital socket and causing a massive haemorrhage in his eyeball. I deliver a second knee to his glabella. The force of the blow shatters the bone, creating a huge dent in his forehead.

I let him fall to the floor and look around the room.

The two other guards have their weapons drawn. One on my left near the bodies and one in front of the forge.

Drago is coming at me with his knife.

He attacks me first, slashing wildly as he rushes towards me. I duck and sidestep, delivering a blow under his floating rib as he passes. He lets out a guttural noise and doubles over.

The other two open fire.

They're panicked, rushing, so they miss.

But they won't for long.

The guard with the shattered larynx is asphyxiating nearby, doubled over, desperately clutching at his throat. His face is blue and eyes bulging and he's making a panicked, wheezing sound.

I grab his shirt at the back of the neck and push him over to my left, using him as a shield from the gunfire of the guard near the bodies. A burst of high-powered projectiles makes mincemeat of the guard's chest and his knees buckle as he goes into death throes.

Fuck it, I've got to keep moving. It's the only way I'm going to survive.

I run at the guard near the table, propping up the mangled Bravatso in front of me. I only make a few steps. The guard I'm propping up is dying, he's having some kind of fucking seizure and his feet drag on the ground, then his legs give out. It's impossible to hold up his dead weight with one hand so I push him at the Bravatso and attack.

The guard sidesteps the corpse and opens fire as I come at him. I hold up my left arm instinctively, for a moment thinking the programmable matter will leap out and protect me.

It doesn't.

The shots pass through what's left of the meat in my forearm and whizz by my ear.

Fucker.

I delver two quick blows. The first to his solar plexus, then I rake at his eyes, clawing and pulling them both from their sockets. He starts screaming, high pitched and traumatised as he desperately tries to shove them back into their sockets.

He's crying tears of blood.

Drago comes up behind me screaming loudly and slashing violently with his knife. I duck, then step behind the blinded guard, deftly avoiding his attack. Drago plunges his knife and buries it deep into the guard's chest.

I'm moving before he can pull it free, running at the guard near the forge.

He opens fire and projectiles scream past me. I keep my head down, shifting right then left, evading as best I can, then leap into the air and deliver a kick to his chest. The force of it sends him sprawling back, knocking the gun from his grip. It clatters to the floor.

As I land, I grab him by the front of his shirt with my right hand, pulling him towards me. He latches onto my arms and I head-butt him in the bridge of his nose. It explodes in a spray of blood and cartilage. He screams loudly, careering backwards, blinded temporarily.

With his arms failing about, he takes one step, then two, then falls backwards into the forge, bursting into flames.

The high-pitched screams of the dying man fill the room.

I look back at Drago as he rips the blade from the guard's chest, throwing his body aside like a rag doll.

He turns to face me.

"Are you ready, little man?" he asks. "I'm going to tear you apart."

He screams a guttural scream and launches at me, lumbering across the room, knife brandished above his head.

I bend down, pick up the gun and level it at Drago Afanasievich.

He looks at me, almost taken aback that I wasn't going to fight him hand-to-hand to the death.

I smile at him and fire.

Drago's chest explodes, one, two. He stops in his tracks, frozen, his mouth opening and closing like a goldfish out of water.

A third shot hits him in the forehead.

Then he's down on his knees.

Then face forward on the ground.

I lower the gun.

I feel like I'm out of my body, looking down on myself.

I can hear shouting, people running. There are more Bravatso on the way.

I'm standing in a pool of blood. My arm is a mangled mess of bone and flesh. Blood pumps from the stump to the beat of my heart.

I need to go. I need to get out of here.

I walk over to the forge and slam the stump of my left arm into the white-hot coals. The flesh blackens and sizzles in the heat as it cauterises.

I think I scream.

The smell is overwhelming.

Darkness dances in my peripheral and I feel like I'm going to black out. But I don't. I can't. Not yet anyway.

I withdraw my smouldering stump and start for the table where my stuff is piled.

I make sure I don't forget the virus.

29.

The Circles of Hell.

They say the average lifespan for a corporate head-hunter is three years.

I've been doing this for seven.

I don't know how many jobs I've done or how many people I've killed. To tell you the truth, I don't like to think about it.

I wonder sometimes if there was another path I could have taken, another direction I could have gone, or if this was always laid out in front of me from the start.

Did I get to decide?

Or did someone decide for me?

Operation Blind Angel. The assassination attempt on Juan Manuel Iadanza, president of the Sovereign States of the Americas was a debacle. Turns out that one of the operatives we were working with was a double agent.

Amon Cherkassky.

He compromised the operation, made sure that everyone involved was either captured or killed. It was only dumb luck that I got out at all.

It took me almost a month to get back to Antarctica. I lived on the streets of Córdoba among the homeless, hiding in plain sight, until I could arrange safe passage out home.

The Black Coats arrested me the moment I stepped off the boat.

From that first night in prison, sitting in a white, square box and staring at the walls, I vowed to take my revenge on Amon Cherkassky one day, make him pay for everything that he'd done.

But I never got the chance.

He disappeared after Blind Angel, and I've been unable to find a trace of him since.

The Antarctician government denied all involvement in the operation. They made up some bullshit story about my unit going rogue, arrested Dr Kyobe and his staff, and charged us all as war criminals.

The trial was televised. It was a farce, of course, held to appease the international community and clean up Antarctica's tarnished image.

Dr Kyobe got the death penalty.

They sentenced me to life in jail without the possibility of parole.

To tell you the truth, I was surprised that was all I got. Antarctica is a totalitarian state and the government pretty much does what they want. I was expecting them to execute me. Or maybe set me up to die in some accident or prison fight.

But instead they made a public example of me.

I suppose it was the only way to save face.

I was kept in solitary confinement, in a specially designed cell made just for me. I was a trillion-dollar weapon. No one wanted me loose in the prison general population.

My cell was a white box, four-by-four-by-four. It had a bed and a toilet, nothing else. I was locked inside twenty-three hours and thirty minutes a day. Half an hour out for exercise each day, an hour on the weekend, under full military surveillance, of course.

I spent a year in that box.

In the end, it wasn't too hard to escape.

Not for me anyway.

I headed north, caught a boat to Australasia. Auckland first, then Melbourne. My escape didn't make the news; I guess the Antarctician government wasn't too keen to tell people I was on the loose. They were keen on finding me though – both cities were crawling with Antarctician agents, so I didn't linger.

A few weeks later I was in the Republic of Mexico.

By then I was almost out of money and desperate. The Antarcticians were still hot on my heels. I found work with the cartels in Phoenix and San Diego, mainly running guns to the warlords in the Louisiana Badlands.

It was good work for a while. But it didn't last.

The cartels were having border disputes with the United States, trying to claim territory in the shanties in southern Utah and Colorado. Things got ugly after they killed an American secret police captain.

When the Americans sent death squads over the border to deal with the cartels, I packed my shit and headed north again.

But I couldn't stay long. The United States wasn't the kind of place you wanted to settle down in. Not then anyway. This is back when the Puritan Party first came to power, back when President Vernon Morrow had passed the new constitution and was holding the first Inquisition trials.

So, I kept going till I hit the Alaskan Free States. Then I headed west. To Korea.

I knew the Antarcticians couldn't follow me there. The Chong-Ro crime syndicate controlled the entire peninsula so I was safe in Seoul. There were no laws, no government extradition, and no police.

A week after I arrived in Seoul, Australasia joined the war against Antarctica. They sent in SAS troops and liberated the Vostok death camp. Thousands of prisoners were rescued and given a new life on the Australian mainland.

My sister's name was not on the list of the people who were saved.

So, I disappeared into the Black Market City and started again.

I did jobs for whoever was paying. It wasn't long before I met someone from Human Resources Management. Actually, it was more like I killed a head-hunter working for Human Resources

Management and they found me. When I got home one night, a small man in dark suit was waiting for me in my room.

He asked if I was interested in some work.

I told him that it wasn't wise to sneak up on me, that I've killed people for much less.

He smiled at this, unperturbed. He introduced himself as 5, then explained who he worked for. I was intrigued. Truth be told, I didn't like the small-time thugs I was working for or the petty shit they had me doing. Truth be told, I thought I was above being some low-level enforcer, I thought I was important, special somehow.

Looking back on things, that was definitely the moment. That was the first step down the path that led me here.

It was my choice to do the things I did.

No one forced me. They offered me a hit and I took it. Simple as that.

The job was in London. They called it the Westminster Job, the assassination of Mothibi Loago, a high-level executive from an African communications company. Just one pull of the trigger led me here.

I wonder where I'd be if I'd said no?

30.

Along the Razor's Edge.

There's a fire exit at the end of the room.

I kick open the door and run up the stairs towards the roof. The car that brought me here was parked up there. At least it was. If it's still there, it'll be my only way out.

If it's gone, I'm dead.

I make it up the first flight of stairs alright but by the second, I stumble and fall to my knees. It takes me a while to get back to my feet. I'm pretty sure I can hear voices somewhere behind me.

I stagger up another floor.

I'm trying not to think of what happened to my arm. What I just did to myself. About my skinned hand lying on the floor. About the blackened stump I'm cradling to my chest. But I can smell it, so it's hard to ignore.

"Two more floors," I grunt out loud.

It's the best I can do to keep from passing out.

I feel like I might be dying. And that's not so bad. I don't mind, I'm not scared. But I'm not done yet, so I need to keep on going. I still need to find out the truth about my sister before I go.

I lumber up another flight and there's one to go before the roof. I can definitely hear footsteps behind me, voices too.

It'd be so easy to fall down here and let it all be over. It'd be quick, one shot, and then forever nothing. All the pain would go away, erased, just like me.

And I'm fine with that.

I'd like to be erased, just like all the identities I've assumed before.

Just like all the people I've killed before.

I come to the top of the stairs and draw my gun. I can see the heat signatures of the two men standing outside through the wall.

I kick open the door to the roof and fire. Two guards, two controlled bursts. The first burst hits the guard on the far side of the roof. He slumps to the ground with a thud. But the second burst misses.

The guard closest, the one leaning against the car, raises the Nettle laser he's holding and stutters "Jesus fuck..." as he fumbles to return fire. I don't miss a second time. Five bursts of charged rounds pepper his chest and midsection.

I start towards the car, discarding the rotary pistol and stopping for a moment to pry the laser rifle from the dead guard's hands.

There's noise of footsteps pounding on the stairs.

They're close.

Coming up behind me fast.

I circle around the car to the driver's side and take cover, then prime the laser and aim it at the darkened stairwell.

Three Bravatso emerge from the darkness, guns drawn. I fire the Nettle laser at them, sweeping the beam wildly across the stairwell entrance. The cold, blue beam slices off the top of the first Bravatso's head like a knife through a soft-boiled egg and sends the other two diving back down the stairs for cover.

Much easier than the pistol.

I jump into the driver's seat, throw the laser rifle onto the seat beside me and pull the door shut.

"Come on, come on, come on...." I'm muttering to myself as I fumble with the ignition, desperately thumbing the button again and again.

Nothing.

I try again.

Nothing.

"Fuck." I glance anxiously towards the stairwell just as the two Bravatso emerge from the dark and open fire.

Gunshots riddle the side of the car.

Instinctively, I duck down in my seat. A round hits the passenger window and it shatters in an explosion of polymer.

"Come on you fucking piece of shit..." I yell as I hit the ignition and turn the engine over one last time.

It comes to life and I rev the car, pulling back hard on the wheel. The anti-gravity engine whines loudly as the car jolts suddenly and starts to rise up from the roof.

More gunshots from the stairwell.

The window behind me explodes. The Bravatso are streaming out of the stairwell now, firing wildly at the car as it ascends above the building.

Rounds begin to shred the underside of the vehicle. They sound like hailstones battering a tin roof. If they hit the fuel cell, the car will fall out of the sky like a stone. Or worse, it'll explode. Either way I'm fucked. I floor the accelerator and the car's engine screams as it begins to pull away. I glance back out the window to the roof below. There's maybe ten Bravatso out on the roof firing up at the car, more of them appearing from the stairwell. Down on the street I can see a mob of Bravatso running from the building, some pointing up towards me, others bolting towards cars and bikes parked nearby.

A barrage of projectiles hits the back of the car.

Something explodes in black smoke and the engine power cuts out. The car drops sickeningly, falling from the sky.

I can feel my stomach rise up into my throat.

"Fucking piece of shit!" I yell as I hit the ignition button over and over again, stamping on the accelerator. "Fuck, fuck, fuck, fuck fuck..."

All of a sudden, the engine sparks brightly and kicks in. A high-pitched whining sound fills the air. My freefall jolts to a stop and the car hovers over the street below, no more than five metres from the rooftop.

I'm fucking dead if I don't get out of here.

I grab the gun from the passenger seat and lean out of the window as high-powered gunfire screams around the car. I fire the rifle, swinging it wildly. The blue beam burns a trail across the rooftop, sending the Bravatso ducking for cover.

And that's when I see them.

The building has back-up battery cells up on the roof. There's a bank of them near the stairwell. If they have charge left in them, even a little bit, then they're explosive.

I aim at the battery bank as the Bravatso open fire again. The laser beam whips across battery cells. They rupture and ignite. I duck back inside the window, drop the gun in my lap and hit the accelerator. The car lurches forward violently, trailing a thick plume of black smoke behind it.

There's a flash of white light, then an explosion.

The roof of the building is vaporised.

Then there's another explosion, this time much larger. The entire building erupts in a fireball.

A deafening blast resonates like a thousand lightning strikes. A rolling set of supersonic shockwaves radiates from the fiery building, picking up the car and tossing it forward like a toy.

I fight for control, desperately trying to keep the car in the air. It shudders and vibrates from the sheer force of the explosion, pitching left then right. It's like catching a tsunami while surfing on a matchstick.

The shockwaves begin to dissipate and I manage to steady the controls. I look back as the car accelerates, speeding across the rooftops. A fireball radiates out, like a miniature mushroom cloud, consuming the entire block.

I slump down in the seat. Cold air buffets the car through the broken windows and rain and wind sting my face. It feels good.

There's dark in my peripherals again.

I drift out, the sound of the engine and the wind become background noise.

Darkness.

Then I wake with a start as my head lolls forward.

I steady the car and shake my head to stay awake, focusing my eyes out at the green cloudy sky. The car streaks west over dark city towards the Rustov Projects.

For a moment it's quiet. For a moment I think I've gotten away clean.

Then the building to my left explodes.

"Fuck," I hiss through my teeth, anxiously checking what's behind me.

In the rear view I can see the sprawl of New Chechnya. The tiny dots of drones and cars and bikes buzz off in the distance. Dozens of them. Closer, I can see two cars and a bike coming up fast behind me.

There's another explosion, this time just behind the car. I'm a sitting duck up here in the open. I bank sharply to the right, steering the vehicle in a sweeping arc down into the dark canyons between the buildings.

I glance back over my shoulder and watch them follow me down into the maze of darkened tenements. I flatten out the car at street level and the two cars and the bike fall in behind as we speed down the pitch-black streets.

They're following closely now.

I can't outrun them.

The car's taken too much damage.

The passengers in each car are leaning out their windows firing automatic weapons. I notice one of the Bravatso is armed with an SRDR 9 anti-personnel cannon.

It's basically handheld artillery. A fucking plasma launcher designed to inflict mass causalities on entrenched enemy forces in an urban environment.

If one round hits the car, I'll be turned into soup.

I floor the accelerator and hit the auto-drive switch on the dash, the beat-up old car hugging the wet streets as it screams through the city.

I sit up in my seat and activate the nanite system in my adrenal cortex, hyper-secreting adrenalin. It dispels the darkness hugging the edges of my eyes. I find the programmable matter discs in my pants pocket and place them in my lap, then grasp one with my right hand and wait as it links to my nervous system and melts around my wrist. I place the other on what's left of my left arm and watch as it liquefies and wraps itself around the stump forming a long, wide blade.

I pick up the rifle and begin to pull myself out through the window, leaning from the side of the car. The wind catches me and almost pulls me out, so I slam the programmable blade into the rooftop to hold on.

They open fire as soon as they see me.

High-velocity projectiles whizz past my head, several slamming into the back of the car. I notice the woman armed with the anti-personnel cannon is priming the weapon. It glows with an ominous green light.

Then she fires.

The dense-plasma projectile shoots past the car and slams into the building ahead, sending huge chunks of nanocrete tumbling to the street below. The car's anti-collision device swerves violently left then right, narrowly avoiding the falling debris.

She missed once. I doubt she'll miss again.

If I'm going to do something, it has to be now.

I turn and fire the Nettle laser at a street light as we fly by. The blue, high-energy beam cuts through the pole, sending it tumbling to the road and into the path of the vehicles behind me. The bike and the first car swerve out of the way.

The second car is not so lucky.

It slams into the pole at high speed. The force of the impact sends it careering off into the façades of one of the tenements lining the street. This crumples the car, bringing it to a sudden stop and ejecting the two Bravatso through the windshield, their bodies cartwheeling through the air before smashing into the road with a wet thud.

I pull myself fully out of the window and hang from the side of the car, the programmable blade anchoring me to the vehicle.

"Come on you fuckers," I growl.

I launch myself into the night, hurtling through the air towards the car behind us.

Time seems to slow.

I can see each and every individual raindrop swell and bulge and collide as they tumble down towards the ground. The flash of lightning in the green clouds above as it slowly forks out across the roof of the dome. The comet-like tails that trail the hundreds of high velocity projectiles tearing through the air around me.

And all the while my purpose seems to be reduced to one simple thing.

Find the truth before I die.

The Bravatso on the bike behind swerves as I leap out from the car, banking up onto the sidewalk. He fires at me and misses. I ignore him and aim the laser at the car trailing close behind, the beam striking the vehicle in the bonnet, just near the windshield. I pull the beam up through the car, slicing through the metal and polymer, cleaving the back section into two. The driver loses his left leg and arm, but I miss the Bravatso in the passenger seat with the anti-personnel cannon.

Her eyes meet mine for the briefest of moments as I fly past. She looks shocked. Scared. Then the car's fuel cell ignites in a flash of white light and she's consumed by the explosion.

I hit the wet road at a sickening velocity, bouncing twice, then sliding before I come to a complete stop.

Then there's silence.

31.

Into the Breach, Mother Fuckers.

My face feels wet.

I don't know if it's from the rain or my own blood.

Spots of darkness have pushed forward from my peripherals and threaten to overtake me once and for all. My body screams in misery. I can barely move, barely breathe. I can't tell what broken or lacerated or burnt or ruptured or anything anymore.

It's all just blinding pain.

So, I stop it. I stop feeling all together and switch off the pain receptors to every part of my body.

The darkness retreats and I push myself up off the ground. My gun's gone. I don't know where it is.

I must have dropped it when I hit the ground.

There's a smell in the air, acrid and bitter, from the burning cars nearby. From the burning flesh and hair.

I get to my feet. There are bodies of several Bravatso sprawled on the street nearby.

Up ahead I can see what's left of my car. It's crushed and broken. Must have crashed after I jumped out. The Bravatso on the bike is stopped near the wreckage, gun drawn, looking inside to see if there were any other passengers.

"Hey," I shout as I start down the road.

My voice sounds strange, hoarse and slurred. I think my jaw might be broken. But I can't tell. Everything feels numb, one step removed. With my pain receptors turned off it feels like I'm watching myself from behind my own eyes.

The Bravatso looks back at me.

"You forget about me, mother fucker?" I yell.

He sneers and revs the bike, turning sharply down the road, and speeding towards me.

I start to run up the street as he levels the sub-machine pistol, aiming carefully. The bike screams towards me. I'm running and watching the gun in his hand, watching his trigger finger, waiting for the moment.

Waiting to strike.

He squeezes the trigger and opens fire as the bike bears down on me. I cut right and activate the programmable matter around my left stump, locking into LASH formation. The long blade unfurls into a razor-edged lash. I turn and crack the programmable matter coil, slicing through rider and bike in one fatal strike.

The bike splits, then the front section lurches forward and flips, sending pieces of the rider tumbling across the wet road.

Then it's silent again.

Just the sound of the rain on the road and the ticking of the engine of the crashed car.

I can't feel anything but I stand and let the rain fall down on me anyway. And the moment feels like forever. Then glance down at myself. I'm a mess. My clothes are tattered and ripped from where I hit the road. Beneath I can see long patches of shredded skin and exposed bone. Dark contusions from some internal rupture.

I can feel my stomach turn.

I start west, limping down the street, leaving the smouldering wrecks behind. There are headlights off in the distance, I can see them glowing in the clouds.

More Bravatso are on the way.

"Shouldn't be far now..." I'm pretty sure I say to myself. "Only a few blocks from the access tunnel."

Overhead a car speeds by through the dense green clouds. I retreat into the shadows of a building and wait for it to pass. They're still looking for me. Not quite sure where I might be. But it won't be too much longer till they spot the smouldering wrecks I left a few blocks back.

Then the streets will be crawling with them.

So, got to keep on moving. Because I'm dead if I stay here.

I stick to the shadows, moving cautiously block after block till I reach the rubble-filled street I first climbed out onto. How long ago was that? How long have I been in this hell hole?

A day? Two? More?

I can see the manhole ahead. I wait in the shadows of a crumbling building, watching till the car circling above streaks off across the sky. Then I move, lurching across the road, until I fall on my knees in front of the circular alloy cover.

I pry it loose. I grab hold of the ladder with my good hand and start down into the tunnel, descending slowly rung by rung, till I reach the bottom.

It's dark down here and the warm air greets me like a friend.

It takes me a second to notice the bodies strewn on the ground.

About five or six near the ladder, then a bunch scattered down the tunnel, all shot in the back like they were running away from gunfire.

I stop and kick one over so I can see their face.

It's a little girl. A refugee. No more than ten.

They must have been part of another group smuggled in by the Yan Brothers. Fuck knows why they killed them.

Maybe they couldn't pay.

Maybe there were Bravatso up on the street and they couldn't get them out without being seen.

Or maybe they're just evil. Maybe they took their money and killed them for the fun of it. Nothing would surprise me in this fucking place anymore.

"Motherfuckers," I say under my breath.

I start down the access tunnel towards the loading docks. Down here in the dark, I move without making a sound. Slowly. Deliberately. Chances are the Yan Brothers and their men will be hanging around at their makeshift camp.

Maybe I can give them a surprise.

I come to the end of the tunnel. About one hundred metres out I can see the fortifications the Yan Brothers have set up ahead, the nanocrete barriers with two Hänsler-28 anti-fortification railguns.

And they're manned.

I can see the radiating heat signature of the two men on the guns and another three nearby standing around in the improvised residence.

But it's dark and they can't see me.

I lock both the programmable matter weapons into BLADE formation and start down the tunnel towards the fortifications, keeping low to the ground, silent.

I get close. I don't recognise the two men on the guns, but I can hear all three of the Yan Brothers laughing nearby. Their cackle is unforgettable.

I get even closer.

I'm next to the nanocrete barricades now.

I can see the Yan Brothers in the dim yellow light of a portable lamp. They're lounging around near the bunk beds in the living quarters past the fortifications. They're all drinking and smoking, laughing at some stupid fucking joke.

Fang is the smart one. Ren is the fat one. Sun is the stupid one.

I strike at the two guards from the dark. Two movements, fluid and silent. They're both dead before they even know they've been attacked.

Then I walk out from the shadows into the light.

I must look like a fucking demon come straight out of hell.

"Remember me, Fang?" I say, smiling at them.

The Yan Brothers all freeze and look in my direction.

"What the fuck?" Sun says.

They all look at me in total surprise. In shock. As if I were the last person they ever expected to see.

I attack before they come to their senses. I punch Sun in the face, the tip of the blade entering just above the bridge of his nose and exiting out the back of his skull, just above the atlas vertebra.

I slip it out before he can blink, ducking as his brother Ren raises his gun. I punch Ren in the gut with the other blade just below the naval and rip up as hard as I can, opening him from pubis to sternum in one quick move.

He staggers and falls dead as his insides empty out.

The shooting stops and it's silent for a moment.

Fang stands backed up to the bed, horror and fear and hatred glowing in his beady eyes. He's shaking, about to cry.

"Please, please don't kill me," he says, looking at his dead brothers.

"I saw what you did to those refugees back there, Fang," I growl.

His voice becomes desperate, pleading. "Please, I didn't do it. It was Ren, I swear it was Ren."

"Bullshit."

"It's true!" he squeals.

I take a step towards him and he cowers. In that moment I can see how much he hates me; how desperate he is to kill me.

"Please, it wasn't me, I swear." He screams so loudly it sounds like his throat is bleeding.

The programmable matter forms into SWARM formation in the palm of my hand. I throw it at him as he tries to scramble away. It leaves my hand like a shot. A thousand tiny needles form and fly through the air, hitting him in the face and neck and chest, like the spray of a riot gun.

He screams his agony and collapses, convulsing on the floor till he's dead.

When he's still, I walk over and place my hand on his chest, waiting till the programmable matter forms and flows like mercury, finding its home again around my wrist. Then I make my way down the loading dock to the long corridor that leads to the docking ports.

The first is empty.

So is the second.

But the third has a ship docked.

I stop and bang on the transport's door, waiting for Radovan Sedlak to answer.

"Who is it?" he asks in a thick Russian accent.

This pisses me off. He can see me. There's a camera above the door.

"Open the fucking door."

"Alright, alright," he says. I can hear him disable the locks and pressurise the airlock. It takes him almost a minute. "It's good you made it, I had to pay those fucking snakeheads a fortune to dock here."

Radovan opens the airlock door. He is tall and lanky with greasy black hair, a scruffy beard and a long nose that's too big for his face.

"To tell you the truth, I'd given up on you," he says smiling. "I was just about to..."

He stops mid-sentence when he sees the state of me.

Then he stops smiling altogether when he notices Xander Odom isn't with me.

"What the fuck is this shit?" Radovan says.

He looks confused.

Then angry.

"Where's the fucking girl? Mr Dougray-Mir said I wasn't to leave New Chechnya without her."

"Change of plans," I growl. "Get this fucking ship moving. I don't have much time."

32.

Really Fucking Small Robots.

They're called nanorobots. Or nanomachines. Or nanites.

Never heard of them before? Got no idea what I'm talking about?

Well, let me try and explain.

Nanites are really small robots. I mean, really small, they're micro-fucking-scopic. To give you some idea of just how small I'm talking about, nanites are measured in nanometres.

That's one billionth of a metre.

Still not getting it? A bacterium is a thousand nanometres long. A strand of DNA is about two and a half nanometres across. A human hair is one hundred thousand nanometres wide.

Now imagine a robot about that size.

It fucks with your head, doesn't it?

Nanorobotics got its start in medicine. It changed the world overnight, saved the lives of millions. It was first used successfully in pharmacokinetics, helping administer drugs with targeted cell delivery. This led to innovations in the treatment of cancer.

This was big news. Huge.

Soon every company in the world wanted to get involved in the field. It was the new arms race, the nanobot race. And the technology exploded.

New developments in imaging and diagnosis, injectable treatments for diseases of the circulatory and lymphatic systems. Then micro-surgical robotics, tissue engineering and cellular repair machines. Then regeneration robotics able to work with stem cells to grow back damaged nerve tissue.

Then organs.

Then limbs.

Soon it was all about reversing ageing.

The technology flourished and the corporations made a fortune. Nothing helps drive innovation more than greed. The nanotech expanded rapidly into environmental clean-up, digital information storage, smart buildings, replicators and biochips that blurred the line between humanity and machinery.

But of course, there was a dark side to all this innovation. It didn't take long to weaponize nanites.

First, Programmable Matter.

Then Smart Guns.

The big innovations came with nanite body armour like the SAUW tactile battle suit. It could form over the body with a neural command, protect the user from almost all forms of small arms weaponry and close combat damage, administer drugs and perform nanite surgery on the wearer. It could even bend light to create near invisible camouflage.

Then came nanite-nuclear weapons. Things got real after they were invented. But they were nothing compared to what came next.

Swarm Weapons or Drexler Particles, named in honour of the man that first theorised their destructive capabilities more than a hundred years earlier.

They were world eaters. Trillions of swarming microscopic bio-machines that were deployed in a gas-like cloud and capable of consuming all biomass in their path, while continually self-replicating.

They were the doomsday machines. Weapons of mass destruction. The worst thing humanity ever invented.

So of course, they were used on civilians.

At the height of the nanobot race, every superpower had developed a Swarm Weapon. Top secret test footage of the weapon's destructive power had managed to find its way out into the media and people were scared, kind of like back in the Cold War, when everyone was terrified of all-out nuclear destruction.

There were a lot of summits. A lot of rhetoric.

Then a border skirmish between Korea and China and reports of Drexler Particles being used on the field of battle. The stories were unimaginable, the suffering worse than you could possibly conceive. Tensions simmered and the world wondered if runaway self-replicating robots would descend like locusts and destroy it before climate change finally did.

Another summit was called, this time in Copenhagen.

For once reason trumped insanity: self-replicating Swarm Weapons were outlawed. They called it the Copenhagen Accord and it was signed by every world power.

After that, nanite technology slowed, its military applications limited to more conventional uses.

But the threat of Swarm Weapons is still real. Superpowers may have agreed to stop producing them, but that doesn't mean they have. Would you believe a promise made by a politician? Or some bureaucratic military lifer or a sleazy corporate executive?

Of course you wouldn't. You're not stupid.

You know that lying is the currency of politics. If there's a dollar to be made or power to be taken, the truth is always the cost.

It's human nature. Look at what we did to the climate.

So, Swarm Weapons never went away; they're just packed up and put into storage in some deep dark vault in the middle of a mountain. Or they're being tested in some secret lab hidden in a facility thousands of metres below the surface of the ocean.

And somewhere, someday, someone is going to use them.

It is not a question of if.

It's only a question of when.

33.

Best Served Cold.

They say before you embark on a journey of revenge, you should dig two graves.

But how I'm feeling right now, it's more like a hundred.

I know I'm not going to live through this, but neither is anyone who gets in my way.

The Azure Habitat glows brightly in distance, brilliant against the grey lunar sea. It's taken us most of the day to get here.

"Bring her down slow and don't try anything," I say, giving Radovan a menacing glare. "Fuck around and I kill you first, got it?"

Radovan nods nervously and banks the transport towards the Azure docking bay. He's sweating. He looks tired and frayed. I suppose I would too if I'd had a gun trained on me all day.

He kicked up a stink after we left New Chechnya, threatened to contact Anatoli Dougray-Mir's people and tell them what was going on. But I let him know just how expendable he was, which seemed to shut him up. Still, I didn't trust him, so I disabled the transport's communication system for good measure. Last thing I needed was for him to contact one of Anatoli's lickspittles and warn them I was coming.

Once we were airborne I went to the back of the ship and patched myself up. The transport was like a long, gunmetal grey RV with a cabin at the front and an open cargo space behind. As this was supposed to be a kidnapping, Radovan had set up the back of the ship to transport a prisoner. It had restraints, a small, lockable detention cell and an emergency triage, just in case Anatoli's prize needed to be fixed up before she was delivered to him.

There was a full nanite surgery back there, everything I needed, but I couldn't afford to be unconscious for hours while an army of tiny robots repaired my fucked-up body. Not with Radovan sitting up the front. He was waiting to kill me, first chance he got.

So, it was graft patches for me.

I found a mirror and did my best to tape myself together, but it wasn't a pretty sight. I'd landed on my face after I jumped from the car. It was a mess and I felt sick looking at my reflection.

When I'd done the best I could do, I sat down beside Radovan and looked out at the stars shining in the black void of space. He tried to talk to me every now and then, but I gave him a look like I was going to break his face and he soon got the idea to keep quiet.

So, we sat in silence until Azure came into view on the horizon.

I look over as we approach and Radovan starts going through the landing procedure, decelerating the vehicle and bringing it down towards the bright yellow lined docking bay. Below, I can see red flashing lights and a squad of heavily armed habitat security coming out to meet the vehicle.

I glare a Radovan and he quips nervously, "It's not my fault. You shut off the communications. We need clearance to land at Azure."

"Bring it in," I say. "Carefully."

Radovan flies the transport into the docking bay. He's nervous, so he fucks it up, coming in too fast and descending rapidly. The transport hits the landing pad heavily and bounces twice before coming to a screeching halt.

"You fucking idiot," I growl. He sinks in his seat.

"You have entered the Azure Habitat illegally. This is a private habitat." A voice drones outside the transport as habitat security surround the vehicle. "Identify yourself. You have thirty seconds to comply or we are authorised to use deadly force."

Red lights flash and alarms sound across the docking bay. There's commotion in the polymer-panelled control room.

The armed squad approaches the transport. They're on high alert, guns at the ready, spread out in attack formation. "Turn off the vehicle and prepare to be boarded."

"Remember," I say as they motion for Radovan to open the door. "Don't try anything or you're a fucking dead man."

He nods and opens the door, trying his best to smile. He looks like a murderer that been caught with a dead body in his trunk.

"Is there a problem?" his voice trembles like a child's.

"Why are your communications off?" the habitat security guard growls.

"Oh, umm, it's broken," he fumbles. "Fucking thing gave out after we left Tycho."

The guard looks at him suspiciously. "Identify yourself."

"I'm Radovan Sedlak."

He looks at me all bloodied and fucked up and levels his AKM needle gun at Radovan's head.

"Who the fuck is that?" he asks, motioning for the squad to open the door next to me. "Both of you, out of the transport, now."

Radovan clears his throat nervously. "Don't worry about my friend. We are guests of Mr Anatoli Dougray-Mir."

The habitat security guard visibly stiffens at the mention of his name. They all lower their weapons, unsure of what to do.

"I should be on the list," Radovan offers with an assuring grin. "He's expecting us."

The security guard pauses and listens to the control room in his ear, then nods and waves us through.

"Sorry for the trouble sir. Mr Dougray-Mir is expecting you, please move along."

Radovan guides the transport through the airlock and into Azure, following the flightpath to Anatoli's lavish residence. He looks terrified as he brings the heavy ship in to land. Tears roll from his eyes and his lip quivers.

He thinks I'm going to kill him.

I probably should. But I won't. Not yet anyway.

"You got a gun?" I ask, as the transport comes to a stop.

He shakes his head no, then looks back down towards the back of the transport. "All I got is an emergency pistol in a cabinet near the rear airlock."

He's lying but I say thanks anyway and walk down the far end of the transport.

There's a cabinet near the airlock, just like he said. I break it open and grab a wide-barrelled, one-shot emergency handgun from inside. It shoots a long-range magnesium flare – should be enough for what I've got planned.

I tuck the gun into the back of my pants and open the airlock, the chamber hissing as it depressurises.

"Don't go anywhere," I say.

Radovan looks at me with a mix of terror and confusion. He's expecting something bad to happen. "You're not going to kill me?"

I turn and look at him. "Do you want me to?"

He shakes his head. "No."

The door opens with a rush of air.

"Then I won't." I walk into the airlock. "But if you move this ship before I tell you to, you're a fucking dead man, you hear me?"

He nods anxiously, his eyes filling with tears, as if he's about to cry again.

"What am I supposed to do till then?" he asks.

"I don't know..." I say with a shrug of my shoulders. "Wait, I guess."

I step of the out of the transport's rear door and into the warm sunlight. The skies are blue and the air smells sweet. A bird's song drifts along on the gentle summer breeze.

This isn't such a bad place to die, I think to myself.

Better than New Chechnya.

I walk towards the pristine white cube, the gravel scattered along the path of the spotless grounds crunches beneath my boots. There are no guards or android security around the building, no sign he's been tipped off that I'm coming.

The building opens as I approach and I walk into the same stark white room I did when I was here last. Just how long ago was that?

A day?

A week?

I don't even know anymore.

The building begins its decontamination protocols, then goes fucking nuts when the scanner picks up the designer virus I've got stashed in the lining of my jumper.

The room goes from white to bright red and alarms begin to sound ominously.

"Warning. Warning. Warning," the disembodied voice tones. "Biological agent detected. Room lockdown commencing in 5, 4, 3..."

"Fuck this," I say to myself.

The programmable matter slips down my wrist and into BLADE formation.

I walk over and slash at the wall, cleaving a gaping hole in the malleable partition. The entrance to the wood panelled hallway opens behind. I make my way to the lift, ignoring the alarms blaring around me, and wait patiently till it arrives and takes me to the top floor of the building.

The doors open out to the same large space as before.

Anatoli is seated at the head of the long dining table on the far side of the room. I see that the rest of the seats are occupied by holograms. One of the holograms is Jensen Gördel.

Anatoli notices me as I step out of the lift.

"Excuse me a moment," he smiles apologetically to his holographic guests, then turns to greet me, leaning back in his chair and crossing his legs casually. "Mr Jones, what a pleasure it is to see you again."

I walk slowly towards him. He should be scared at the sight of me, terrified actually. But he's not. In fact he seems smug, almost amused.

"My, my, my," he says mockingly. "You look frightful Mr Jones. Are you alright?"

I don't answer. I keep my eyes locked on him as I move across the room.

Anatoli turns to the guests at the table and smiles apologetically. "Something has come up. We're going to have to cut this short, I'm afraid. Let's reschedule this meeting for the same time tomorrow."

He dismisses them with a wave of his hand and the holograms flicker, then disappear.

"And you've returned alone I see," he shakes his head, feigning disappointment. "How very unfortunate."

"I came to tell you it's over, Anatoli," I growl as I move slowly towards him. "I know what's really going on in New Chechnya."

He smiles at me. It's a dead smile that doesn't even spark in the vacuum of his eyes. "Do you?"

"Drago Afanasievich is dead and the Bravatso are fucked," I say. "So's your little science experiment. Xander Odom has escaped the city, along with all your research."

"I see."

"She's got evidence on the bacteriophage you've been developing to destroy the Bennetto Reactor. Proof of the human experimentation you've been conducting on the refugees in New Chechnya," I spit out at him. "She's going to expose you, show the world how you tried to fuck it over just so you could keep your little monopoly."

"Is that right?"

"You're finished," I say as I reach the end of the table. "SPM is finished."

He sits back in his seat, pretending to be concerned.

He should be terrified right now.

But he's not.

Why?

"Well, I must say, this is all very disappointing," Anatoli shakes his head at me, like a parent scolding a child. "I expected more from you Mr Jones. I thought you valued your sister's life a little bit more than that."

"Enough!" I shout back at him, the sudden fury in my voice making him sit up in surprise.

Our eyes meet. He looks at me with an amused indifference, like a cat might look at a mouse it's toying with, right before it rips it to shreds.

"You don't get to use her anymore," my voice is shaking, my body filled with rage. "I know she's dead. I know you used her memory so I would cover up your fucking crimes and release that virus. And I'm going to kill you for that."

"Really? Is that what you think, is it?" he chuckles, shaking his head. "It seems I misjudged you. I thought you were smarter than that. What a shame, for your sake, and your sister's."

What the fuck is he talking about?

His face grows cold, the faint amusement replaced by a grim, soulless mask. "Your sister is very much alive, Mr Jones. Well, at least for the moment, that is."

What the fuck is he talking about?

"And the best bit is, you found her for us." Anatoli motions with his hand. "Kobayashi, bring out Mr Jones's sister, please. I'm sure he's dying to meet her."

A wooden panel near the fireplace on the far wall slides open and Kobayashi emerges from the shadows, dragging a woman behind him. He pushes her roughly to the floor and she falls to her knees, hands bound at the wrists, her head bowed.

It is Xander Odom.

My mind reels. I don't understand what is happening.

Nothing.

Makes.

Sense.

Xander can't be my sister. She can't be.

"You didn't know, did you? After so long, I can't say I'm surprised," Anatoli continues, chuckling and shaking his head as if he's just said the punchline to some elaborate joke. "All the prisoners liberated from the Vostok death camps were given new identities by the Australasian government. New names, new faces, all to protect them from reprisals by the Antarcticians."

She's my sister. Sakura.

"Not all that dissimilar to the Antarcticians giving you a new face and a new name. It's no surprise you didn't recognise her."

She's been beaten badly. Her face is a mess of red and purple welts, her lips split. Our eyes meet. They're my sister's eyes.

My sister's eyes.

I should have known. All this time, I should have known.

"Don't feel too bad, she thought you were dead as well. The Antarctician government listed you as deceased when you entered Project Daybreak."

"Why the fuck would you do this? Why the fuck would you go to all this trouble?"

He looks surprised by the question.

"Really Mr Jones? I thought that was obvious. You killed my executives."

Red in the fucking ledger. All this to settle a score.

"I simply can't allow that. Can you imagine what would happen if I did? SPM would be destroyed. You needed to be appropriately punished for your actions, so, I had our intelligence look into your past. It took a while for HEARST to put it all together, but when he did, well, I just couldn't resist the irony."

"You're a fucking monster..." I snarl.

He pays me no heed and keeps on talking.

"Now, Mr Gördel had his doubts. He actually thought you would figure it out. But I knew you would find your sister." He smiles. It's more horrible than you could ever imagine. "What's more, you eliminated Mr Afanasievich and dismantled the Bravatso operation as well. Well done Mr Jones, well done."

I look back at her. She's crying. She looks broken, as if her entire world has come crashing down around her.

I feel the same.

"My operatives picked her up in Lunar City while she was attempting to get passage back to Earth. To tell you the truth, I expected to find you with her. We sent an entire detachment to ensure you didn't get away."

I try to ignore the drone of his voice, but I can't. His words cut like knives. This is all my fault. Everything is all my fault.

"And now we finally have her, it's just a matter of getting the research she stole from the drive in her head."

This gets my attention. I tear my eyes from my sister's face and stare at the soulless monster at the end of the table.

"Kobayashi tells me we can simply download the information and wipe the drive in her head. But I'm not so sure about that. Data retrieval is such a fickle industry. I think it would be much more prudent to remove your sister's head altogether. It's the only way to be sure."

Anatoli's eyes twinkle and hellfire dances in them.

"Touch her and I'll tear you apart." I warn.

The programmable BLADE slides from my arms.

"I tire of this," Anatoli Dugray-Mir whispers, his eyes never leaving mine. "Kobayashi, please see to Mr Jones."

34.

A Propensity for Violence.

Kobayashi nods curtly at his master and takes off his expensive suit jacket. He folds it carefully and drapes it over the back of a nearby chair.

Then, he starts towards me.

As he does, the nanite battle-suit he's wearing beneath his clothes activates. Curls of what looks like thick, black smoke begin to surround him as the nanite swarm emerges.

This is not good.

Clouds of millions of microscopic robots form around Kobayashi as he continues across the room. They shimmer like an oil slick on water as they swarm across his entire body, endlessly shifting and reforming until he is entirely consumed by a swirling vaporous suit of nanites.

Nanite battle-suits are cutting edge. Military grade technology. They make wearer almost impervious to attack, heighten their abilities to superhuman level.

I kick my system into overdrive, pushing everything further than it's meant to go. My heart races, nerve endings crackle with energy, almost like there's a nuclear reaction inside my body.

Kobayashi quickens his pace and forms the nanites into what resembles a long-bladed katana, then leaps into the air, attacking me with an overhead downward strike.

His movement is so fast he is on me in the blink of an eye.

My reaction is instinctual.

I raise the programmable matter weapons at the speed of my firing synapses, just managing to block his attack, barely deflecting the blade. The pure force of his assault sends me reeling across the room.

He's fast and strong.

He stands at the ready in *sha no kamae* stance, then advances with three quick forward strikes, the nanite sword flashing through the air. The blade slices down at my torso then up in one fluid movement, barely missing the tip of my nose. I stumble back, trying to raise my defences as he brings it down in a blur of strikes, then, I'm impaled as he thrusts the blade forward through my shoulder.

Kobayashi withdraws the blade as quickly as it goes in. I feel nothing but an uncomfortable pressure in what remains of my left arm.

I'm stunned.

Xander gasps in horror as I stumble backwards.

"Outstanding Kobayashi, simply outstanding," Anatoli Dugray-Mir claps as his assistant circles me. "Don't make it too quick. I want to enjoy this."

He's too fast.

Too strong.

Even before New Chechnya chewed me up and spat me out, I doubt I could match him.

Kobayashi strikes at me again. This time I manage to block the blow, swatting the nanite blade to the side as I counteract the attack, darting forward and stabbing at his torso.

The battle-suit seems to anticipate my attack, like a fly might see a clumsy attempt to shoo it away.

Millions of nanites positionally reorganise as I stab at him. The swarm forms around the blade, engulfing it and slowing the strike, before hardening into an impenetrable shield that deflects my blow.

It all happens in a micro-second.

We circle each other.

The nanite weapon dissolves in Kobayashi's hand. He forms them into two short blades. He feigns, then counters my defensive reaction, striking faster than I can see.

One.

Two.

Three.

I block the first. The next two hit me in quick succession under the rib cage, mincing my internal organs.

Suddenly, I can barely breathe.

Suddenly, I can taste blood in my mouth.

In the background I can hear Xander screaming.

I turn, trying my best to remain upright, and rush at him before he can attack again, slashing at him in a fury of blows. Kobayashi avoids the attack with ease, blocking my first blow with his hand before pushing me aside.

I land on the hard, cold floor hard to the sound of Dugray-Mir's hyena-like laugh.

"Oh my," Anatoli cackles. "This is better than I could have ever hoped for."

I'm going to die here, fighting like an animal in a cage. All for the amusement of that monster.

My eyes meet Xander's. She's going to die here too unless I can do something about it.

I push myself up and scramble to my feet. I don't know if I scream or not, it's hard to tell. There's a large pool of blood on the floor where I was just lying.

Kobayashi is standing, patiently waiting for me to get to my feet. When I turn to face him, he bows his head and assumes an open hand fighting stance. The nanite battle-suit begins to change. It swirls around him, shimmering. Then it becomes almost mirror like, refracting the electromagnetic light. The shimmering surface seems to warp as the nanite suit ripples, then bends the light around it and disappears into the background.

He's invisible.

"Fuck."

It's all I get to say. I try raise the programmable matter blades in a vain attempt to defend myself as Kobayashi strikes.

All I hear is a rush of air.

Then I look down and notice that the stump my left arm, still covered in the programmable matter blade, is laying on the floor in front of me.

I stumble back, in shock. It's been completely severed just above the elbow. Blood pumps from the appendage in great red gouts. I retract the blade in my right hand desperately try to stem the flow of blood, falling to my knees, defeated.

I can't beat him.

"Bravo, Kobayashi, bravo." Anatoli cheers, getting to his feet and walking towards me. "I hope now you understand, Mr Jones, that every action has a consequence."

I'm not listening to him.

I've got to stop the bleeding.

The programmable matter morphs and shrinks, forming a small ball in the palm of my right hand. I press it against the bleeding stump of my left arm, watching as the black, viscous matter forms around what is left of the limb and stems the flow of the blood.

"You owed me a debt when you took the lives of my SPM employees," Anatoli continues, almost floating across the floor towards me like the spectre of death. "I will consider taking your life as fair payment."

"Fuck you," I growl. I can barely raise my voice above a whisper.

"Once we are done with you, I am going to see to your sister. She will give back what she stole from me, but not before she learns the consequences of her actions, too. Just like you have. But let me assure you, hers will be a fate much worse that you could ever possibly imagine."

I can barely breathe. Kobayashi must have punctured my lung.

"And then, I will release the bacteriophage and put an end to the Bennetto Reactor. And with no competition, I will control every source of energy available to mankind. Which means, I will control the world..." Anatoli smiles at me, it's like a skull, like death. "And everyone in it."

I cradle my wounded arm and look up at his hideous face, knowing that this is going to be the last thing I ever see.

Then I feel something inside my pocket, like a small lump of clay.

"This is all thanks to you, Mr Jones." His horrible laughter fills the room again.

It's the DED. The last of the deflective grenades that piece of shit Abram Nikolayevich gave me back in New Chechnya.

I'd forgotten about it.

"Kobayashi will kill you now," he smiles. "But not before he cuts you down to size."

The old man is close now, no more than five metres from where I'm kneeling.

"When your other arm and your legs are scattered on the floor beside you, then, and only then, will I let Kobayashi end your misery," he continues.

My hand slips inside my pocket and grasps the small explosive round of putty. It links to my neural network.

He turns to Xander.

"Watch what happens to your brother, dear," Anatoli sneers at her. "It's going to be nothing compared to what I'm going to have Kobayashi do to you. I am going to make your suffering last..."

At that moment, Kobayashi passes between where I am kneeling and Anatoli is standing. The nanite battle-suit is still invisible, still bending light around itself, but as the light refracts it ripples around the reflection of Anatoli's moving mouth as he speaks.

This is my chance.

My only chance.

So I strike.

The programmable matter around the DED forms into a short spike, and I lunge forward, plunging it into the nanite cloud like a dagger. The microscopic robots anticipate the blow, believing the explosive to be a sharp melee weapon. They react accordingly. The cloud forms around the object to halt its velocity before hardening and deflecting the blow.

Except it shouldn't do that.

Not with a DED.

If I'd thrown it, the nanite cloud would have recognised it as a DED, remained intangible and simply let the explosive pass through the swarm. Perfect defence. But because I used the DED like a bladed weapon, the nanites reacted like it was. It slowed the weapon's velocity, then hardened to deflect it.

DEDs are programmed to adhere to solid surfaces.

And explode.

The particle collision explosive flashes as the reaction ignites, the close quarter tera-electron voltage consuming Kobayashi and the nanite cloud before it can counter the denotation, disintegrating them both in a burst of bright white light.

I leap back as a supersonic shockwave blasts across the room, the force of the explosion sending everyone hurtling through the air. I hit a wall and I come to a sudden, violent stop, landing face first on the ground.

There's only spots in my eyes and ringing in my ears.

I get up.

Slowly.

I'm dazed. Shell shocked.

I'm badly burnt. I can smell it.

My right hand looks mangled; only my index finger and thumb remain.

The rest is gone.

I can't see so well. I reach up and touch the right side of my face. It feels wet and ragged, like mince.

My right eye is missing.

I actually laugh out loud at this. I don't know why.

The room is badly damaged. Smoke fills the air. The only evidence that Kobayashi ever existed is a smouldering pile on the floor.

"Xander..." I hear myself say. "Xander. Are you alright?"

I hear coughing.

"I'm over here," she groans.

I make my way across the room to her. I can barely walk. My right leg is shredded. There's a large chunk of cauterised quadriceps muscle missing. Xander is laying in the foetal position on the far side of the room.

She has flash burns on her face and arms.

"Are you okay?" I bend down beside her, she looks at me, her face contorting in alarm at the horrific state I am in.

"Look what they did to you..." she stutters, her eyes wide with concern. "Your face."

She reaches out to touch what's left of my face. I try to smile.

"I'm okay," I say. "Are you hurt?"

"I'll live." I help her to her feet.

She stands wobbly at first before gaining her footing.

"I didn't know," I say to her. "I thought you were dead. If I'd known you were alive I would have done anything to save you. Anything."

She smiles and hugs me.

"It doesn't matter," she whispers. "Not now, none of it matters."

I return her embrace. For a moment, everything is perfect.

One perfect moment.

Not far away, I can hear Anatoli coming to.

I find a shard of metal on the floor and help Xander out of the restraints around her wrists, then smile at her as best I can.

"You need to go," I say. "Right now."

"Are you serious?" she looks at me with disbelief. "No. I can't go..."

I talk over her.

"Please Xander, please listen."

"Sakura," she says.

I smile at that.

"Sakura, you know this place will be crawling with police after that explosion. I can already hear the alarms. This place will be in lockdown in fifteen minutes. There's a transport downstairs right now that can get you out of here before they come."

"Come with me then."

"I can't. Believe me, I wish I could. The only way you escape clean is if they're not looking for you. That means they need to find me."

"You can't do that, we just found each other..."

I cut her off.

"Then we'll find each other again. I promise." I look back over at Anatoli. He's trying to use one of the chairs to get to his feet. "Please, make him pay for what he's done. Make sure no one can ever do it again."

She looks at him, then back at me and nods.

She embraces me one more time and whispers in my ear. "Thank you, Jurou. I hope you know that our parents would have been so proud of you."

I look at her. My sister's eyes looking back at me. "They would have been proud of you too, Sakura."

She walks to the lifts and then she's gone.

I retrieve the positioning transmitter from my pants pocket. It's hard to operate with only a finger and a thumb. All the while I'm watching Anatoli struggling to his feet. The old man can barely move.

"Radovan," I say over the static blare of the communicator. "Are you there?"

White noise. Then his voice crackles back at me.

"I'm here. What the fuck is going on? It sounded like an explosion in there."

"Shut your mouth and listen, alright?" I snarl back at him. "There's a girl on her way down to the transport. I need you to get her out of here, safe, okay? Take her anywhere she needs to go."

"Sure, sure, no problem. Anything you say," he replies, almost too enthusiastically.

"Good. Because if anything happens to her, I'm coming to find you. Understand?"

"I understand," he answers. He doesn't sound enthusiastic anymore. He sounds fucking terrified.

I drop the positioning transmitter on the stone floor and crush it under my boot. Then I turn my attention to Anatoli Dougray-Mir.

He's shuffling away towards the far end of the room.

The emergency gun I took from the transport is still stashed in the back of my pants. I fumble and grasp it in my ruined hand. Anatoli looks over his shoulder and sees me.

This time he's not smiling.

This time he looks scared.

"Please, no. Don't." He's facing me now, hands up, backing away slowly. He's badly burnt, wobbly and unsure on his feet, ready to collapse. "I can pay you a lot of money more than you could ever imagine."

His voice trembles as he speaks. His dark vacuum eyes are wide and filled with panic.

"Like you said, every action has a consequence, Anatoli." I shuffle forward slowly. "This is for what you did to my sister."

"Wait..." is all he gets to say. I level the handgun and fire the magnesium round into his knee.

The blinding blue projectile strikes him in the left patella, burning through the bone and the knee joint behind it and separating the femur from the tibia. His leg collapses beneath him, folding like a cheap table, and it sends him sprawling to the floor screaming in agony.

The kneecap is the most painful place you can get shot.

Ask Anatoli.

I stand there, just watching him for a while. I'm not a sadist but there is something cathartic about watching him writhe in pain. When enough time has passed and I know Sakura would be clear of Azure, I walk over to the lift and wait till it arrives. Then I turn and look at Anatoli Dougray-Mir for the last time.

"I wonder Anatoli..." I begin.

I hold up the Chimera weapon in the little glass vial that he gave me so he can see what's about happen. His face, already contorted in agony fills with dread and horror and panic all at once.

"No please, no don't. I beg you..."

"...what will you say when it comes time to meet your maker?"

I toss the vial into the air and step into the lift.

It spins forever in the air, end over end over end, until at last it hits the stone floor and shatters.

As the lift doors close Anatoli screams like I have never heard anyone scream before.

By the time I get to the ground floor the building is going ballistic.

"Pathogen level 5 detected," the disembodied voice tones. "Biosafety protocols engaged."

Slowly, I walk down the wood-panelled hall towards the exit. My right leg can barely hold my weight and drags behind as I walk.

"Upper levels contained. Full building lockdown imminent."

I limp outside into the bright sunlight and start back towards the Azure airlock. The walk down the tree-lined gravel driveway takes quite some time. I can barely hobble.

But it's beautiful all the same.

I can hear birds singing.

The sky is blue.

The air smells sweet.

By the time I make it out onto the road, alarms are sounding across the dome.

Drones begin to dart across the sky.

Far off in the distance, I can hear the sound of panic and screaming.

Soon, I can see black security vehicles circling above.

I put that out of my mind.

The summer wind feels good on my face.

Warm sunlight on the back of my neck.

And I can't help but smile.

I make my way up the road. One shaky step after the other.

The Azure airlock is a blockade. An army of androids is set in attack formation, deployed in strategic positions along the roadway, weapons trained on me.

I approach with what's left of my arms in the air and surrender.

"Down on your knees," a voice booms. "There's nowhere left to go."

A gunship buzzes loudly overhead. More Lunar Security, men in HAZE suits.

As I get down on my knees they move in on me, guns drawn, ready to shoot at the slightest sign of resistance.

It's over. It's all over. There's nothing left for me but just to be. And so, I activate my pain receptors and let myself feel again.

Just one last time.

A wave of white light crashes down upon me as every nerve ending comes to life and screams at once.

But I don't feel the pain. Not because I can't. It's because for the first time in forever there's something else to fill the void.

My sister.

She safe. So nothing hurts anymore.

Darkness dances in my peripherals. This time, I don't fight it. This time, I let it take me.

This isn't such a bad place to die, I think to myself.

35.

Contagion.

They called it the Lunar Flu.

It was deadly.

The authorities spun the release of the virus as a terrorist attack by DAWN. They painted me as a fanatical extremist, intent on killing innocent women and children.

But I knew the truth.

I knew it was the Chimera weapon Anatoli Dugray-Mir had created to wipe out the inhabitants of New Chechnya.

But no one else knew, well maybe Sakura. But that was it.

So, no one got the irony when a virus designed to kill refugees, the poor and destitute, ended up being released in an exclusive community reserved for the richest of the rich.

But it was never supposed to get out. It was never supposed to spread.

Anatoli was a germaphobe. His home was designed to keep germs out, it was hermetically sealed for exactly that purpose. When I released the virus the death toll was supposed to be one.

Him.

I would never have released it if I thought it would infect thousands of people.

But it did.

And that's on me.

You see, I didn't know that Anatoli had an escape route, a final getaway plan in case the shit ever hit the fan. He had a secret panic room in his home and it was fitted with an escape vehicle to get him the fuck out of there if something like that ever happened. And although he was badly injured, Anatoli somehow managed to drag himself into the room and blast out of there before Azure was quarantined.

He had some help, mind you.

AI HEARST ensured he made it out.

It manipulated the habitat-wide lockdown and saw that he made it all the way to the Via Lactea low-orbit habitat, so he could receive the best medical treatment money could buy.

But when he escaped, the virus escaped with him.

No one knew what the disease was at that stage.

Anatoli was non-symptomatic and by the time the authorities on the Moon had breached his house, AI HEARST had rendered the premises completely decontaminated – all evidence of wrongdoing was destroyed.

Anything else incriminating was conveniently pinned on me.

When Anatoli Dugray-Mir's escape pod docked at Via Lactea he was met by a team of doctors. AI HEARST had already started working on a cure for the virus in secret and made arrangements for Anatoli to be placed in isolation till it could produce a vaccine to save him. But, because AIs are so closely monitored by authorities, it couldn't divulge he was infected with the disease to anyone. So, all it could do was work on a cure and allow the virus to spread. It reasoned the only way it could adhere to its programming was to save Anatoli while not incriminating SPM.

So, the virus spread.

Like wildfire.

Anatoli Dugray-Mir was met by a team of twelve medical workers and a compliment of twenty-five security. Out of those thirty-seven people, thirteen were infected upon contact. Because HEARST had destroyed all information about the disease, and it was non-symptomatic for seven days, no one knew they were sick.

In an enclosed environment like an orbital habitat, disease spreads fast.

HEARST ensured Anatoli was placed in isolation at an exclusive medical facility and began monitoring the habitat's hospitals for patients presenting with symptoms, including high fever, convulsions and bleeding of mucous membranes, skin and organs.

Three other people came into contact with the virus on that first day. Another doctor and a nurse, as well as the head of SPM Orbital who came to visit Anatoli at the hospital.

All in all, sixteen people were infected from the time Anatoli Dugray-Mir arrived at the Via Lactea habitat till he was placed in medical isolation.

The next day, the number was forty-eight.

The day after that, it was just over two hundred. And by then, eleven of the two hundred had left the habitat, spreading the disease to Earth and the Moon.

Four days later, when Anatoli Dugray-Mir finally became symptomatic, almost fifty thousand people were infected.

He never breathed a word about the disease.

Not one word.

Now, normally a virus spreading like this would result in a pandemic. Death toll in the millions. Billions maybe. But one thing saved everyone from the hell this Chimera weapon was ready to unleash on humanity: the outbreak had occurred in a rich, hyper-elite community.

And super rich people don't mingle.

They stay in their own exclusive communities.

Lavish seascrapers in the middle of the ocean.

Private habitats on the Moon.

Restricted arcologies cut off from the cities that surround them.

It was like self-imposed quarantine.

So, when the virus was identified and contact tracing began, AIs EVE and ADAM were able to contain the outbreaks with hours.

Lockdowns, isolation and travel restrictions were implemented.

Four days after the Lunar Plague was first diagnosed, it was totally contained.

Five days after that, there was a cure.

But the cost was enormous.

The virus was just as horrible as Anatoli had planned. It did its job, just as it had been designed to. The death toll was close to one hundred thousand people. I'll never be okay with that.

Never.

How could you be?

The only solace I took from this was that for once the rich paid the price, not just the poor. For once the trillionaires that spent their lives taking more than they need finally got what was coming to them.

For once they couldn't walk through the raindrops without getting wet, just like everybody else.

It may not sound like much, but was enough for me.

Anatoli Dugray-Mir died in a private hospital in Via Lactea from total organ failure a week before the cure was found.

It was recorded that his cryptic final words were, "Was it worth it?"

They meant nothing to anybody else, but when I heard that, I had to smile.

36.

Cyanide Jones.

They say you see a tunnel of light right before you die.

I didn't.

I didn't see anything, just darkness. Oblivion. A never-ending nothing, as incomprehensible as it is to contemplate your own existence before your birth.

It was like that for the longest time.

Then it was light again.

I woke up in an intensive care facility in an ultramax prison on the Moon. Apparently, I was in a coma for eight months. I'm surprised they just didn't let me die, but they needed a scapegoat.

So, I lived.

A week after I woke up I found out about what had happened. I was charged with acts of terrorism in relation to the release of the Lunar Flu.

Mass murder.

It made me sick. But there was nothing I could do. I could have told them about the operation in New Chechnya, how Anatoli gave me the Chimera weapon to cover up his crimes, but they would never have believed me.

I was the fall guy. And to tell you the truth, I deserved to be.

So, I kept my mouth shut.

I didn't really care. Sakura was safe. That was all that mattered.

It took me a while to find out what had happened to her. It's kind of hard to come by information when you're locked down in an ultramax prison. My lawyer eventually told me Xander Odom was in the news about a week after the vaccine for the Lunar Flu was released. She leaked evidence of SPM colluding with the Bravatso crime syndicate and conducting human experimentation in New

Chechnya.

Then she disappeared without a trace.

There was a major investigation into the allegations. New Chechnya was annexed by the Lunar government and what was left of the Bravatso in the city were rounded up and arrested. The media had a field day. But, by then Anatoli Dugray-Mir was dead, so AI HEARST and some high-level SPM directors came up with a scheme to blame him for the entire scandal and mitigate the damage to the company.

And it worked.

In the end a few executives, including Jensen Gördel, were arrested and given lengthy prison sentences, and SPM was hit with fines for anti-trust breaches.

And that was all that happened.

SPM came out of it clean and it was business as usual.

Except it wasn't.

Because the Bennetto Reactor came online. And it worked, just like they promised. Cheap and reliable power for everyone. Pretty soon there were other reactors and the stranglehold SPM had over the world dwindled.

Don't get me wrong, the world's still a shitty place.

Just not quite as shitty as before.

Which was good.

Then it was my turn. Surgery after surgery, grafts and cheap shit prosthetics, then months of rehabilitation. All to get me healthy and presentable enough to stand trial. After all, the monster has to look his best for the cameras.

It took about a year.

As you can imagine it was big news. International in fact. Fuck that, it was interplanetary, beamed out from the Earth to the Moon, the settlements on Mars and the colonies orbiting Jupiter and Saturn.

The trial was drawn out, like all trials are. It took two days just to read the charges. I kept my head down and didn't speak unless I was told to. Every day they brought in another expert to testify. Every day they presented more and more fake evidence of how I colluded with other members of DAWN to spearhead a co-ordinated terrorist attack against the habitats of Azure and Via Lactea. And every morning I was paraded in front of the media and public on the way into the courtroom like I was the devil incarnate.

I never reacted. Not once.

That was until I saw her in the crowd. My sister, alive and well.

She was towards the back of an angry mob. I saw her one morning from the back of the prison transport on my way into the International Court of Justice in Stockholm. She looked completely different. She had undergone radical cosmetic alteration. But I knew it was her. The eyes. They couldn't change who was behind the eyes.

I smiled at her and she smiled at me. Then she was gone.

I pleaded guilty. It was the least I could do for the families of all the people who had died. After all, it was my fault and everyone needs a villain, someone they can hate.

If not me, then who?

Am I the hero or the villain? I've asked myself the same question over and over these past months and for the longest time I didn't know.

Then I realised something. Maybe I'm both. Maybe we're all both.

Maybe that's the point.

After the circus was over they sentenced me to be incarcerated for the rest of my life in the Terra Australis prison facility in North-west Australia.

It's the most dangerous prison on Earth, in the most dangerous place on Earth, reserved for the most dangerous criminals on Earth.

A prison without walls, in the middle of the desert, surrounded by wasteland on every side. It was impossible to escape. In Terra Australis there was no law, there was nothing.

Kill or be killed. Only the strong survive.

So that's it. I'm sitting in a prison transport now, a shiny metal box, in full body restraints under military guard on my way to Australia, waiting to be dumped out in the middle of nowhere.

And that's alright. I'm okay with it.

Maybe I'll like it in Terra Australis. Maybe I can make a new life there, one where I'll be happy. Or maybe some fucker might kill me the moment I arrive and I can be finally free of all this shit, once and for all. Maybe I can disappear back into nothing, like I was before they so rudely woke me up.

But I've got a feeling my story isn't over just yet, that Terra Australis is just another pit stop along the way. I've got a feeling that even though I'm still fucked up whoever or whatever is waiting for me down there better steer clear.

Because I don't look like a threat.

But I am.

I'm the most dangerous fucking person you'll ever meet.

I look at my face, reflected in the shiny metal box that I'm sitting in. They did a shitty job replacing my eye. My arm, too, for that matter. The prosthetic they gave me is a piece of crap. They didn't do a very good job on my face either – it's a totally fucked up disaster, but at least I look like someone now, not just a face that blends into a crowd and is forgotten.

I stand out. I'm me and I like that.

My name is Cyanide Jones... and that's who I'm going stay.